My mother had begged m
work to look at Streetmar
Holiday Extravaganza fo

I tried to be objective,
an overstuffed grape if you
patio door. Does he need to go out?"

"He's not a grape. He's an acorn. He'll look better once I get the hat on him. When he stops biting. And no, he doesn't need to go out. We were just out a half hour ago."

"I think he wants to go. He's frantically pawing at your patio door."

My mother turned and walked to the patio door. "Maybe you're right. Hold on. I'll grab his leash."

At the instant the sliding glass door opened, Streetman yanked my mother across the patio and straight toward the Galbraiths' backyard barbeque grill.

"I should never have taken the retractable leash!" she shouted. "I haven't learned how to use it yet. It's new." Her voice bellowed across the adjoining yards as she approached the Galbraiths' grill. "Streetman, stop that! Stop that this instant!"

The dog zeroed in on the tarp and gripped the edge of it with his teeth. My mother stood directly behind him and fiddled with the retractable leash.

"Now see what you've done," she said to the dog. "You've uncovered the bottom of the grill. I'll just shove those black boxes back a bit and put the tarp back down."

"Don't move, Mom!" I screamed. "They're not boxes. They're shoes." I bent down to take a closer look and froze. "Um, it's not shoes. I mean, yeah, those are shoes, but they're kind of attached to someone's legs."

* * *

Praise for the Sophie Kimball Mysteries!

"An entertainingly funny cozy that will tickle
the fancy of readers."
—*Library Journal* on *Booked 4 Murder*

"Funny, great cast, great plot—readers will absolutely love this
one!"
—*Suspense Magazine* on *Booked 4 Murder*

Books by J.C. Eaton

The Sophie Kimball Mysteries

BOOKED 4 MURDER
DITCHED 4 MURDER
STAGED 4 MURDER
BOTCHED 4 MURDER
MOLDED 4 MURDER
DRESSED UP 4 MURDER

(and coming in November 2020:
BROADCAST 4 MURDER)

And available from Lyrical Press

The Wine Trail Mysteries

A RIESLING TO DIE
CHARDONNAYED TO REST
PINOT RED OR DEAD?
SAUVIGONE FOR GOOD

Dressed Up 4 Murder

J.C. Eaton

KENSINGTON BOOKS
www.kensingtonbooks.com

This book is a work of fiction. Names, characters, places, and incidents either are products of the author's imagination or are used fictitiously. Any resemblance to actual persons, living or dead, events, or locales is entirely coincidental.

KENSINGTON BOOKS are published by

Kensington Publishing Corp.
119 West 40th Street
New York, NY 10018

ISBN-13: 978-1-4967-2458-8 (ebook)
ISBN-10: 1-4967-2458-5 (ebook)
Kensington Electronic Edition: March 2020

ISBN-13: 978-1-4967-2455-7
ISBN-10: 1-4967-2455-0
First Kensington Mass Market Paperback Printing: March 2020

10 9 8 7 6 5 4 3 2 1

Printed in the United States of America

For our backyard neighbors, the Carlini and Gabert families, whose covered grills always made us wonder, "What's really under those tarps?"

Acknowledgments

From the moment we came up with the idea to plot a murder around a grill and a pet parade, our "behind the scenes supporters" were always there to help out. They proof our drafts, listen to us whine, and come to our rescue when technology fails us. Thank you, Larry Finkelstein, Gale Leach, Susan Morrow, Fran Orenstein, and Susan Schwartz from "Down Under." And a big thank-you to the "Cozy Mystery Crew" of authors who work together to support one another. You're incredible: Bethany Blake, V. M. Burns, Sarah Fox, Lena Gregory, Jody Holford, Jenny Kales, Tina Kashian, Libby Klein, Shari Randall, Linda Reilly, and Debra Sennefelder.

We realize that none of this would be possible without our tireless and capable agent, Dawn Dowdle from Blue Ridge Literary Agency, and our thoughtful and skilled editor, Tara Gavin from Kensington Publishing. The fact that they "get" our humor makes all the difference for us. Thank you, Dawn and Tara, for continuing to seek out the best in us and push us forward.

And to production editor Carly Sommerstein, we genuinely appreciate your eagle eye! The staff at Kensington Publishing deserves a huge shout-out, from its brilliant art department to its outstanding marketing team. We are humbled that you've taken us under your wing.

And to our readers, thank you so much for bringing Phee, Harriet, Streetman, and the gang into your lives.

Chapter 1

Harriet Plunkett's House
Sun City West, Arizona

"Doesn't he look like the most adorable little dog you've ever seen?" my mother asked when I walked into her house on a late Wednesday afternoon in October. Signs of autumn were everywhere in Sun City West, including pumpkins on front patios, leaf wreaths on doorways, and someone's large ceramic pig dressed like a witch. Of course, it was still over ninety degrees, but that wasn't stopping anyone from welcoming the fall and winter holidays.

My mother had begged me to stop by on my way home from work to look at Streetman's costume for the Precious Pooches Holiday Extravaganza for dogs of all ages and breeds. And since her dog was a Chiweenie, part Chihuahua, part Dachshund, he certainly qualified. The contest made no mention of neuroses.

I tried to be objective, but it was impossible. "He looks like an overstuffed grape or something, if you ask me.

And what's he doing? He's scratching at your patio door. Does he need to go out?"

"He's not a grape. He's going as an acorn. He'll look better once I get the hat on him. When he stops biting. And no, he doesn't need to go out. We were just out a half hour ago."

"Maybe he's trying to escape because you're about to put the hat on him."

"Very funny. It's not easy, you know. There are three separate category contests, and I've registered him for all of them—Halloween, Thanksgiving, and Hanukkah/ Christmas. And just wait until it comes time for the St. Patrick's Day Doggie Contest in March. The prize for that one is almost as good as a pot of gold."

St. Patrick's Day? That's months away. And what's next, dressing him up as "Yankee Doodle Dandy" for the Fourth of July?

"Like I was saying, Phee, Shirley Johnson is making the costumes. You're looking at the Thanksgiving one. I can't make up my mind if I want Streetman to go as a pumpkin for Halloween or a ghost. Goodness. I haven't even given any thought to the winter costume. Maybe a snowflake . . ."

"Right now, I think he wants to go. Period. Look. He's frantically pawing at your patio door."

"He only wants to sniff around the Galbraiths' grill. A coyote or something must've marked the tarp, because, ever since yesterday, the dog has been beside himself to check it out. I certainly don't need him peeing on their grill. They won't be back until early November. I spoke to Janet a few days ago. She really appreciates Streetman and me checking out her place while they're up in Alberta. You know how it is with the Canadian snowbirds.

They can only stay here for five months or they lose their health insurance. Something like that."

"Uh-huh."

"Anyway, how are you and Marshall managing with your move? That's coming up sometime soon, isn't it?"

"Not soon enough. I feel as if I'm living out of cardboard boxes, and Marshall's place is no different. We won't be able to get into the new rental until November first. That's three weeks away and three weeks too long."

Marshall and I had worked for the same Mankato, Minnesota, police department for years before I moved out west to become the bookkeeper for retired Mankato detective Nate Williams. Nate opened his own investigation firm and insisted I join him. A year later, and in dire need of a good investigator, he talked Marshall into making the move as well. I was ecstatic, considering I'd had a crush on the guy for years. Turned out it was reciprocal.

"Do you need any help with the move?" my mother asked. "Lucinda and Shirley offered to help you pack."

Oh dear God. We'd never finish. They'd be arguing over everything.

Shirley Johnson and Lucinda Espinoza were two of my mother's book club friends and as opposite as any two people could possibly be. Shirley was an elegant black woman and a former milliner while Lucinda, a retired housewife, looked as if she had recently escaped a windstorm.

"No, I'll be fine. The hard part's done. I can't believe I actually sold my house in Mankato. Other than autumn strolls around Sibley Park, I really won't miss Minnesota."

"What about my granddaughter? Did she get all nostalgic?"

"Um, not really. In fact, she had me donate most of the stuff she had in storage to charity. She's sharing a small apartment in St. Cloud with another teacher and they don't have much room. Besides, Kalese was never the packrat type."

My mother had turned away for a second and walked to the patio door. "Maybe you're right. Maybe he does need to go out again. Hold on. I'll grab his leash. We can both go out back." With the exception of the people living next door to my mother and busybody Herb Garrett across the street, the other neighbors were all snowbirds. Michigan. South Dakota. Canada.

"Dear God. You're not going to take him outside in that outfit, are you?" I asked.

"Fine. I'll unsnap the Velcro. Shirley's using Velcro for everything."

At the instant in which the sliding glass door opened, Streetman yanked my mother across the patio and straight toward the Galbraiths' backyard barbeque grill.

"I should never have taken the retractable leash!" she shouted. "He's already yards ahead of me."

"Can't you push a button or something on that leash?"

"I haven't learned how to use it yet. It's new."

I was a few feet behind her, running as fast as I could in wedge heels.

Her voice bellowed across the adjoining yards as she approached the Galbraiths' grill. "Streetman, stop that! Stop that this instant!"

The dog zeroed in on the tarp and gripped the edge of it with his teeth. My mother stood directly behind him and fiddled with the retractable leash.

"Now see what you've done," she said to the dog. "You've gone ahead and uncovered the bottom of the grill. I'll just shove those black boxes back a bit and put the tarp back down."

"Don't move, Mom!" I screamed. "Take a good look. They're not boxes. They're shoes."

"What?" My mother flashed me a look. "Who puts shoes under a grill where snakes and scorpions can climb in them?"

I bent down to take a closer look and froze. Streetman was still tugging to get under the tarp and my mother seemed oblivious to what was really there.

"Um, it's not shoes. I mean, yeah, those are shoes, all right, but they're kind of attached to someone's legs."

"What??"

If I thought my mother's voice was loud when she was yelling at the dog, it was a veritable explosion at that point. "A body? There's a body under there? You're telling me there's a body under that tarp? Oh my God. Poor Streetman. This could really set him back."

Yes, above all, the dog's emotional state was the first thing that came to my mind, too. "Mom, step back."

At that moment, she scooped Streetman into her arms and ran for the house. "I'm calling the sheriff. No! Wait. We have to find out who it is first. Once those deputy sheriffs get here, they'll never let us near the body."

"Good. I don't want to be near a dead body. Do you?"

"Of course not. But I need to know who it is. My God, Phee, it could be one of the neighbors. Can't you just pull the tarp back and take a look?"

Streetman was putting up a major fuss, squirming in my mother's arms and trying to get down.

"Okay, Mom. Go back to the house. Put the dog inside and come back here. I won't move until you do. Oh, and bring your cell phone."

My mother didn't say a word. She walked as quickly as she could and returned a few minutes later, cell phone in hand. "Here. Take this plastic doggie bag and use it as you pull the tarp away. Don't get your fingerprints on the tarp."

"I'll pull the tarp back and take a look, but I won't have the slightest idea if it's one of your neighbors. I don't know all of them."

"Fine. Fine. Oh, and look for cause of death while you're at it."

"Cause of death? I'm not a medical examiner." I bent down, put my hand in the plastic bag, and gingerly lifted the tarp. I tried not to look at what, or in this case who, was underneath it, but it was useless. I got a bird's-eye view. Male. Fully clothed, thank God, and faceup. Middle aged. Dark hair. Jaundiced coloring. Small trickle of blood from his nose to shirt. No puddles of blood behind the head or around the body.

My mother let out a piercing scream. "Oh my God. Oh my God in heaven!"

"Who? Who is it? Is it someone you know?"

I immediately let go of the tarp and let it drape over the body.

"No, no one I know."

"Then why were you screaming bloody murder?"

"Because there's a dead man directly across from my patio. A well-dressed dead man. Here, you call the sheriff's office. I'm too upset. And when you're done, give me the phone. I need to call Herb Garrett."

"Herb Garrett? Why on earth would you need to call Herb?"

"Once those emergency vehicles show up, he'll be pounding at my door. Might as well save us some time."

I started to dial 911 when my mother grabbed my arm and stopped me. "Whatever you do, don't tell them it was Streetman who discovered the body."

"Why? What difference does that make?"

"Next thing you know, they'll want to use him for one of those cadaver dogs. He's got an excellent sense of smell. Don't say a word."

"You're kidding, right? First of all, the law enforcement agencies have their own trained dogs. *Trained* being the key word. No one's going to put up with all his shenanigans. And second of all, how else are you and I going to explain how we happened to come across a dead body under the neighbors' tarp?"

My mother pursed her lips and stood still for a second. "Okay. Fine. Go ahead and call."

The dispatch operator asked me three times if I was positively certain we had uncovered a dead body. I had reached my apex the third time.

"Unless they're starting to make store mannequins in various stages of decomposition, then what we've discovered is indeed a dead body. Not a doll. Not a lifelike toy. And certainly not someone's Halloween decoration!"

Finally, I gave her my mother's address and told her we were behind the house. Then I handed my mother the phone. "Go ahead. Make Herb's day. Sorry, Mom, I couldn't resist the Clint Eastwood reference."

My mother took the phone and pushed a button. "I have him on speed dial in case of an emergency."

All I could hear was her end of the conversation, but it was enough.

"I'm telling you, I had no idea there'd be a body under that tarp. Sure, it was a huge tarp, but I thought it was covering up one of those gigantic grills. . . . Uh-huh. . . .

Really? A griddle feature? . . . No, all I have is a small Weber. . . . Uh-huh. Behind the house. . . . Fine. See you in a minute."

"I take it Herb is on his way."

My mother nodded. "Do you think I should call Shirley and Lucinda?"

"This isn't an afternoon social, for crying out loud; it's a crime scene. No, don't call them. It's bad enough Herb's going to be here any second. Maybe we should go wait on your patio. We can see everything from there."

Just then I heard the distant sound of sirens. "Never mind. We might as well stay put."

My mother thrust the phone at me. "Quick. While there's time, call your office. Get Nate or Marshall over here."

"Much as I'd like to accommodate you by having my boss and my boyfriend show up, I can't. Marshall's on a case up in Payson and won't be back until the weekend. I think he took the case so he wouldn't have to be stepping over cartons. And as for my boss, Nate's so tied up with his other cases, he certainly doesn't have time to interfere with a Maricopa County Sheriff's Office investigation."

"Humph. You know as well as I do those deputies will be bumbling around until they finally cave and bring in Williams Investigations to consult."

Much as I hated to admit it, my mother was right. Not because the deputy sheriffs were "nincompoops," as she liked to put it, but because the department was so inundated with drug-related crimes, kidnappings, and now a highway serial killer in the valley that they relied on my boss's office to assist.

"Look, if and when that happens, I'll let you know."

The sirens were getting louder and I turned to face my mother's patio.

From the left of the garage, Herb Garrett stormed across the gravel yard. "Where's the stiff? I want to take a look before the place is plastered in yellow crime tape."

"Under the tarp." I failed to mention the need for a plastic bag.

Herb made a beeline for the Galbraiths' grill and lifted the tarp. "Nope. Don't know him. Damn it. I forgot my phone."

"Don't tell me you were going to snap a photo. And do what? Post it on the internet?"

Herb let the tarp drop and positioned himself next to my mother. "How else is poor Harriet going to sleep at night knowing some depraved killer is depositing bodies in the neighborhood? If I post it, maybe someone will know something."

My mother gasped. "Depraved killer? Bodies?"

"Herb's exaggerating," I said. "Aren't you?"

Suddenly it seemed as if the sirens were inches away from us. Then they stopped completely.

"Oh no," I said. "This can't be happening. Not again."

My mother grabbed my wrist. "What? What's happening?"

I took a deep breath. "Remember the two deputy sheriffs who were called in to investigate the murder at the Stardust Theater?"

"Uh-huh."

"Looks like they're back for a repeat performance. Deputies Ranston and Bowman. I don't know which one dislikes me more."

Well, maybe "dislike" wasn't quite the word to describe how they felt about me. "Annoyed" might have summed it up better. Over a year ago, when my mother and her book club ladies were taking part in Agatha

Christie's *The Mousetrap* at the Stardust Theater, someone was found dead on the catwalk. And even though I wasn't a detective, only the accountant at Williams Investigations, I sort of did a bit of sleuthing on my own and might have stepped on their toes. What the hell. They're big men. They needed to get over it.

"Miss Kimball." Deputy Ranston's feet crunched on the yard gravel as he approached us from the side of my mother's house. "I should have taken a closer look at the name when I read the nine-one-one report. Seems you're the one who placed the call."

"Nice seeing you again, Deputy Ranston." I turned to his counterpart and mumbled something similar before reintroducing my mother and Herb.

"So, was it you who found the body?" Ranston asked.

I honestly don't know why, but for some reason, the man reminded me of a Sonoran Desert Toad. I kept expecting his tongue to roll out a full foot as he spoke.

"Um, actually it was my mother's dog. Streetman. He found the body."

Deputy Bowman cut in. "Just like that? Out of the blue?"

My mother took a few steps forward until she was almost nose to nose with Bowman. "For your information, Streetman and I cut across the Galbraiths' yard every day while they're still in Canada. We keep an eye on the house for them. Usually the dog is more concerned with the quail and the rabbits that hide under the bushes. He never as much as made a move toward the grill. Until yesterday afternoon. That's when he started whining to go over there. I thought a coyote might have marked it or left a deposit there."

"So you lifted the tarp up to check?" Bowman asked.

"Of course not. The dog was on a retractable leash and

got to the grill before I did. He nuzzled the tarp aside, and that's when we saw the body."

Bowman gave his partner a sideways glance. "How big a dog is this Streetman that he could lift an entire tarp off of a body?"

"He's less than ten pounds," I said, "but very strong."

Bowman wasn't buying it. "Look, Miss Kimball, I know you have a penchant for unsolved crimes and I'm more likely to believe it was you who lifted the tarp."

My mother responded before I could utter a word. "Only for a split second and only because she happened to see someone's legs attached to the shoes that were beneath it. And she used a plastic bag so she wouldn't get fingerprints on the material."

Then the deputies turned to Herb and Ranston spoke. "Were you here as well when the ladies discovered the body, Mr. Garrett?"

"No. Harriet called me after dialing nine-one-one."

"I see."

Ranston wrote something on a small notepad and looked up. "The nine-one-one dispatcher gave us the Plunkett address. Would any of you happen to know the Galbraiths' address?"

"Of course," my mother said. "Something West Sentinel Drive. It's the small cul-de-sac behind us."

I could hear both deputies groan as Bowman placed a call.

"In a few minutes," he said, "a forensic team will be arriving as well as the coroner. I suggest you all return to your houses and stay clear of this property until further notice."

"Will you at least tell us who it is?" Herb asked. "For all we know, it could be one of our neighbors. Or a cartel drug lord who was dropped off here."

"Here? In Sun City West? That's what we have the desert for," my mother said.

Deputy Bowman forced a smile and repeated what he had told us a second ago. "Please go back to your houses. This is an official investigation."

"Will you be contacting the Galbraiths?" I asked.

Bowman gave a nod. "Yes."

I tapped my mother on the elbow and pointed to her house. "He's right." Then I whispered, "If you hurry, you can call the Galbraiths first."

Chapter 2

My mother charged across the two adjoining yards, with Herb at her heels.

I was a few feet behind. "Hold up for a minute. I need to ask the deputies something. I'll meet you inside the house."

Herb patted my mother on the arm. "I'll stay with Harriet until you get back."

She shrugged, shook her head, and kept walking. Two more emergency vehicles pulled up to the front of the Galbraiths' house as I reached the deputies.

"Um, I know you don't want me poking around the crime scene, but I think it's in everyone's best interest if you can at least tell me what identification you found on the body. I know you've already looked."

Actually, I didn't know, but it was a good guess.

"Miss Kimball," Ranston said, "you work at a detective agency. You should know as well as anyone that we cannot divulge that kind of information. We need to notify next of kin and—"

I crossed my arms and glared at him. "Let me put it

this way. All I need to know is if the person is a resident of Sun City West. Given my cursory look at the body, I don't believe this was the scene of his death. It's too staged. Too neat. He was dumped here, and I'm banking he's not from this area. Um, too young."

Ranston cleared his throat and I continued, "You've met my mother. *And* her friends. I guarantee within fifteen minutes, twenty if we're lucky, she'll be on the phone with the nosiest cadre of gossips from every retirement community in the Greater Phoenix Area. And you know what she'll be telling them? That the residents of Sun City West are being murdered in their own backyards. If you can at least clarify that this particular body came from anyplace but here, we can avert that disaster."

Ranston turned and faced Bowman. "What did that ID say?"

I was too far away to hear the rest of the conversation, but I could read body language, and Bowman wasn't pleased. I stood still and waited for Ranston. After what seemed like an inordinate amount of time for the deputies to confer with each other, Ranston motioned me over.

"I'm doing this as a professional courtesy, Miss Kimball, and nothing more. And this is *not* public knowledge. The driver's license in the victim's wallet shows a Peoria address. That's all I'm at liberty to say. And until the medical examiner and the forensic team complete their process, we can't really be sure the name and address on the ID belong to the victim."

"But you're pretty sure, right? I mean, as sure as you can be, considering the jaundiced coloring and the dried blood on the face. Do you think he was poisoned? I know rigor mortis set in, but that could mean anywhere from four hours on."

"Good God, Miss Kimball. You seem to be quite familiar with the body, considering you only took a split-second look. And let me warn you not to confuse any of your Google meanderings with a medical degree in forensic pathology."

I bit my lower lip and smiled. "You can relax, Deputy Ranston. The only thing I'll convey to my mother is that the body doesn't belong to any of her neighbors."

"Good. Last thing we need is a full-blown panic on our hands."

No sooner did he say the word "panic" when the sheriff's forensic team cut across the Galbraiths' front yard and were immediately ushered to the crime scene by Deputy Bowman.

There must have been at least six people on duty. If that didn't spell out "panic," I didn't know what would. The only saving grace was the fact that the houses next to the Galbraiths' all belonged to snowbirds and my mother's next-door neighbor was on a seven-day cruise that began three days ago.

I thanked Deputy Ranston and walked back to my mother's patio. She and Herb were at the sliding glass door watching the crime scene. Streetman was chomping on a rubber chew toy a few feet away in one of his dog beds.

"What took you so long?" My mother slid the door open. "I called Janet Galbraith and told her what was going on. She wanted to know if there was a lot of blood on her patio, because if there was she asked me to call one of those disaster cleanup companies to have it removed."

I rolled my eyes and stepped inside. "I hope you told her we didn't see any blood."

"I told her the truth. We don't know what's under the body. Maybe the guy was shot in the back."

"I don't think so, Harriet," Herb said. "He looked as if someone poisoned him."

"That's what I thought, too," I blurted out. Then another thought occurred to me. "Mom, when was the last time you checked the outside of Janet's house? Front door, windows . . ."

"The day before yesterday. The day before Streetman—Oh my gosh. There could be other bodies strewn all over the place for all we know. Janet covers up those huge planters in her front courtyard. You've seen them, Herb. The ones with those hideous fake flowers."

"Well, I—"

"It doesn't matter," I said. "Those deputies will be combing the entire property. Did Janet leave you a key to her place?"

My mother shook her head. "No. I only check the outside. Janet and her husband have one of those emergency key boxes on their front porch. The sheriff's office can unlock it and get the key. She signed the permission form. Besides, they're probably calling her right now."

"Good. You can relax. So, other than worrying about the blood, how did Janet take the news?"

"I'm not sure. But I did hear her screaming to Al. Something about buying a new grill."

"I don't know about you or Herb, but I'm going to sit down in the living room for a few minutes. That crew out back will be here for hours. And they'll have to set up temporary lighting. It's going to be dark in a few minutes." I walked out of the Arizona room, across the kitchen, and to the couch, glancing at the street through the front windows. A bright blue van sped past, and I was about to say something about speed limits when I realized what it was. Rushing to the window, I saw the bright letters on its rear bumper—KPHO.

"I can't believe it! It's channel five. They must've picked up the dispatch and sent a news crew."

I was facing my mother and Herb, who were on their way into the living room, when Herb announced, "Take another look, cutie. There goes channel fifteen and channel ten. In another two minutes, channel twelve's bound to show up."

"Dear God! This is insane."

"Now can I call Shirley and Lucinda?" My mother was already picking up the phone.

I sank down in the comfy cushions. "Sure. Knock yourself out."

Herb rubbed the back of his neck. "If you're calling that book club of yours, I might as well head home. No sense in all of us being here at once. Of course, I'll check in later with you, Harriet."

My mother put the receiver to her ear and waved him off. "Honestly. You're not fooling anyone. You're going home to call that pinochle crew of yours—Kevin, Kenny, Wayne, and Bill. You're worse than a bunch of old hens."

"Someone has to stay on top of things around here. I'll call you later. Oh, and nice seeing you again, sweetheart." He cast me a wink.

I tried not to grimace.

Herb went out the front door and my mother quickly locked it behind him. "I might as well take something out of the freezer. It's going to be a long night. You're staying here for a while, aren't you?"

"I'll stay, but only for a little while. I'm sure you'll be fine with all the ladies. Listen, while you're about to play Paul Revere on the phone, I'm going to make a few calls myself. To Marshall and Nate. I'll use the guest room so our conversations don't interfere with each other."

My mother hadn't dialed the first number when her

phone rang. I paused as she answered. "It's Louise Munson, Phee, from around the corner."

"Okay. I'm going into the bedroom."

I figured I'd better give Nate the heads-up first since he'd be likely to catch the news and head over here. The phone rang four times before he picked up.

"Hey, it's me. You wouldn't happen to be near a TV, would you?"

"As a matter of fact, I stopped at Ray's, picked up a sub for dinner, and just got in the door. Why? Is there something you wanted me to watch?"

"Oh yeah. My mother's dog found a dead body in the yard behind her house. Every news station from here to San Diego is on the street."

"Oh geez. I can be there in a few minutes. Your mother must be past hysterical by now."

"Uh, actually she's doing quite well. Surprisingly well, if you ask me."

"Whoa. That *is* a surprise. Considering the last time a dead body was found in the neighborhood. That time she insisted on a twenty-four-hour security patrol. And that body was a few blocks away. On a golf course. Not in the yard behind her house."

"Give it time. It will sink in. And when it does, she'll want Homeland Security and every local, state, and national government agency on the case, not to mention law enforcement."

"Give me a second to stash my sub in the fridge and I'll be right back."

I held on while Nate put his dinner on hold. Even with the door shut, I could hear my mother talking to Louise.

"It's worse than the golf course body. It was inches from my house. Inches!"

I rolled my eyes and tried not to laugh.

"I'm back, kiddo," Nate said. "Give me all the details."

I went on to explain how I was with my mother at the time and how Streetman pulled her across the yard and straight to the Galbraiths' grill, where he yanked off part of the tarp.

Nate didn't seem too surprised. "Dogs have an incredible sense of smell. I think I read somewhere that while humans can smell a stew cooking on a stove, a dog can smell each separate ingredient. So, I take it you got a good look at the body?"

"Uh-huh. Unnerving, if you must know. It was a man who looked younger than middle age, with dried blood trickling from his nose and a pasty yellow coloring on his face. He was dressed well. Not that it matters to him anymore."

"Jaundiced, you said?"

"Yeah. Herb and I think he might have been poisoned."

"Herb Garrett? Your mother's nosy neighbor? He saw the body, too?"

I let out a long sigh and explained how Herb came barreling across the street because my mother just *had* to call him.

"Oh brother. So, who's on the case?"

"Deputies Ranston and Bowman."

"Yeesh. At least they'll be thorough. I don't suppose you were able to find out anything from them."

"As a matter of fact, yes. I think they were afraid of a full-blown neighborhood panic, so once they checked the victim's ID, they told me he wasn't a Sun City West resident. That's all I know. You don't have to skip dinner and rush over. Everything's fine."

"All right. If you're sure I'm not needed over there,

I'll make some calls and see what I can find out for you. Tell your mother not to go off the deep end. Chances are this was a drug-related crime and the perpetrator dumped the body in Sun City West because they didn't want to drive the extra few miles to the desert."

"Okay. I'll call you later if anything comes up. If not, I'll see you in the morning."

"Does Marshall know?" he asked.

"Not yet. I'm about to call him. I thought I'd call you first since you were most likely to catch it on the news."

"Turning the TV on now. Tell Marshall I'll touch base with him later, will you?"

"Sure thing. And thanks, Nate."

"Are you still on the phone, Phee?" my mother yelled. "Louise is on her way over and she's calling Myrna and Cecilia. I've got to call Shirley this instant. Too bad all the snowbirds aren't back or we could have the entire Booked 4 Murder book club here."

Sure. Why not make this a Ringling Brothers event while you're at it? "I'm about to call Marshall!" I shouted back. Then I dialed.

Unlike Nate, he picked up immediately. "Hi, hon. Is everything okay? I saw your name pop up, but we usually don't talk with each other till later at night."

"Um, everything's fine. Well, not really. Long story. I'm not sure if you can get the Phoenix TV stations where you are, but there's a dead body across the yard from my mother's house. The sheriff's forensic crew is on the scene."

"Oh my gosh. I can't imagine your mother's reaction when she turned on the TV."

"Uh, about that. She was the one who discovered the body. Well, Streetman actually. And me. I stopped by her house and we took the dog out and he ran for the Galbraiths' backyard grill and that's when he sniffed it out."

"Holy Hell."

For the next five minutes, I gave Marshall all of the details, including my earlier call with Nate and my observations about the body. I also told him what Deputy Ranston said about the victim's identification. "I suppose, in some bizarre way, it's kind of comforting to know the body didn't belong to one of the neighbors. Still—"

"I know. I know. Listen, I was about to let you know I finalized this case and was planning to drive back first thing in the morning, but I can head out in less than an hour."

"No. Don't. That beeline is awful in the dark. All those curves and no guardrails. The last time I was on that god-awful Route 87, it was with my aunt Ina and she was screaming her lungs out. 'Use the brakes! Use the brakes!' Promise me you'll wait till the morning."

"All right. If you're going to be that worried about it. I'll leave first thing and see you in the office. I'll call you later tonight once you get home. You are going home, aren't you? Or will you be staying with your mother?"

"Home. Most definitely. She's got a zillion book club friends. One of them can stay."

Marshall laughed and we said our good-byes. I walked into the kitchen to find my mother hand-feeding what looked like small meatballs to Streetman.

"The poor dog must be absolutely traumatized," she said.

"He looks more ravenous than traumatized, if you ask me."

"Louise should be here any second. I wonder what's

keeping her. Oh, and I called Shirley. She was going to call Lucinda and offer to drive her here."

"Is there anyone else in the West Valley you've forgotten to tell?"

"Oh my God! Your aunt Ina! In all the fuss, I completely forgot to call my sister. Here. You feed Streetman his special dinner. I'd better call Ina before she turns on the TV and pitches a fit."

Terrific. Not only Ringling Brothers but, with Aunt Ina, a Wagnerian opera to boot.

My aunt could take the most mundane situation and turn it into a Lady Gaga spectacle before anyone knew what was happening. I grabbed the small bowl of meatballs from my mother and held one up for the dog. "Go ahead, Mom. Might as well have a full house tonight."

Chapter 3

The dog snatched the morsel of meat from my hand and swallowed it in one gulp. As I reached for another, the doorbell rang and I could hear Louise's voice.

"It's me, Harriet. Open the door. Myrna's with me."

I looked over at my mother, who was waiting for Aunt Ina at the other end of the phone line.

"I'll get it." I left Streetman staring at the small bowl I had placed on the counter.

Louise and Myrna rushed in, nearly knocking me down. Both of them were talking at once and all I could do was nod and mutter "uh-huh."

"Cecilia will be here any second. Poor Harriet. Did they tell her who it was?"

"Forget who it was; how was he killed? Your mother said it was a man."

"Never mind *how*; do those deputies have any idea who?"

"Did either of you look at the body? Recent or decomposed?"

Finally, Myrna grabbed Louise by the arm. "Give the girl a break. She's probably still in shock."

I ushered them into the living room, making sure they had closed the door behind them, but it swung open and Cecilia stepped in. Dressed in black from head to toe, with the exception of a white dickie under her sweater and her hair tousled about, she looked as if she had made a hasty retreat from a funeral.

"Er, hi, Cecilia," I muttered. "Make yourself at home."

She plopped herself in one of my mother's floral chairs, while Myrna and Louise took over the couch. Streetman assessed the situation from the kitchen and made a mad dash to the master bedroom.

"My mom's on the phone with my aunt Ina," I said. "She'll be right in."

"Ina's coming?" Louise's voice sounded somewhat panicky.

"I'm not sure. Would any of you like something to drink? I know there's juice and water in the fridge."

The ladies shook their heads and continued talking at once.

"I thought Shirley and Lucinda would be here by now."

"Maybe that's them pulling up. I just heard a car."

I walked to the front window and took a look. No such luck. It was a sheriff's deputy car, and Ranston had just slammed the passenger door.

"Excuse me, ladies. I'm going to step outside for a minute and speak with one of the deputies. I'll be right back." I didn't wait for a response. I hustled as fast as I could so I didn't have to let Deputy Ranston into the house. Not with the sideshow taking place in my mother's living room.

"I'm doing you a favor," I said as I met him on the walkway. "If I let you inside, you'll be besieged with questions. Three of my mother's friends are in there, and two more are on their way. Not to mention my aunt. She may be coming, too."

Ranston was expressionless. "Oh, hell. I wanted to ask your mother if she had noticed anything strange in the neighborhood the past few days, but I suppose it can wait. Here's my card. Have her call me first thing in the morning. You won't forget, will you?"

I took the card. "Of course not. Say, do you have any idea how long that team is going to be working in the Galbraiths' yard?"

"Until they secure the scene and gather evidence. The sheriff's office will be sending a forensic crew into the house tomorrow. We got the Galbraiths' consent. Shouldn't take too long. Unless, of course, the victim was murdered inside the house."

"What? That's preposterous. If he was killed inside the house, why wouldn't his assassin leave the body right there?"

"I'm not saying the guy was killed inside their house; I'm just saying."

"Your team secured the premises. The house didn't look broken into, did it?"

Of course, that really didn't mean anything, considering the murderer could've gotten a key.

Ranston shook his head. "No. Not broken into. I'm telling you this because I don't need you snooping around there tonight. It's a crime scene."

"Got it. A crime scene."

"Your mother mentioned something about the neighboring houses belonging to snowbirds. We're still going to canvas the area and speak with any of the residents who aren't out of the state at the moment. Maybe one of them noticed something."

"Um, I'm not sure if you have the authority, but I'm hoping you do. . . ." I let the rest of my thought dangle.

"The authority for what?" Ranston began to tap his foot, and I knew I'd better get to the point.

"The authority to have the sheriff's posse patrol this neighborhood tonight. I really don't have to tell you that—"

"It's been taken care of. And don't think for a minute the department is granting your family special favors. There's a slight possibility whoever dumped the body might decide to return in order to retrieve something from the deceased. Something they may need. Oftentimes these street criminals are kind of short in their planning."

"Like what? ID? Money?"

Suddenly headlights appeared in front of the house, and I knew, without a doubt, Shirley and Lucinda had arrived. I couldn't believe it was dark already. The time had whirled by so quickly.

"Uh, never mind. Looks like more of my mother's friends are showing up."

"When you go back inside, be sure to tell everyone to stay inside. This isn't Arizona Broadway Theatre out here."

"I understand. And thanks."

Ranston got back in his vehicle and the driver, most likely Bowman, pulled away from the curb and down the block, freeing the parking space for Shirley's large Buick. I stood still and waited for the car to come to a complete stop. Shirley was out the door in a matter of seconds, and Lucinda wasn't far behind. The two of them rushed me like offensive tackles for the Cardinals.

Shirley was waving her arms in the air and trying to catch her breath. "Lordy, Phee! Lordy! This is dreadful. Simply dreadful. Your poor mother."

"Yes," Lucinda added. "I imagine Harriet is beside herself."

Actually, she's in there like the Queen of the May surrounded by a full court. "Um, she's doing okay. Come on in and make yourself at home."

I followed the two women into the house and scanned the block. So far, so good. Nothing else on the horizon. I was positive Herb had called his pinochle buddies, but, knowing that crew, they were busy downing their first beer at Curley's. The place had more lotharios than the entire romance section of the library, and if Bagels 'N More was my mother's "go to" spot, Curley's bar belonged to the senior men in the community.

"Ina and Louis are on their way!" my mother shouted from across the living room as I closed the door behind me. "Shirley, Lucinda, help yourselves to some juice or water. I'm so flustered I can't think."

Shirley walked over to where my mother was standing and put her arm around her. The two of them headed to the kitchen when my mother turned around.

"I was going to take something out of the freezer for us, but Ina insisted on bringing food. Louis was going to call one of those fast-food places to pick it up from. Thank goodness. I can't think. I must be losing my mind."

"You'll be okay, Harriet," Lucinda said. "It's the shock. Your mind is trying to process the fact a dead body was dropped so close to your patio door. I thought Wanda and Dolores had it bad when they found out a killer trampled through their side yard a year or so ago, but this is much worse. Much worse."

My mother grabbed her chest with one arm and sighed.

She would've made a great silent-screen actress. I clamped my teeth together and tried not to laugh.

Thank you, Lucinda, for bringing up Wanda and Dolores. And thank you, Wanda and Dolores, for staying in Portland until Thanksgiving.

For the next forty minutes, the book club ladies dissected the crime scene and offered up their own versions of what might've transpired. That was when they weren't all standing around the patio doors looking out at the ongoing investigation in the Galbraiths' yard.

The sheriff's investigators seemed to be walking back and forth, conferring with each other and talking on their phones. The body had been removed, along with the tarp, and only the grill remained.

Just then, the doorbell rang.

"It's Ina and Louis," my mother said from her vantage point by the patio. "Will one of you get it?"

"I'm on it, Mom." I opened the door, expecting to see my aunt and uncle, but instead, I was face-to-face with two delivery guys from Jimmy John's Gourmet Sandwiches. They looked as if they hadn't reached puberty yet.

"Is this the Plunkett residence?" the blond one asked. "We've got a delivery. All paid for. The tip, too. Mixed subs. Turkey, ham, roast beef, and vegetarian with cheese. Just in case. Where do you want them?"

I couldn't believe what I was staring at. "Um, you can go ahead and put the trays on the kitchen table and the counter."

"Good deal," the kid said. "We got paper plates, napkins, and canned soda."

The few women who were standing got out of the way quickly as the guys brought in the trays and drinks. I had to admit, no matter how flaky my aunt and uncle were, they could always be counted on in a pinch. I watched the delivery truck pull away when another vehicle pulled up. My uncle's new sapphire blue Lincoln Navigator.

"The Melinskys are here!" I yelled. "Perfect timing."

My aunt immediately flung herself into my mother's arms, while Louis stood like a statue against the living room wall.

"Louis," I said, "you remember the book club ladies. Shirley, Lucinda, Louise, Cecilia, and Myrna."

"Yes, of course. Nice to see you again."

The poor man looked totally out of his element and I felt bad. Especially since he had gone out of his way to bring this crew some needed refreshments. Then, before I could say a word, Myrna insisted he sit between her and Louise on the couch and all but yanked him onto the seat cushion. Everyone thanked him for the impromptu meal. Myself included.

My aunt flung her orange paisley duster onto a chair and, with a sweeping motion, pointed to the kitchen. "Eat, everyone! Eat! The food's not going to serve itself."

My mother miraculously regained her composure and reiterated what her sister had just said. "Yes. Come eat! Sit anywhere."

At the sound of the word "eat," Streetman emerged from the master bedroom and scurried under the kitchen table.

"He can have small pieces of the meats, but don't give him the cheese," my mother said. "He gets a loose stomach."

I munched on half a turkey sub as my mother told everyone exactly what we had discovered and how "absolutely brave and fearless" Streetman was. I thought I'd gag.

Shirley wiped the corners of her mouth with a small

cocktail napkin and sighed. "Oh, Lordy, Harriet. I wasn't going to say anything to you. Not tonight anyway. But you'll find out soon enough."

My mother sat bolt upright in her favorite armchair and leaned forward, not to miss a single word. "What? What will I find out? It can't possibly be any worse than this."

"Not worse. But bad enough. I was at the rec center admin building this morning to pay my dues and I overheard the most dreadful woman speaking. She was talking about the Precious Pooches Holiday Extravaganza and she told whoever was listening that she hired professional designers from New York to create the costumes for her dog. My gosh, Harriet, how can we compete with something like that?"

"Did you catch the name of her dog?" my mother asked.

"Sir Breccki something."

"Not Sir Breckenthall the Third?"

Shirley shrugged. "Could be. Why?"

"He's a third-generation Cavalier King Charles Spaniel and his owner is a first-generation—"

"More sandwiches, anyone?" I bellowed.

Then the doorbell rang and everyone froze.

"Did you call anyone else, Mom?" I asked.

"No. Don't open the security door. And only open the front door a teensy bit."

"You can relax. It's Herb."

"If I didn't know any better"—he marched himself across the living room and into the kitchen—"I'd swear you were holding a wake for that guy."

My mother motioned to the sandwiches. "Help yourself. Phee and I figured you'd be yammering with the pinochle men at Curley's."

Herb looked at his watch. "I will be. In about twenty minutes. That's why I came over here first. I'm only going to stay for one beer at Curley's. Maybe two, but I'll be back by quarter to ten the latest. I figured you always take that dog out around that time, so I thought I'd keep you company. You know, so you won't be alone outside."

"That's a very sweet gesture, but I'll be fine. Streetman is extremely protective."

Protective? Of what? His chewy bones? "That's a yes. My mother will expect you between nine forty-five and ten. And thanks."

Herb nodded and walked over to the tray of subs.

"What did you do that for?" my mother whispered.

"So I don't have to drive back and watch while the dog takes his evening wee-wee."

Even though there were ten of us in the living room and kitchen, it sounded as if thirty different conversations were going on at once. I caught bits and pieces as I moved about the place. Sir Breckenthall's designer costumes and the corpse behind the house were neck and neck.

Then, out of the blue, my aunt stood up and clasped her hands. "You shouldn't stay here alone tonight, Harriet. You can stay with Louis and me. Phee can take the dog with her."

What? How'd this happen? I opened my mouth, but the only thing that came out was a small squeak.

Then everyone began to offer up their own houses. Amid the cacophony, I heard things such as "on Cecilia's couch," "on Myrna's futon," and "in Louise's guest bedroom."

"Enough, everyone." my mother said. "I'll be perfectly fine right here. Herb's across the street and the sheriff's posse will be patrolling. Isn't that right, Phee? Isn't that what Deputy Ranston told you?"

"Uh-huh. Patrolling."

"So there. I'll be absolutely safe."

Myrna stood up and walked to the patio door. The deputies had left for the night, and it was dark out there. She cleared her throat and spoke as if she was delivering a proclamation. "Unless the murderer returns to the scene of the crime."

Chapter 4

I awoke the next morning to the sound of my phone and not the blare from my alarm clock. Seven forty-one. It couldn't be good news. My thoughts raced from Marshall leaving at some obscene hour and winding up in a horrific accident on the highway to the sheriff's office calling me to tell me someone broke into my mother's house. I lunged for the receiver and sat up.

"Phee!" My mother's voice was sharp and loud. "I thought you'd be up hours ago. Have you seen the morning news? It came on at four thirty."

"Uh, I haven't even seen my morning cup of coffee, let alone the news. Are you all right?"

"Yes. Of course I am. I turned on the news as soon as I got up. Every station is covering the Galbraiths' dead body. And not one of them mentioned who found it. All they said was 'authorities have discovered a dead body belonging to an unidentified male in his thirties or early forties.' No mention of Streetman whatsoever. Can you believe it?"

"Uh, yeah, well . . ."

"And another thing. The sheriff's office has cars all over the block. They're checking the neighboring yards with some sort of large hound dog. Presumably looking for more bodies. Streetman could barely do his business outside with all the commotion."

"Mom," I lied, "I don't think they're looking for more bodies. I think they're seeing if the killer left any evidence elsewhere. You know. Maybe the Galbraiths' house wasn't the first choice when they dumped the body."

The last thing I needed was for my mother to take the situation to the extreme.

"See what you can find out when you get into work. I know Nate's probably made some calls. Make one more and tell me what's going on."

"Okay. Okay. I'll call you sometime this morning. In the meantime, please stay out of their way. The sheriff's deputies, that is. I'm already on shaky ground with Ranston. By the way, that was really nice of Aunt Ina and Uncle Louis to bring that spread last night."

"Louis was grateful we got him out of that mess last year. He was the prime suspect in a murder, for heaven's sake. And as for your aunt, well, you know Ina."

"Anyway, it was nice of them and I made sure to thank them."

"Yes, yes. Me, too. Honestly, Phee, I don't know what's more upsetting at this point. The fact a killer was behind my house or the thought that some obnoxious woman is paying a New York designer to ruin Streetman's chances of winning that contest."

I was about to brush off her last comment when something occurred to me. If I could keep my mother focused on that pet parade or whatever the heck it was, she'd have less time to mull over yesterday's unfortunate discovery.

"Shirley Johnson is an absolute genius when it comes

to designing costumes. You've seen that handmade Teddy bear collection of hers. I'm sure the two of you will outdo and outclass any fancy New York designer."

My mother sighed. "I suppose so. Besides, Streetman has a natural charm, not a snotty pedigree."

"Good. Good. Look. I've got to get going if I'm to be at work on time. Call you later."

I made myself a quick cup of coffee, took an even quicker shower, and selected an outfit that was bound to make Marshall wish he hadn't been away on a case for the past few days. Nothing like a silky top and slim-fitting slacks to say "I've missed you."

Augusta, the office secretary, was at her desk when I got in the door, but Nate hadn't arrived yet and I wasn't expecting Marshall until midmorning.

"Good morning, Augusta. I suppose you've seen the local news."

"Please don't tell me that dead body in Sun City West has anything to do with your mother's book club. I don't think I can stand much more of that drama. Every few months it's something."

"It's something, all right. It was my mother's dog who found it. Right behind their house, too."

"Yikes. Anyone she knew?"

"Thankfully, no."

"Someone got lazy and didn't want to drive into the desert, that's all. Nothing for your mother to be worried about. Then again, knowing your mother, I'm not too sure."

"That's what I told her. At least it didn't appear to be one of those drug-related crimes where the gangs or cartels dump the body. My mother would have packed up with Streetman and moved in with my aunt Ina or, worse yet, me! Anyway, those drug cartel victims usually have gunshot wounds or stab wounds. Well, according to the news anyway. But I saw this body. Up close. Unfortunately. Long story. Anyway, he looked poisoned. Yellow face, dried blood from his nose. Say, do you know anything about poisonings?"

"Can't say that I do." Augusta adjusted a small floral clip in her bouffant hairdo and steepled her fingers. "Back home we usually shoot them. Faster that way."

I had momentarily forgotten Augusta was raised on a farm out in the Wisconsin boondocks, where justice was served hot and fast.

"Anyway, I called Nate yesterday when it all happened and he was going to see what he could find out. Geez, that'll teach me not to stop by my mother's house on the way home from work."

Augusta grinned. "Or any other time."

"Very funny. Give me a shout when Nate gets in, will you?"

"He usually beats me to it, but I'll try."

I walked into my office, booted up the computer, and picked up where I left off yesterday on some spreadsheets. One of the things I liked about accounting was that numbers and figures didn't lie, unless someone was manipulating them. And there were ways to figure that out. Clean, direct, and simple. Unlike murder investigations.

My eyes moved from column to column, and I was so engrossed I jumped when I heard Nate's tap on my doorjamb.

"Hey, kiddo. I see you survived the night."

"Barely. I left there a little past nine, with most of the crowd. Shirley and Lucinda stayed to help my mother clean up. According to her phone call this morning, Herb showed up to walk the dog so she wouldn't have to be alone outside. As it turned out, Streetman had a four-person security entourage. Anyway, she said the deputies are swarming the neighborhood. What were you able to find out?"

Nate pulled a chair over to my desk and sat down. Leaning on one elbow, he smiled. "More than I wanted to know, I'm afraid. In the pit of my stomach, I have a feeling Marshall and I will be called into this case on a consult. I'll know for sure in a few days. I gave your boyfriend the heads-up late last night. After he got off the phone with you. Next time, have shorter calls, huh?"

I grimaced. "What makes you think they'll ask for your help? And more pressing, what did you find out? Was I right? Was the guy poisoned?"

"Maybe. No gunshot wounds. No stab wounds. No blunt trauma wounds. They're running toxicology tests and that could take a while. Blood. Urine. Stomach contents. You name it. Not unusual for a four- to six-week wait time."

"Four to six weeks? That's ridiculous."

"That's reality, I'm afraid. But, in this case, they may hurry things along. Seems the victim worked in middle management for a major food distributor in the valley. If he was poisoned, it may have something to do with that entire industry. The Maricopa County Sheriff's Office needs to rule out other scenarios and, since they're so inundated, they may reach out to us like they've done before."

"Huh? What? What scenarios?"

"The usual motives for murder: love, revenge, power, money—"

"Quit being so general, Nate. You know what I mean. What did the sheriff's office say? Did you get stuck with Ranston?"

"Bowman. They need to rule out family, friends, and acquaintances in Sun City West, but right now they're concentrating on his job. The sheriff's office surmised the guy's death had something to do with the division he managed—seafood."

I opened my mouth slightly and then closed it. Seafood. None of this was making sense.

Nate made some sort of *humrph* sound. "Apparently, there are some major issues with the seafood industry. Glad I never gave up red meat."

"Issues? What issues?"

"Bowman wasn't specific. All he told me was they'd had a similar case a few months ago. Still unsolved. That body was found in a riparian preserve in Gilbert."

"Gilbert. Good. That's about two hours from here if you factor in the traffic. Um, you said something about family and friends. If the guy's death didn't have anything to do with his job, then maybe it wasn't a coincidence he was dumped in my mother's backyard. Come on, you must know more."

Nate shrugged. "All we have is a name and address from his driver's license. And an insurance card. Blue Cross Blue Shield of Arizona. Good luck getting information out of them. The sheriff's office is trying to track down next of kin. I imagine they've already secured a warrant to go inside the guy's residence, but since it's in Peoria, they'll have to work with the local police department."

"Ugh. I remember what a pain in the neck that was when we had to work with the Surprise Police Department last year. Thank goodness they were friendly."

"I'm sure Peoria will be the same."

"So, who's the victim? We can't keep referring to him as 'the body.' "

"Cameron Tully. Age thirty-eight. And until the sheriff's office releases that information to the press—"

"I know. I know. Mum's the word."

Nate went back to his office and I concentrated on my accounting. At midmorning, I gave my mother a call and found out the sheriff's deputies had walked through the Galbraiths' house.

"They didn't find anything," my mother said. "Streetman and I happened to stroll by in front of the place and ran into Deputy Ranston as he and his partner were leaving."

"*Happened* to stroll by?"

"I can't help it if we decided to take our walk as they pulled up to the house. It's not my fault I can see what's going on from the back patio. I had Streetman leashed and we enjoyed a leisurely walk in front of the Galbraiths' house. Not my fault the dog takes his time sniffing around. We were standing on the sidewalk when the deputies came out."

"So, just like that, they saw you and told you the crime wasn't committed in the house?"

"Not exactly. I overheard them saying, 'That's an all clear,' so I asked, 'Does this mean the body was dumped?' and Bowman, the one who looks like Grizzly Adams, said, 'Mrs. Plunkett, you can't keep interfering.'"

My neck began to stiffen and I rolled it from side to side. "Oh brother."

"And that's when I said, 'Maybe I should just push the "Call Us Button" for KPHO.' Bowman threw his hands in the air and told me nothing was touched in the house. I told him it wouldn't've mattered really because I was going to call Janet Galbraith anyway."

"Oh geez."

"Not that it's any of my business, but that man should have his blood pressure checked. I've never seen anyone turn so many colors of red in so short a time. So, was your boss able to find anything else out?"

"The name of the victim and that's all I can tell you. And let me reiterate what you already know—he's not a resident in Sun City West."

My mother went on to tell me she was meeting Myrna and Shirley for lunch, but Lucinda had a dentist appointment and Cecilia was volunteering at her church along with Louise. I told her I'd call again in the evening and we left it at that.

Frazzled from the call, I stood up, shook my head like a punk rocker, and groaned. That was the second Marshall came in.

"Remind me not to be gone so long."

"Oh my gosh. I didn't even hear you. I've been on the phone with my mother. A veritable nightmare. Worse than the golf course body. Although he turned out to be a resident. Lucky you were still in Minnesota for that one. What am I babbling about? I'm so glad you're back."

Marshall kicked the door closed with his foot, pulled me close, and gave me a sweet but short kiss. "Okay. Break time's over."

"What? No coffee?"

"I've got some news that might put a smile on your face and, from the looks of things, you could use one."

"Don't keep me waiting. What news?"

"I got a call from the Realtor. We don't have to wait until November first to move into the new place. The current tenants are moving out this weekend and a cleaning crew will be there during the week. The owner says we've got the green light next weekend."

"Next weekend? That's less than ten days away. We've

got to notify the electric company and the cable, and what about a phone? Should we keep a landline? And water. The water company. We've got to tell everyone the dates have changed."

"Relax. We've got plenty of time. Usually they require a five-day notice. We can figure all of this out tonight. The good thing is my place came furnished. Essentially I'm moving in with the clothes on my back."

"And cartons of miscellaneous."

"I'll have you know miscellaneous is highly underrated." He gave me a quick peck on the cheek and darted out. "I've got a lunch meeting on that missing relative case from Phoenix. Smile. This is great news."

Of course it was great news. Marshall and I were practically counting the days until we were able to move into our own house. We found one in Vistancia, a wonderful multi-generational neighborhood not far from where I was currently renting a small semi-furnished casita. Small and cozy for one. Cramped and impossible for two. I should've been ecstatic, but instead, I was jittery. Too many things at once. Especially the latest fiasco in Sun City West. I took a deep breath, returned to my computer, and forced myself to focus on numbers and figures.

I grabbed a ready-made sandwich at the Quick Stop during my lunch break and spent the rest of the day in my own little accounting world. I had made lasagna a few days before and stuck it in the freezer. That, along with a tossed salad, was going to be our dinner. Unfortunately, the lasagna never made it out of the freezer and into the microwave to defrost. That's because my mother phoned at six forty-five insistent we drive over there.

"I'm not kidding you, Phee. I'm positive I saw someone poking around the back of the Galbraiths' house. I saw beams from a flashlight."

"Maybe it was one of the investigators from the sheriff's office. Did you call them?"

"Of course I did. They sent a posse car over, but that was after I used my Screamer on whoever was behind the house."

"The Screamer? That loud alarm device Myrna got you?"

My mother's voice got softer. "In retrospect, using it might not have been such a good idea. I mean, I didn't see the flashlight beacon, so they may have already left when I went to get the Screamer. I closed the patio door behind me, but the noise must have scared poor Streetman, because he peed all over the kitchen floor."

I squelched a laugh and handed the phone to Marshall. "Here, you talk to her."

Ten minutes later we were in his car and on the way to Sun City West. My mother felt bad we hadn't eaten dinner yet and insisted we try some of the tuna salad she bought at the supermarket.

"Have a bite to eat, first." She motioned to a table with toasted bagels and assorted store-bought salads. "Then you can go see what they were after at the Galbraiths'. The posse volunteers took a quick look and left. They're probably spending more time on paperwork than they did checking the place. And by the way, that crime tape is still up. How long before they take it down?"

Marshall lifted a bagel top from the plate and spread some tuna salad on it. "Thanks, Harriet. As long as the crime tape is up, the place is off-limits. Tell you what. First thing tomorrow, I'll give the sheriff's office a call and ask if they'd be willing to send someone over to have a look-see. I'll even meet them. We've got a solid working relationship, and I'm sure they'll want to keep it that way."

"Maybe Ranston was right after all," I said. "He told me criminals are sometimes short in the planning department. Maybe whoever they killed had some information on him that the killer meant to get and then, in his haste to dump the body, forgot about it until later."

I was careful not to mention the name or my mother would be Googling every Tully in Sun City West.

She nodded in agreement. "That's probably why they came back this evening. Oh dear God! That means I was only a few yards from a cold-blooded killer."

"You don't know that, Mom."

"I know this much. Something fishy's going on and it's not the tuna."

Chapter 5

Deputy Ranston agreed to meet Marshall at a little past nine the following day. Neither of them was sure what they'd find, considering the forensic team had spent hours scouring the place, but if it meant placating my mother, they were more than happy to oblige.

Meanwhile, I spent that morning complaining to Augusta and Nate about how this recent murder was driving me crazy.

"At least they released the name," Augusta said. "It was on the morning news. Who names their kid Cameron? Whatever happened to old-fashioned names like Robert or James?"

"They released the name? The full name? What else did they say? Darn it. I should've turned on the news this morning."

Nate popped a K-cup into the Keurig and motioned for me to slow down.

"You don't understand," I said. "Now that my mother and her friends know the victim's name, she'll be relentless about tracking down any relatives. And by 'relentless' I'm not referring to her. I'm talking about myself. She'll insist I investigate. Good grief. I've got enough on my plate. Marshall and I have less than ten days to move into our new place and we haven't even hired a moving company. Not that we have all that much stuff, but what we do have adds up. Even if we used both our cars and yours and Augusta's, we'd still need someone to move the living room chairs I bought and my desk. Oh, and the kitchen table. I can't forget that. It's a gorgeous southwestern oval-style table with—"

"Got a pickup truck you can use," Augusta said, "but first you'd have to unload the hay bales I've got in it."

Nate put his coffee cup down and scratched his head. "Hay bales? What'd you do? Buy a farm in the country?"

"Not me. A friend of mine. She's raising donkeys and goats. Also bought some guinea hens for ambience."

"Um, uh, well, that's really nice of you, Augusta. Really nice," I said, "but I'm afraid Marshall and I will need something bigger. We were thinking of hiring the retired firefighters who run a small moving company."

"Good plan," Nate said. "If I were you, I'd get right on it. It's October. All those snowbirds are coming back, and, from what I've heard, they're buying property, not renting. Those moving companies are going to be pretty busy."

"Yeah, you're right. When Marshall gets in, I'll let him know. Meanwhile, I'd better start on some of the billing."

I had completed four invoices when I heard Augusta shout, "Marshall's coming in. I can see him from the window. Good thing, too, because his eleven o'clock should be here any minute!"

His eleven o'clock was an elderly priest who had lost contact with one of his relatives. Something about finalizing a will. I figured I'd better wait until after Marshall's appointment before pouncing all over him regarding this morning's escapade at the Galbraiths'.

Augusta was spot-on about the timing. Father Obernon and Marshall nearly collided with each other at the door, according to her. "By the time he gets out of there, he'll be starving." She leaned inside my office door. "I'll see if Mr. Williams wants me to order a pizza for the office. You in?"

"Absolutely. Last night we ate the worst tuna salad in creation."

"One of your recipes?"

"Very funny. No. Something my mother bought."

"Hmm, that's interesting."

"How so?"

"I ordered a tuna steak at the Mall Grill last week and it was dreadful. Abominable really. It didn't even taste like seared tuna."

"Maybe it was a bad catch."

"I'll tell you one thing. It was a bad meal."

The pizza arrived moments after Father Obernon left the office. Good thing Augusta thought ahead, because the four of us were practically starving. We sat around the workroom table hoping the phones would be quiet and no walk-ins would interrupt us.

"A whopping zero at your mother's place this morning," Marshall said. "Of course, we really didn't expect to find anything. Those forensic teams are damn thorough. Still, there's the off-chance possibility whoever was snooping around found what they were looking for and left."

I shook my head. "More likely that Screamer of my mother's scared the daylights out of them and they'll be back."

"Funny, but Ranston had the same thought. They're

boosting up patrols in her neighborhood. I'm glad I've got a decent relationship with the guy, because he's certainly willing to share information with me."

"He should be." I reached for a napkin. "If it wasn't for this office, half of their cases would be stone cold."

Augusta took a gulp of her Coke and cleared her throat. "Speaking of stone cold, any news on what kind of poison killed Cameron Tully?"

"They won't know for weeks," I said. "Something about a zillion bodily fluid tests and stomach contents."

Nate laughed. "Someone's been listening."

Just then the phone rang and Augusta got up to answer it. "I don't want it to go to the answering machine."

Two seconds later she shouted, "Phee, it's your mother!"

I looked at Marshall. "Aargh. She's probably calling to find out what you and Ranston uncovered, or didn't uncover, this morning."

"No. We already spoke with her. She and Streetman were sitting on her back patio watching us. I'm telling you, if we ever need a surveillance team, we can always hire those two."

"Okay, Augusta!" I yelled back. "Tell her I'll be right there. I'll pick up in my office."

Nate gave Marshall a poke in the elbow and snickered. "Looks like Phee and Augusta found a way to get us to clean up."

"Hey! I'll trade places with you if you'd like. You can placate my mother."

"No way, kiddo. Putting a pizza box in the trash is the far better deal."

I hustled to my office and grabbed the phone. "What's up? I thought you already spoke with Marshall."

"That's not why I'm calling. The TV stations released

the name of the dead man. Cameron Tully. From Peoria. I spent most of the morning looking up all the Tullys in Sun City West, but I couldn't find anyone with that last name. I suppose I should be relieved, but what if the deceased does have relatives here? So, I was wondering—"

"Oh no. We're not starting this again. The sheriff's office has a good handle on it, and I'm sure that's exactly what they're doing. Checking for any possible connections."

"Good for them. But it wouldn't hurt for Nate and Marshall to see what they can dig up."

I tried to keep from screaming and took a long, slow breath. "They're not even on this case, and I'm not about to bother them with something I'm positive the authorities are already doing."

"Fine. Then if you don't want to do that, the least you can do is see if Cindy Dolton from the dog park knows anything. Ever since you first contacted her regarding the book curse, she's been more than willing to pass on the information she gets."

It was true. I had developed a pretty neat relationship with Sun City West's number one source of gossip. Deep down, I thought Cindy knew I was really investigating and not contributing to the rumor mill. I wasn't so sure the same could be said for my mother.

"I'll see what I can do." *My God. I've lost my mind.* "Maybe after work. On my way home. She's usually there right before dusk. But this is the last thing I'm doing. I've got way too many things to deal with right now."

"That's right. Ina said you're moving this coming week. Then she babbled on and on about color schemes. That reminds me. Cecilia said she's willing to go over to your new place and sprinkle holy water around it. She sneaks it out of the church when no one's looking. And Gloria Wong, you remember Gloria Wong? My former neighbor who moved in with her daughter? Gloria said she'd be happy to help you arrange the furniture according to feng shui. It'll create a sense of calm and an overall harmonizing effect."

Great. Maybe she can get together with Aunt Ina and the two of them can battle it out for wackiest design of the year. "The only calm I need right now is the quiet joy of working in my office. I really have to get back to work."

"Call me when you find out something from Cindy."

"Okay. Okay."

"Want me to keep you company?" Marshall asked when I told him about my plans to drop by the dog park on my way home from work. He had stepped inside my office to make sure everything was all right. Even though my mother was behaving relatively calmly, he and I were both on edge, waiting for that to change. Maybe it was because my mother realized Cameron Tully wasn't actually killed in the house behind hers that she was able to function without bursting into histrionics every few seconds. This wasn't like the last time a body surfaced in her neighborhood. That victim was a resident, and rumors of a serial killer were rampant. Thankfully, this time it was merely a "body drop-off."

"Nah. You're wearing good shoes. You might as well go straight to my place and put the casserole that I made in the oven. I'm trying to use up all the food I have so we don't have to take it with us to the new place. Besides, I don't plan on being at the park for more than a few minutes."

Marshall gave me a peck on the cheek and went back to his office. The next time I would get another kiss wouldn't be until later that evening. Unless I counted the dog slobber from Bundles, Cindy's white poodle. Or Maltese. I always got those confused.

Cindy was standing by the fence at the dog park when I pulled up. Her short gray hair looked as if it had been permed, and she was wearing new glasses. I rolled my car window down and waved. Then I shouted, "Don't move. I need to ask you something!"

If I thought the dog park had been crowded on other occasions, this balmy evening in early autumn had brought out every canine owner from one side of the municipality to the next. Clusters of small dogs jumping on one another were everywhere. The benches were full and it was SRO by the fences.

"Wow!" I walked toward Cindy. "This place is worse than senior citizen day at the supermarket."

"Wait till the snowbirds come back. You'll have to bring your own chair. Where's Streetman? I thought you came here with him."

"I've been spared. Actually, I stopped by hoping to catch you. It's regarding the body that was found near my mother's house."

"It was *her* house? Harriet's house? Oh my gosh, I didn't know that. She must be going crazy by now."

I shrugged. "Yeah. You can say that. Between the dead body and that pet parade extravaganza she signed Streetman up for, she's like a lunatic. Even though the sheriff's deputies have no reason to believe the victim had any association whatsoever with Sun City West, my mother isn't all that sure. That's why she was hoping you might have heard something. Anything."

"I hate to say it, but I haven't heard a thing. Not a blasted thing. And believe me, I've heard plenty of other stuff. I think what they're saying on the news is true. The killer or killers stashed the body where they thought no one would find it right away. Uh-oh. You don't suppose they meant it as a message for the homeowners? Like in *The Godfather*? With the horse's head?"

"Oh, heck no. My mother's been on the phone with the homeowners and they've never heard of Cameron Tully."

"Well, that takes care of one rumor. By the way, I heard your mother signed Streetman up for all three costume contests. I enrolled Bundles in the Halloween one, and that's enough for me. He's going as Casper the Friendly Ghost. With all his white fur, it's a no-brainer. What about Streetman?"

"I saw one costume. An acorn or something. My mother will be lucky if he doesn't tear off his costume until after the parade. Or worse, become too amorous with the other dogs in the lineup. Listen, if you do hear anything about Cameron Tully, would you please give me a call? You've got my office number."

"Sure thing. Are you going to the pet parade?"

"If I don't, my mother will run me out of town."

Cindy laughed and I made a beeline for my car. It was a short visit, and I made it home in time to help Marshall set the table. I'd packed most of my plates and utensils, so we were down to two place servings and lots of paper products.

"I can't believe we've only got nine days," I said. "Or is it eight? Unless we get ahold of a moving company, we'll be stuck with Augusta's livestock transport."

"What?"

"Her truck. She's helping a friend. Don't ask."

"As soon as we're done eating, I'm calling those retired firefighters."

Marshall and I downed the ham and cheese casserole and did a bit more packing before calling it a night.

I was amazed at how much stuff I had managed to cram into cabinets, drawers, and closets. *Dear Lord. I've become my mother. Partial boxes of God-knows-what, just in case.*

He was already in bed and half-asleep when I remembered I had promised my mother I'd give her a call regarding Cindy Dolton. I mumbled something to Marshall and walked back to the living room. I knew my mother would still be awake because the late-night news was still on. I placed the call and took a breath. "Hi, Mom. Sorry I'm calling so late. No news from Cindy Dolton."

"Give her time. If that Cameron what's his name has any friends or relatives here, she'll find out before the sheriff's office. Of course, that's not saying much. You know how they bumble around."

"I don't think they actually bumble around. It's not a TV show where, all of a sudden, the fingerprints match something in a database."

"It's the twenty-first century, Phee. They have technology. They just need to use it."

I didn't want to get into a long-winded discussion with my mother about the Maricopa County Sheriff's Office, so I simply said, "Uh-huh," and let her continue.

"It's not bad enough there was a corpse behind my house, but that horrid woman who owns Sir Breckenthall sent a letter to the rec center demanding they line up the dogs with the pedigreed ones first and then have 'those mixed-breed gutter mutts' at the tail end. And don't you dare laugh at her pun."

"No. I wouldn't. Um, how did you find out she did that? Whoever she is."

"I heard it firsthand. Myrna did, too. She and I were having our nails done this afternoon when, all of a sudden, this pompous overbearing woman seated across from Myrna began to tell Jeong, that's one of the manicurists, about the letter she sent. And that misery of a woman was none other than that too-much-money-in-my-life Phyllis Gruber."

"Hmm, what did Jeong say?"

"Nothing. She doesn't speak English."

"What did you and Myrna do?"

"We didn't want Phyllis to think we were eavesdropping, so we didn't say anything. Now I'm sorry I didn't open my mouth. I've been fuming about this all night. Well, this and that dead body. Cameron what's his name."

"Try not to think about it and get some sleep." *Try not to think about it? That's like an open invitation to dwell on it. Why on earth did I say that?*

"The murder investigation is one thing, Phee. The matter of discrimination is another. There are laws against that, you know. Constitutional laws. Or maybe Supreme Court decisions. Something like that. Anyway, I refuse to have my Streetman at the end of the line because some prissy snob insists her purebred canine get special treatment in that parade. So help me if the rec center tries to pull a stunt like that, I'll hire a lawyer. There are laws, I tell you."

Every nerve in my body was on high alert. "For people, yes! Not dogs!"

It had finally gotten to that point. My mother refused to recognize her little Chiweenie as a dog and not a human. I tried to be understanding. "I know this is upsetting, but I'm sure the people at the rec center will be sensitive to everyone's feelings. They must be used to wacky, demanding people by now."

My mother groaned and we ended the call. I tried to crawl under the covers without making too much fuss so as not to wake Marshall.

No luck. He leaned on his side, propping up his head with an elbow. With the dim hall light behind me, he looked even more adorable than ever. "Everything okay, hon?"

"As long as the Supreme Court doesn't try to reinterpret any decisions."

Chapter 6

The following week was a blur. Work and moving prep had morphed into a strange reality of phone calls, packing, labeling, account keeping, and placating my mother. No headway on the Cameron Tully case and only a cursory toxicology report, according to Nate and Marshall.

"Give it time," Nate reminded me. "It takes weeks, not days."

That conversation was sometime during the middle of the week and nothing had changed by the weekend. Except for me. It felt as if my mind was spinning all over the place with the big move scheduled for Saturday.

Marshall had hired the retired firefighters from Sun City West, and I was expecting a somewhat geriatric crew to show up at my house that morning. Instead, four men who looked as if they'd stepped out of a *Playgirl* magazine came to my door. They had already been to Marshall's house and had loaded up his paltry boxes so he could get over to the new place for some last-minute cleaning. Miraculously, the utility companies had turned on our electricity and water and the cable company set up our TVs and internet a few days before.

Our rental house was only a few blocks from the casita I had called home since I first moved out west. I had chosen to rent a place in Vistancia, having fallen in love with the mountain vistas and the easy access to major highways and shopping. Other than my address, very little would change. I'd still be able to meet my friend Lyndy for late-night swims at the development pool or hour-long coffee shop visits on weekends.

Unlike my predictable schedule, Marshall's schedule meant out-of-town surveillance at times or unexpected late nights. Still, he managed to work out at the fitness center or go for a quick run when the mood struck him. Juggling two residences this past year had gotten tiresome, but most of all, we wanted to spend our lives and our time together.

I followed the moving van to our new residence and couldn't believe the street when we pulled up. The house next to ours had a giant plastic spider on its roof and an assortment of graveyard "bones" in the yard. Across the street was another makeshift cemetery and a splattered witch on a tree. For a minute I panicked, knowing there'd be trick-or-treaters and I would be stuck at the Halloween dog parade. Then I remembered my mother telling me all three events were to be held on Fridays. I was in luck. Halloween was a few days later.

The movers were unbelievably fast and careful. Nothing broke and nothing was lost. By midafternoon the furnishings were in place and the boxes neatly piled up in their respective rooms. It was definitely worth the trouble labeling each box. Only one dilemma remained—the new bed.

Marshall and I had spent an agonizing week in the

summer testing out mattresses until we could finally agree on one that wouldn't torture us. The delivery was scheduled for later in the month since we weren't expecting the early move. And neither was the mattress store. Later in the month was when our bed would arrive. Apparently, the mattress we'd selected was still at the factory in North Carolina. That left us with two choices, an air mattress or the small folding couch I had brought with me from Mankato. Both options stunk.

In the end, we decided to opt for the air mattress because "no coils will kill us," according to Marshall. It was a long and tedious day, broken up only by short treks to fast-food places for lunch and dinner.

"Brace yourself for a long morning at the supermarket," I said as we tossed a sheet on the air mattress and scrambled to find the pillowcases. "Other than some canned goods and paper products, we're down to one box of crackers."

"At least your mother didn't offer to give us something from her freezer."

"Not yet. She did offer to help us unpack, along with Shirley and Lucinda, but I managed to talk her out of it."

Marshall let out a sigh of relief and stretched out on the mattress. "Coffee. We don't have coffee. Tomorrow morning both of us are going to be like zombies. Good thing I can get us to Dunkin' Donuts on autopilot."

My head hit the pillow and I was fast asleep before I knew it. The next day was equally frenetic, but we were able to load up the fridge, stock our pantry, and unpack the necessities. Things like hanging pictures and putting up shelves would have to wait until we had more energy.

"Hmm," Marshall said as we took a midafternoon break to munch on some cold cuts and cheese, "I imagine your mother is still boiling over Sir Wrecking Ball or whatever that dog's name is."

"Sir Breckenthall *the Third*." I placed the emphasis on the last two words.

"Oh brother," he moaned. "You know what that means, don't you? She'll be driving poor Shirley crazy to make costumes—the likes of which Broadway has never seen."

"Good. Anything to keep her mind off that murder. You have to admit, it *is* kind of strange. Having a body dropped off behind a neighbor's house and using their own tarp to conceal it. Lucky break or what?"

"The house sits on a cul-de-sac with no through traffic. Ranston's first thoughts were maybe it was their landscaper, but it turns out the Galbraiths do their own landscaping. Not much work with a gravel yard and cacti."

I put a slice of Havarti on a cracker. "Someone from a utility company, maybe?"

"The deputies looked into that as well. None of the companies were at that house in years. The gas, electric, and water meters are read by a computerized system, along with the cable."

"Well, someone had to know about that tarp and the large grill."

Marshall took a quick bite of his mixed cold-cut sandwich. "Oh my gosh. We're forgetting the obvious. The grill! It's enormous and had to be delivered and installed. I'll call Ranston first thing tomorrow morning when we get into the office."

We let Olive Garden take care of our dinner and called it an early night. I checked in with my mother to see how she was doing, and so far so good. The sheriff's patrols were monitoring the area and she didn't seem as distraught as she had been the other day. But all of that was about to change when the official toxicology report was released four days before the Halloween pet parade.

Deputy Ranston called our office on that Tuesday

morning to inform Nate and Marshall of the findings but, more important, to ask if they'd be willing to consult on the case. So much for the perfect little nirvana I imagined we'd enjoy.

"Must be real bad," Augusta said. "Whatever killed that man. Or the sheriff's office wouldn't be bringing our office into the case."

I bit my lower lip and popped my second K-cup of dark roast into the Keurig. "Nah. I think it has more to do with that serial killer in Phoenix. Everyone's on edge. The police department . . . the sheriff's office. They're thin on resources, that's all. I wouldn't read too much into it. By the way, did Nate or Marshall say what time they'd be back from their meeting at the sheriff's office? I forgot to ask. Um. Not that it's my business."

"Uh-huh. And no, they didn't. Well, I might as well take my break along with you. Hold on a second. I'll pull up the local news on the computer and see what they have to say about the killer in our own neck of the woods."

I pulled a chair over to Augusta's desk and took a sip of coffee. She unwrapped some sort of a muffin and took a bite. "Want one? They're bacon and maple syrup muffins. Family recipe."

"Thanks. No. I like bacon. And I like maple syrup. But not together."

Just then she looked at the screen and put the muffin down. "Well, Holy Hell. I'll be darned. I was only kidding when I thought the news was going to have an update on the body dumper in your mother's neighborhood. They released the toxicology information. Can you read the ribbon on the bottom of KPHO?"

"Yeah. Sort of. I'll move in closer."

"You're going to have to get bifocals one of these days, you know."

"Don't remind me."

We stared at the headline ribbon at the bottom of the KPHO website and didn't say a word.

Finally, Augusta spoke. "You wouldn't see this kind of poisoning back in Wisconsin. We stick to normal toxins. Antifreeze, lead, mercury—"

"This is Arizona. Nothing's normal here. Not even the palm trees, apparently. I had no idea those things were so dangerous. I see them all over the place. Every fancy landscape has at least one of those sago palms with the feathered plumes."

"Yep. Keep reading. It says ingesting the most minuscule leaf or seed can cause vomiting, diarrhea, jaundice, bleeding, and death."

"We know about the death part. Um, at least Cameron did." I was still staring at the screen. "Oh no. Oh no, no, no! I've got to call my mother before she sees this. She's going to go crazy checking all over the neighborhood for those things. Quick. Hand me your phone."

Augusta shoved the clunky office phone toward me and I dialed as fast as I could. Maybe my mother hadn't turned on the news. Oh hell. Who was I kidding?

My mother pounced on the phone before it completed the first ring. "Phee! I can't stop and talk to you right now. Herb is on his way over. We've got to scrutinize the neighborhood for any of those poisonous palm trees. That's what killed the man we found under the Galbraiths' grill. It was on the news. Nate and Marshall should've known and you should've called me sooner. I had to hear it from Herb. Of all people."

"Slow down, Mom. It'll be all right."

"It'll be all right when Herb and I are done canvassing the neighborhood."

"I don't think any of your neighbors' trees killed Cameron Tully."

"Cameron Tully? Who cares? All I care about is my poor Streetman. Now I have to create a new walking map for him in case you or one of the ladies takes him out. I can't risk having him anywhere near one of those god-awful sago palms. Those things should be removed from every greenhouse and warehouse immediately."

And here we go. . . .

The walking map. I had completely forgotten about the walking map. My mother put more effort into Streetman's map than National Geographic did with any of theirs. She had painstakingly noted every rock, bush, pole, and mailbox he liked to lift his leg on. In addition, she had circled all of the yards that were off-limits to him and had included anecdotal notes on the bottom of the map with such tidbits as "Crazy screaming lady will come out of the house if the dog so much as steps foot on her gravel."

"Okay, Mom. I won't keep you. Maybe you can just put in a few small notes instead of creating a new walking map for the dog. Anyway, I wanted to let you know Nate and Marshall will most likely consult on the case."

"Enough with the consulting. Tell them to solve it already."

Augusta started to laugh the minute she heard me say "walking map for the dog." I used my free hand to "shush" her, but we both started giggling and I needed my hand back to cover the receiver.

"Um, gotta go, Mom. I'll talk to you later."

"A walking map," Augusta said. "That's a first."

"Don't even get me started."

I went back to my office and plodded along on my spreadsheets until lunchtime. I needed some fresh air, so I volunteered to pick up Augusta's and my lunch at the Quick Stop. Nate and Marshall didn't make an appearance until after three, and they looked exhausted.

"I know you're both dying to find out if it's official." Nate took the seat next to Augusta's desk and leaned back. "I'll make it fast. We're on the case. The type of poisoning has everyone stymied."

"Any suspects?" I asked. "The only thing on the news was the toxin Cameron ingested."

Marshall walked over to me and gave my shoulder a squeeze. "The sheriff's office did a pretty thorough check into the guy's background, his work, and his personal relationships. No red flags anywhere."

"There must be something," Augusta muttered. "There always is. Angry ex-wife? Lunatic ex-girlfriend? Secret ex-boyfriend? Money trouble?"

Nate chuckled. "Are you plotting a novel or what? And no, none of the above. Cameron Tully was employed by Coldwater Seafood, one of the top twenty-five North American seafood distributors. His territory was the Greater Phoenix area. The company supplies seafood to major supermarket chains and restaurants. He was one of its managers."

Augusta stared directly at Nate. "Could be someone had it in for him. Maybe they wanted his job."

"According to the employees the sheriff's office interviewed, including top management and subordinates, Cameron was well liked and didn't have any problems with anyone. They got the same story from the CEO, as well as from Cameron's customers."

Augusta remained unmoved. "People have been known to lie. Especially when it suits them."

"Um, what about his personal life?" I asked. "Does he have family in the area?"

Marshall shook his head. "Nope. He was single. Not celibate, mind you, but single. Had a few girlfriends here and there but nothing serious and none of them carried any grudges. I'm telling you, the sheriff's deputies cast a pretty wide net on this one."

Augusta propped an elbow on the table and rested her head on her fist. "Not wide enough, if you ask me. What about his relatives? Lots of deep-rooted anger and resentment can be found in all sorts of families."

"You're watching too many late-night dramas," Nate said. "Cameron was an only child. He grew up around here and had a pretty normal, uneventful life until, well, you know. Anyway, his father and mother ran a small mom-and-pop grocery in Tempe up until the mid-nineties. His father had a heart attack and passed away a few years ago. His mother is in an Alzheimer's facility in Chandler."

My eyes moistened up and I ran the tips of my fingers over them. "Oh, how sad. I almost wish I didn't hear all of that. A nameless body is one thing, but this almost feels personal."

"I wouldn't go that far," Marshall said. "But yeah, it *is* really sad. Sad and confounding."

I looked at him and then at my boss. "So, where do you begin?"

Nate smiled. "Same place we always do—motive, means, and opportunity. The sheriff's deputies may have interviewed a number of sources, but I agree with Augusta. People lie. We just have to find out who. Beginning tomorrow, Marshall and I are going to reinterview a number of workers at Coldwater Seafood in Phoenix and see if we can get anywhere."

"Funny, but sometimes people are more apt to share information with private investigators than with law enforcement," Marshall said.

I clasped my hands together. “I hope you’re right. If this case isn’t solved soon, there’s no telling what any of us can expect from my mother. Right now, she’s honing her skills as a cartographer.”

“It’s a long story,” Augusta said. “I’d leave it at that, if I were either of you.”

Nate and Marshall took the cue and headed to their respective offices.

Marshall gave my shoulder another squeeze. “You can tell me later, Phee, when we get home.”

When we get home, the last thing on my mind will be my mother’s mapmaking skills.

Chapter 7

While Nate and Marshall spent the next three days interviewing coworkers and acquaintances of Cameron Tully, my mother used all of her available time to drive me nuts. Endless phone calls about doggie designer clothes and the Halloween pet parade. I was looking forward to this first spectacle of the Precious Pooches Holiday Extravaganza as much as a root canal.

It was late Thursday night and Marshall was taking a shower when my mother called. "Make sure you get to the dog park no later than four or you won't get a good spot in front of the knoll. The program ends at six. It'll be dark by then."

Granted, it was a stretch to consider the pet parade part of the Cameron Tully investigation, but Nate was as open-minded as anyone and, rather than incur my mother's wrath, he insisted Marshall and I leave the office early on Friday so as not to miss any part of "yet another reason to stay away from senior citizen communities."

The Halloween pet parade was to take place at the RH Johnson Complex, smack-dab in the center of Sun

City West. The staging area was the dog park, adjacent to the tennis courts and across the way from the bocce courts and miniature golf. In the middle stood a large grassy knoll that led to what the locals referred to as "Meeker Mountain," a man-made stone structure with picnic tables and a view of the Hillcrest Golf Course. The residents had once considered fencing it in for dogs, but the idea met with so much opposition they tossed it.

"You'd think the damn hill was Stonehenge," Herb once told my mother, "the way they guard that property."

The program was to begin promptly at four thirty. Each contestant had received a randomly chosen number for their dog's spot in the parade. Streetman's was seventeen. The dogs were to walk out of the staging area, leashed and with their owners, around the circular knoll. They were to stop at the top of the hill so the judges, who would be seated in front, could take a good look at the costumes. One dog at a time. When their number was called. It sounded simple and organized. It wasn't.

Someone had gotten the bright idea to decorate the trees surrounding the knoll with Halloween bats, witches, werewolves, skeletons, and every kind of macabre object remotely associated with the holiday. In addition, they ordered yards and yards of fabric cobwebs that stretched from one tree to the next. If that wasn't ludicrous enough, they set up sound machines in the background that emitted groans, squeaks, and the occasional shriek.

I spotted Streetman and my mother as soon as Marshall parked the car in front of the tennis courts. She was standing near the gate and waved us over. "What do you think of his costume? Shirley really outdid herself this time."

My God! My mother must've spent more money on his

costume than she did for my senior prom dress. "It's spectacular. It really is."

Streetman was dressed as a vampire. And not just any run-of-the-mill blood sucker, but a stylish nineteenth-century version, complete with a burgundy vest, black cape, high satin collar, and black ankle booties. It was one step below ostentatious and a million steps above anything I could imagine.

"Holy Cow!" Marshall said. "Is he wearing a gold watch on a chain? It looks like it was sewn into the vest."

My mother lifted the dog's cape slightly so we could get a better look. "It's not real gold, mind you, but Shirley managed to find a vintage watch fob and chain that went perfectly with the ensemble."

The ensemble. I can't believe she used the word "ensemble." "Um, we'd better go stand with the rest of the audience."

My mother gave her hair a little tousle. The movement accentuated the red streaks in her new blondish color. "All of the book club ladies are over there, but I can't tell where they're standing. Too bad my sister couldn't make it. Something about allergies. Or was it crowds? Never mind. Meet me back here in the dog park when it's over. The park is the staging area as well as the waiting area when the dogs finish with the judges."

"Okay, fine. Good luck, Mom. You, too, Streetman."

The dog looked up for a second and then licked his tail. The only part of him that wasn't covered up. Marshall and I made it to the viewing area just as the announcer introduced the program, explained the procedure, and went over the rules for spectators. Essentially, no feeding dogs.

The first dog to be called was a tan pug named Lola. She was dressed as Belle from *Beauty and the Beast* and looked adorable. She walked calmly up the knoll and past the judges. Following her was a reddish Pomeranian by the name of Wexley. He was dressed as a pirate, complete with a paper sword attached to his outfit. With the exception of growling at the goblins in the trees, Wexley was a model canine.

Unfortunately, the same couldn't be said for the five dogs who followed him. Maybe it was the sound effects or the fact that the wind had started to pick up, but once the cobwebs and Halloween "creatures" started moving about, the dogs went wild. Barking. Jumping. Pawing. One of the owners was all but yanked to the ground when his dog decided to attack a tree skeleton. It took a good ten minutes to calm everyone down and continue with the parade.

And while the next few dogs weren't exactly what I'd consider to be model citizens, they weren't as wild as the ones who preceded them. I noticed Cindy Dolton with Bundles, who made a perfect Casper. She was right. The white fur helped.

"You don't think Streetman is going to go berserk when he sees those Halloween figures in the trees, do you?" Marshall whispered.

"Oh my gosh. Do any of them have teeth? Quick. Try to get a good look."

"Uh, no. I don't see teeth. Why?"

The year before, when my mother and the book club ladies decided to take part in Sun City West's theater production of *The Mousetrap*, they were convinced a ghost was haunting the place. Streetman was brought in to check it out but instead ruined some vintage mink stoles when he spied taxidermied teeth on them.

"Never mind," I said. "He might be okay."

We held our breath until number seventeen was called

and then held perfectly still so as not to do anything that would spook him. So what if we were yards away. Heaven forbid we jinxed anything.

Streetman walked up the knoll nonchalantly as if nothing was going on. When my mother stopped in front of the judges, he stood absolutely still.

"Only five seconds more, little buddy," Marshall mumbled, reaching for my hand.

I gripped his tight and held on. Five seconds seemed like hours, but finally the judges gave a nod and my mother moved on.

"Did she pop him a Xanax or what?" Marshall asked. "I've never seen that dog so calm."

"Yeah, well, look again."

As soon as my mother completed the route and was in sight of the dog park, Streetman made a mad dash toward the first female dog he spied. An English Bulldog dressed like a fairy princess. Streetman dismantled her wings in a matter of seconds and began to pounce on her as if nothing else in the world mattered.

We watched as my mother immediately scooped him up, returned the wings to the owner, no doubt with sincere apologies and an offer of restitution, and raced back to the dog park.

Marshall gave me a nudge. "How many points off for that?"

I was about to answer when I heard someone shriek and whipped my head around. Apparently, the wind had loosened the cobwebs from their fasteners on the trees and a large swath of that gauzy material landed on top of the owner of dog number eighteen. She stumbled and fell, rolling down the knoll completely covered in enough gauze to resemble The Mummy.

Her dog got so flustered he picked his leg up and peed

all over her. The audience was beside itself. Marshall included.

"It's not funny," I said. "Someone needs to help her."

Marshall took the not-so-subtle hint and charged toward the knoll. He was able to remove most of the cobwebs, leaving only a small portion that was still wrapped around one of her arms. Another bystander picked up the dog and held him while Marshall helped the woman stand. Then all of a sudden he shouted, "Someone call nine-one-one. Call nine-one-one immediately!"

I had no idea what was happening, and it was impossible to tell. The woman collapsed on the ground again and I thought she might be having a heart attack or a seizure. The announcer told everyone to remain where they were and make room for the emergency responders.

A Sun City West fire truck arrived in a matter of minutes, followed by an ambulance. Surprisingly, the crowd did as they were asked and the program resumed a few minutes later.

"What do you suppose happened to her?" I asked Marshall.

"I'm no expert, but it wasn't a stroke or a heart attack. Crap. I think the woman was poisoned. Her nose was bleeding and she kept grabbing her stomach. Listen, I'm almost certain this has nothing to do with Cameron Tully, but I'm going to head over to the hospital and have a chat with the folks in the emergency room. If the program ends before I get back, hitch a ride with your mother to her house and I'll see you there. Meanwhile, any chance you can do a bit of sleuthing and find out who that woman is?"

"I thought you'd never ask. You're getting as bad as my mother. Yeah, I'll nose around for you."

Marshall gave me a peck on the cheek and darted off to his car. I maneuvered my way to where I was originally standing when I caught sight of the man who had grabbed the woman's dog. Number eighteen. A Yorkshire Terrier who couldn't have weighed four pounds dripping wet. And that included his pumpkin costume. The poor thing was shaking and nuzzling the man's arm.

I elbowed my way through the crowd as the parade continued. We were on number twenty-one by now. The man didn't seem a whole lot better than the Yorkshire Terrier.

"Excuse me," I said. "Are you friends with that woman? The one who was rushed to the hospital?"

"No. My wife and I own a big dog. A yellow Lab. We usually take him to the dog park in Surprise, but she thought it would be fun to enter Bouncer in this contest. He's still in the staging area. I have no idea who the owner of this little guy is, and I'm not sure what to do."

I looked at the trembling dog and began to pet him. "I'm positive they have the names and contact information for all of the entries. You can check once the parade or contest or whatever they call this is over. If not, I'm sure the dog club will know someone who's willing to watch him until the family can be notified."

"Bouncer gets along with everyone, so that won't be a problem. I just feel bad for this dog's owner. I thought the woman got tangled up in those ridiculous cobwebs and fell. But something was off. The way she was gasping and holding her stomach. It wasn't a fall."

Suddenly I had an idea. "Why don't you let me hold him for a while? That way you can get a better look at Bouncer once his number is called. The people at this dog park seem to know each other's dogs and can contact the owner's family."

The man was more than willing to relinquish the dog to me. "Sure you'll be okay?"

"I'm sure. By the way, I'm Phee, and my mother's Harriet Plunkett. She's back in the staging area with—"

"Harriet Plunkett? The woman who played Mrs. Boyle in *The Mousetrap*? We saw that play last year and she was wonderful. I'm looking forward to more of her performances."

You can catch them every day. Rain or shine. "Um, I'm not sure if she'll be trying out for more plays, but I'll let her know you enjoyed her performance."

Just then we heard the announcer. "Number twenty-two, Snowy."

"I'd better hurry," the man said. "Bouncer's number twenty-three, and I want a good view."

As he made his way to the front of the crowd, I milled around, stroking the little Yorkie, hoping someone would recognize him and say something. No luck. I decided to go back to the dog park and see if my mother could offer any suggestions. No sooner did I open the gate when I heard her.

"Phee! What are you doing with Mrs. Meschow's dog?"

"Is that who the woman was? Mrs. Meschow?" Not that I had any idea who Mrs. Meschow was . . . "Didn't you see what happened? They took her to the hospital."

"I saw them taking someone in an ambulance, but I didn't know it was her. I had my own problems. Streetman apparently likes English Bulldogs."

"We saw. Face it, Mom, Streetman likes any dog he can jump on. But enough about the dog for a moment. I need to tell you something." I talked as fast as I could so as not to let her interrupt me. "Marshall went to the hospital to speak with the ER staff. He thinks Mrs. Meschow might have been poisoned."

"Oh my God! Oh my God! What if we've got a serial poisoner on the loose? They don't even have to go into a drugstore or hardware store to buy the stuff. Those palms grow like grass around here."

"Calm down, will you? Just because the lab identified the sago palm as the poison that killed Cameron Tully, it doesn't mean that's the same thing Mrs. Meschow ingested. *If* she ingested anything. She might not be poisoned. It might be something else entirely. What do you know about Mrs. Meschow?"

"Only that her husband left her well off financially. Who knew you could make so much money in the natural dog food business? That's what he did, you know. Before he passed away. His company manufactured and sold natural dog food. You know. The kind I wouldn't feed Streetman no matter what. Ingredients like goose, rabbit, salmon, cod, tuna, ocean whitefish, herring, duck, and venison. He's a dog, mind you, not a wilderness trapper!"

Suddenly we heard the announcer. The parade had ended and they were about to award the winners.

"Let's move to the fence," my mother said. "As soon as the winners are announced, they're supposed to go back to the judges for their ribbons and certificates."

"That's nice," I mumbled, shifting the Yorkie into my other arm. He had stopped shaking and was dozing off.

"Not just ribbons," my mother continued, "they have terrific prizes. Dog grooming, doggie day spas, gift certificates at pet shops, and a grand prize for whoever wins the overall top placement in all three contests. It's a three-night weekend stay at the JW Marriott resort in Scottsdale. For the dog and the owner. They allow dogs, you know, and they have special programs for them. Streetman and I could really enjoy a weekend of being pampered."

"The dog's pampered already, Mom. He won't know the difference."

Suddenly a woman about my age rushed over to us. "Prince! There you are. Oh, poor, poor Prince."

She reached out her arms and the dog immediately jumped in.

"You know this dog?" I asked.

"I should. He belongs to my mother, Elaine Meschow. I've been looking all over for the dog ever since they called me from the hospital. I drove here as fast as I could. Luckily, I was only a few miles away in Surprise. With one of our accounts. I work for our family business. We manufacture and sell natural dog food. Grain free, non-GMO, antibiotic-free natural foods. Maybe you've heard of us. Spellbound Naturals. Our plant is in Chandler. I'm Bethany Cabot."

I kicked my mother in the ankle and gave her one of those "Don't you dare say anything" looks.

Apparently, it didn't work. She squinted and took a step toward the lady. "My dog prefers food that's a little less natural."

Before Bethany could respond, I jumped in. "Did the hospital say how your mother was doing?"

She nodded. "It wasn't a heart attack or a stroke. Or a seizure. They think it might've been food poisoning. They're doing blood and urine tests, and they're treating her for dehydration. If it turns out to be another kind of poisoning, they'll administer activated charcoal. Honestly, I can't, for the life of me, understand how my mother could've been poisoned. Most likely it's simply food poisoning, like from E. coli or one of those horrid things."

"I'm sure she'll be okay," I said.

Bethany half-smiled. "I hope so. Meanwhile, Prince will be fine staying with my husband and me if they have to keep my mother overnight. Anyway, I'd better get over to the hospital. Good thing this dog is small enough to fit in a tote bag."

"You're not going to stay to see if Prince wins the doggie costume contest?" my mother asked.

I didn't think anyone's eyes could open that wide, but Bethany's did. "The rec center can email us. I really need to go." She tucked the dog under her arm, thanked us, and tore out of the dog park.

I turned and glared at my mother. "I can't believe you asked her if she wanted to stay to hear who won the contest. Of all things."

"Maybe it didn't matter to her, but it might to her mother."

"What matters is whether or not Elaine Meschow had food poisoning or—"

"Oh, so now you want to admit it, Phee? Sago palm poisoning. Maybe Elaine Meschow had sago palm poisoning."

"Shh!" someone shouted. "They're calling the winners now!"

My mother and I moved closer to the fence and listened. The announcer thanked all of the area businesses for their generous donations, as well as extending his appreciation to the canine club and the recreation centers of Sun City West. His words glossed over until he announced the third-place winner—Bundles Dolton.

Cindy went running up to the judges' bench with Bundles under her arm. She won a twenty-five-dollar gift certificate from the Pet Land Pet Shop.

"Those judges always have a thing for fluffy white dogs, no matter how they're dressed," my mother whispered. "Still, if one of them had to win, I'm glad it was Cindy's dog."

I rolled my eyes and didn't say a word.

"In second place, Streetman Plunkett."

"Mom!" I shrieked. "Streetman took second place. Go! Go get his prize!"

My mother made a mad dash for the judges' table, with Streetman at her heels. I followed her out of the dog park and waited with the rest of the audience in front of the knoll. A sudden tap on my shoulder and I jumped to see Shirley Johnson standing right behind me.

"Lordy, Phee. I didn't mean to scare you. Isn't this the most exciting thing ever? Streetman took second place. If he keeps this up, he might stand a chance of winning the grand prize."

I couldn't tell who was more exuberant. My mother or Shirley.

"It was your costume that did it," I said. "It's magnificent."

We waved to my mother as she made her way toward us. This time, carrying the dog. "My little man won a twenty-five-dollar gift certificate from Pet Land Pet Shop and a free grooming at their doggie salon. Maybe that groomer will have better luck with him."

By "better luck" she meant not having the poor person's fingers bitten off. Streetman enjoyed getting groomed as much as he probably liked getting neutered.

Before I could say anything, the final announcement was made.

"And now, ladies and gentlemen, the moment we've all been waiting for. Taking first place in today's Halloween extravaganza is Sir Breckenthall Gruber."

"Ugh!" my mother exclaimed. "I could just spit. Not that I have anything against the dog, mind you. It's not his fault his owner is an *s-n-o-b*."

"You can say the word, Harriet," Shirley said. "It's not one of those other words that have to be spelled out."

Sir Breckenthall took home the twenty-five-dollar gift certificate, the free grooming, and a Martha Stewart doggie bed, compliments of the Pampered Pooch kennel. The crowd dispersed as soon as the announcer thanked everyone and reminded them of the upcoming Thanksgiving pet parade the following month. Same place. Same time.

"I'm getting his certificate framed and I'll hang it in the kitchen," my mother said the minute Myrna, Lucinda, Louise, and Cecilia approached. We were off to the side of the parking lot. A number of cars were already headed out.

The ladies all began to talk at once (no surprise there) while Streetman tried furiously to yank his vest off.

"Wait a second," my mother said. "I'd better get him out of this costume before he ruins it."

She bent down to remove the Velcro fasteners when who should walk by but Phyllis Gruber. Streetman bared his teeth at Sir Breckenthall, and the Cavalier King Charles Spaniel let out a nasty growl.

"Come along, Breccki," Phyllis said. "You're the winner here. Don't waste your time with that street mongrel."

"That's one Halloween witch who doesn't need a costume," Myrna said, "and I don't mean the dog."

Chapter 8

The next morning my mother called at her usual time—early. "Streetman's acorn costume will have to be even more dazzling for the Thanksgiving event."

Marshall had been right all along. If we could keep her focused on the Precious Pooches whatever, then she wouldn't be obsessed with Cameron Tully's murder. Or food poisonings, for that matter.

Marshall had more interviews to conduct with some of the people associated with Coldwater Seafood. Mainly restaurant owners in the Phoenix area. Four of them agreed to meet with him today. Two restaurants downtown, one in Tempe and one in Scottsdale. Nate had a similar Saturday morning lined up, only instead of interviewing restaurant owners, he had to discuss Cameron's demise with supermarket chain managers.

Deputy Ranston also called us at an ungodly hour. Well, not us. Marshall. Apparently, Mrs. Meschow hadn't responded to the usual protocol for food poisoning, so the hospital was beginning to think it might be a more serious situation. She was now being treated with activated charcoal while they waited for a complete toxicology report.

"This isn't how I expected my Saturday morning to pan out." Marshall reached an arm around my waist, pulling me closer. "Don't go too crazy with the unpacking. Tomorrow's another day and those boxes aren't going anywhere. Try to give yourself a break."

He kissed my cheek lightly and then moved his lips to mine. "On the other hand, maybe you should unpack. Then we can have all day tomorrow for other things."

This time it was me who nuzzled his neck and returned the kiss. "I'm not letting you off this easy. The boxes can wait. Halloween is tomorrow night, and I need to buy candy for the trick-or-treaters. The only entertainment we're going to have is answering the doorbell. By the way, does Ranston think Mrs. Meschow's poisoning has anything to do with Cameron Tully?"

"Doubtful. But until the official lab results are in, his guess is as good as anyone's. Maybe today's interviews will get us closer to figuring this out. I should be home before five. If not, I'll call. Want me to pick up dinner?"

"I've got to be at the supermarket anyway, so I'll take care of it. What are you in the mood for?"

Wrong question but a great answer. A long, sweet kiss that left me with goose bumps on my arms.

"Get going, before I block the door and force you to cancel those appointments."

Thank goodness we were able to hire the retired firefighters for our move. The days had flown by and we were thrilled to be in our new place. Other than our having our own leaning tower of cardboard boxes between our living and dining areas, and an air mattress that could qualify for torture in most civilized countries, the house was really beginning to feel like home. What really felt good on that particular Saturday was not getting coerced into joining my mother's book club at their favorite breakfast haunt, Bagels 'N More, across the road from Sun City West.

The women decided to skip the Saturdays following the pet parades because "We're not fifty-something Boomers anymore with all that energy," according to Lucinda. Besides, they'd still have three other mornings each month to criticize the food and haggle with the waitresses.

I spent my morning cleaning and unpacking two boxes of books before making myself a cheese sandwich and driving to the nearest supermarket. And while I had every intention of buying the kind of candies I'd never put in my mouth (sour worms, Swedish fish that stuck to the teeth, gumballs, and caramels), in the end, I broke down and bought my favorite stuff. It wasn't my fault. Not really. I was obeying a mantra I had been taught at an early age: "Don't let anything go to waste." I knew uneaten gummies and jawbreakers would only wind up in the trash, but leftover mini chocolate bars wouldn't suffer that fate.

By midafternoon, all my errands were done and I started on dinner. A real easy fix—stir-fried chicken that could quickly be microwaved when Marshall got back. My culinary skills were more in the "preparation" column than the actual one reserved for cooking.

I had placed the large bowl of chicken, broccoli, mushrooms, and onions in the fridge and loaded the dishwasher when the phone rang. Expecting it to be Marshall, I answered on the first ring.

My mother barely took a breath. "Phee! I hope I'm not interrupting anything, but I just got off the phone with Janet Galbraith. They're not coming back until after

Thanksgiving. And they're still arguing over the grill. Janet wants that thing removed from their property, but her husband refuses. He told her 'the body was found under the grill, not cooking on top of it.' And then he told her to 'get over it.'"

"Um, he does have a point. I mean, Cameron's body was shoved under the grill and covered with their tarp. I can understand her not wanting to reuse the tarp, but the grill? That's going a little overboard, don't you think?"

"I don't know what to think. Janet's a basket case. She kept saying, 'The sheriff's office took the tarp for evidence; why can't they take the damn grill?'"

"After Thanksgiving, huh? You think it has something to do with the murder?"

"Of course it does. She's scared to come back. I'm telling you, Streetman and I still have nightmares about some crazed killer poking around the yard behind ours. And now that they've removed the yellow crime scene tape, it's open season once more."

Hats off to you, Janet Galbraith, for getting my mother all riled up again. "I'm sure Cameron Tully's case will be solved soon. Nate and Marshall are interviewing everyone who did business with Cameron. If something's the least bit off, they'll figure it out. Stop worrying. I'm sure no one will be in the Galbraiths' backyard anymore. Except the Galbraiths. And that won't be for another month. Relax, will you?"

My mother groaned, so I changed the subject. "Uh, you mentioned Streetman's acorn outfit. What did you have in mind?"

"Swarovski crystals."

"What?"

"I already talked with Shirley and we have it all worked out."

The uptick in my mother's voice was a good sign, so I let her continue. "By the time Shirley is done, Streetman won't look like an ordinary acorn. His hat will be rimmed in shades of orange, yellow, olive, and topaz. And the stalk will be a blend of greens and yellows. As for the body itself, well, Shirley will fuse some of the colors together to create an overall dazzling effect. When Streetman takes the runway, every eye will be on him."

I pictured one of those street thugs decked out in enough bling to blind someone. All the dog needed was a solid gold chain around his neck. I tried to get the image out of my mind, but it was impossible.

"So, uh, Swarovski crystals, huh? Aren't they a tad expensive?"

"My little man is worth it. And I'll be gosh darned if that Sir Breckenthall tries to upstage him."

Ah-hah. The real reason behind the lunacy. "It's going to be awfully hard to upstage Industrial Light and Magic."

"Industrial what? What are you talking about?"

"It's a visual effects company that specializes in spectacular graphics. George Lucas was the founder. You know, *Star Wars*?"

"I don't know what any of this has to do with Streetman."

"Forget it. It was an exaggeration. I was comparing your dog's outfit to the stuff that company does. Anyhow, I really should be going. Marshall will be back any second." Another exaggeration.

"Before you hang up, have you heard anything about Elaine Meschow? Was she really poisoned?"

I should've known my mother wouldn't let this go. "They're still waiting for a toxicology report."

"They can run those things in twenty minutes on *Elementary* or *Hawaii Five-O*."

"I'll be sure to remind Nate and Marshall of that. Listen, if I do hear anything, I'll call you. Promise."

"Mark your calendar for the Friday before Thanksgiving. At the dog park."

"I did already. Same for December. Love you, Mom."

My head was spinning by the time I got off the phone, and I had to do a few neck rolls and stretches before I felt human again. The TV receiver said four forty-one, and I knew Marshall would be coming in the door at any minute. I changed into something less frumpy and was giving my cheeks a bit of blush when I heard him.

"I'm back, hon, and you're not going to believe this. Jocelyn Amaro, the restaurant owner at La Mar Maravillosa in Tempe, used to date Cameron. And I'm not talking ancient history. I mean recently. Can you hear me okay from the bedroom?"

"Loud and clear. I'll be right there." I put down the blush and walked into the living room.

Marshall was still talking. "He ditched her a few weeks ago. No explanation. No nothing. And worse than that, he dropped her restaurant's account at Coldwater Seafood."

"Can he do that?"

"I guess so. Because he did. She found another seafood distributor and said everything was hunky dory. Her words."

"Hmm. Think she could be responsible for his death?"

"She said she didn't have any animosity toward him, in spite of his behavior. Said she found out about the homicide from the local news sources and was shocked. Told me Cameron was one of those guys who got along with everyone. Even-tempered. Hardworking. Her only issue with him was his roving eyes. Followed by his—"

"I get it. I get it. He was a womanizer. What about the other restauranteurs?"

"All men and none of them had issues with him. But, in all four inquiries, including my conversation with Jocelyn, I got the feeling they were hiding something. One of them even went so far as to say, 'If you need to look over our accounts, I'll have to put you in touch with our restaurant's legal firm.' Phee, I never even mentioned the accounts for the seafood. Now I'm beginning to wonder if there isn't something going on."

"Like what? Price wrangling?"

"I don't have the authority to look into their accounts. And neither does law enforcement. There's nothing whatsoever that would point them in that direction. Not yet anyway."

"So now what?"

"Well, Nate and I will share what we find and look for possible connections. Oh yeah, one more thing. Two of the restaurants, the ones in Phoenix, had sago palms in their lobbies. Strange, but I never gave those things a second thought until now. Yikes, those things are more plentiful around here than the hanging peppers we see in every Mexican restaurant."

"Maybe one of those things was more than a decoration. You told me there isn't a part of that plant that's not toxic. The leaves, the seeds, the roots, everything. A good chef would know how to add a dash of palm poisoning into someone's food."

"Yeah, if they worked for the Borgia family, maybe. It's not exactly a skill they teach in culinary school. And no chef in his or her right mind would risk poisoning customers. I seriously doubt the sago palm concoction originated in a restaurant."

"Maybe not the restaurant," I said, "but that doesn't exonerate one of those chefs or the restaurant owners, for that matter."

"They would need a motive. A darned good motive. And if I take Jocelyn at her word, we don't have one. Not yet anyway."

I shrugged. "Give it time. Anyway, I made us stir-fry for dinner. All I need to do is boil up some rice."

"And all I need to do is kiss the cook and offer to wash the dishes."

It was one of those warm, cozy evenings at home, followed by a full morning of hiking at White Tanks Mountain. We picked up takeout chicken on the way home and got ready for a slew of trick-or-treaters.

"We'd better portion out the candy slowly," I said, "or we'll run out."

"Then we can shut the lights, hide in the bedroom, and hope no one eggs the house."

The trick-or-treaters began to arrive shortly after five. Toddlers and little kids accompanied by their parents or older siblings. By seven, the marauders were older—ten and up, judging from their costumes. We still had a full bowl of candy, but if the pace didn't slow down, I would be forced to rummage through the kitchen for granola and yogurt bars. Somehow, I always had a bountiful supply of those.

It wasn't until eight thirty when we caught a breath between the knocking on the door and the sound of the doorbell. We decided to call it a night at nine fifteen, but a few minutes later three groups of older kids arrived. No costumes. Just kids holding out pillowcases, demanding we fill them with goodies. I was half-tempted to find a fiber bar, but Marshall talked me out of it.

"They know where we live. Might as well part with those Hershey miniatures."

"I can't believe I'm actually extolling the virtues of

Sun City West, but they don't have trick-or-treaters. It's a boon that comes with living in a senior development."

Marshall froze and I laughed. "It's also home to Shirley, Lucinda, Cecilia, Louise, and Myrna. Oh, and let's not forget Herb." I laughed again. "Need I say more?"

"How'd your aunt Ina get out of living there?"

"She and Louis fell in love with a house in Sun City Grand. And that house is only a stone's throw from my mother's place, so it's kind of the same thing when you think of it."

At the end of the evening we were left with ten Hershey miniatures, three Kit Kat bars, and two Nestlé Crunch miniatures. The fiber bars would be safe after all.

"You know, the condo pool is still open," I said. "They don't close it until eleven and it's heated. What do you think?"

"I think I can get my swimsuit on quicker than you. Let's do it."

I thought Marshall and I would be the only crazy ones in an outdoor swimming pool on Halloween, but as it turned out, I was wrong. We were met by two other couples who swore they'd never have children and another guy who told us he was counting the days until he turned fifty-five so he could move to Sun City.

Surprisingly, the air mattress actually felt good an hour or so later when I stretched out and closed my eyes. Good for all of three or four minutes. Then the phone rang and every muscle in my body cramped up.

Marshall picked up the call, but all I heard him say was, "You're sure? . . . Okay. Stay put. We're on our way."

"What? What was that all about? And who? Who called us so late?"

He winced before the words could form in his mouth, and I knew right away it was my mother.

"What happened? Is she—"

"She's fine. As she was leaving the kitchen, she looked outside and there were lights on at the Galbraiths' house. Someone's inside."

"Did she call the sheriff's office?"

"Uh-huh. After she changed out of her housedress. That's too much information, if you ask me. Anyway, the sheriff's office is sending a car over right now, but we'd better get moving, too. I'll drive."

I threw on a sweatshirt and my old jeans and slipped into some sneaks, and I was ready to go. It wasn't a fashion show, although I had to admit Marshall looked a heck of a lot better in his pale blue button-down shirt and khakis.

We were racing so fast I didn't even remember buckling up my seat belt.

"Geez," I said, "you don't suppose it's the same person who was snooping around the last time, do you?"

"Not after your mother unleashed that Screamer device on the guy. I imagine he's waiting to regain his hearing. *If* it's a he. I don't want to sound sexist. Truthfully, I think it was an ordinary break-in. Bowman told me a while back that there've been a number of burglaries in the Sun Cities. Mostly electronics and small appliances. Easy stuff to grab and fence. Some of those homes have expensive artwork, but it wasn't touched. Whoever's stealing the stuff is dealing with a younger market. Look, it doesn't take a mastermind to figure out which houses are empty. Even if the flyers and newspapers are picked up. Some of those snowbirds are pretty lax when it comes to lawn maintenance."

"The Galbraiths' place looks pretty good, though."

"Good for a robbery. That house got so much publicity as a result of Cameron's body on the back patio that every thief and petty criminal from here to Yuma knows the place is empty. It was all but advertised. And once the crime tape was removed and the deputies moved on, it was only a matter of time before a burglar would seize the opportunity."

"You really think that's what it is? A robbery?" I asked.

"Uh-huh. Up until now, no one knew its owners were gone. Nothing had been touched in that house when the forensic team went through it. That thin layer of red dust on the tile didn't so much as yield a footprint. The place was undisturbed."

"Ugh. That red dust. The stuff is everywhere. I used to drive myself crazy wiping the sliders on the windows, but now, not so much."

"That's good to know. I was beginning to think compulsive cleaning was a family trait."

"Oh, don't get me wrong. It is. It most definitely is. Only Aunt Ina uses an extended family—her cleaning service."

Marshall had exited the 303 onto Grand Avenue. From there he signaled to make a left-hand turn when blue and red flashing lights shone from the car behind his.

"That must be the sheriff's car. I can't believe we made better time than they did. Not unusual, with all the calls they get. I'll pull over and let them pass. Whoa. Looks like there are two cars."

"Two cars. That's not sounding good."

"Could be protocol. Could be—"

"Look! They're not turning on my mother's block. And now there's a third car coming from that intersection ahead. That's right near Louise Munson's house. Across from the golf course. Maybe they caught the thieves and it's down to a chase."

"Um, about Louise Munson. Isn't that her over there by the light pole? The woman with the long robe and curlers?"

"It's hard to tell in the dark, but yeah, it sure looks like her."

"I'm pulling over. We might as well make this a real night to remember and see what's going on."

Chapter 9

"Oh my gosh! Phee and Marshall! What are you doing here?" Louise pulled the belt on her red chenille bathrobe and gave it an extra tug. "There are more sheriff cars around the corner, by the other side of the golf course. The lights woke up my poor bird, and he's been squawking ever since."

I suddenly remembered all about Louise's African parrot. Up until I moved to Arizona, I never gave birds a second thought. Especially parrots. But my boss had acquired one, albeit on a temporary basis, and Louise Munson owned the most pernicious one imaginable. However, the thing did help solve a murder case when I first came out here, so far be it for me to say anything against them.

Marshall had rolled down the windows and Louise continued to talk as she leaned farther into the passenger side where I was seated.

"A naked man is running around the streets and on the golf course. They're trying to catch him. The Pearlmutters from across the street saw him, but they went back inside to get jackets. It's chilly out. Same for Mrs. Friekin.

She went to get her coat, too. You see, I stepped out when I saw the first sheriff's car. It was the Pearlmutters who phoned it in."

A sharp shrill voice interrupted us and a heavyset woman in a hooded parka approached the car. I assumed it was Mrs. Friekin. "Louise, did you see him? Did you catch a glimpse of him?"

"No, darn it. He's probably on the golf course again. What kind of lunatic runs around butt naked in the middle of the night?"

I tapped my teeth, a habit I was trying to break, and took a breath. "Are you sure it was a naked man? I mean, this *is* Halloween night. Maybe it's a prankster all dressed up to look that way."

Mrs. Friekin shook her head. "Not according to the Pearlmutters. Not enough stuffing to fill a butt that large."

Marshall put the car in park and turned off the engine. "The first sheriff's car? How many of them are out there chasing this guy?"

"Oh, I imagine quite a few," Louise said. "We don't get action like this all the time. Oh, look! Here come some more neighbors."

Sure enough, Louise's street was beginning to look like the Macy's Thanksgiving Day Parade route. At least eight or nine more people stepped outside.

"So," Louise asked, "what brings you here?"

"I got a call from my mother. She saw lights on at the Galbraiths' empty house. She called the sheriff's office. That's why we thought those cars were headed over there."

"I'm afraid your mother will have to wait her turn." Mrs. Friekin turned up the collar on her coat. "A man in his birthday suit is certainly cause for more attention."

I looked at Marshall, but it was too dark to see his reaction in the car.

"Tell Harriet to call me later," Louise said. "I'm going to be up for hours. Maybe that man will make an appearance on this block."

"Um, sure," I muttered as Marshall put the car in drive and we headed out.

"Have a nice evening!" he shouted, and I burst out laughing.

"'Have a nice evening'? Honestly?"

"Well, what was I supposed to say? 'Hope you see the naked guy'? Can you believe those women? I'm speechless. Truly speechless."

"Yeah, it's unbelievable, isn't it?"

Unfortunately, Mrs. Friekin was right. When we got to my mother's house, the sheriff's deputies hadn't arrived yet. Streetman took one look at Marshall, grabbed a gnawed-on chew toy, and made a beeline for the master bedroom.

"He's become quite possessive about his toys," my mother said, "especially if he hasn't seen you in a while."

Dear Lord. Is that her way of saying we'll have to visit the dog more often? "We saw him at the pet parade."

"That doesn't count. He was preoccupied. Anyway, I've been watching the Galbraiths' house and it's pitch black over there. Whoever was inside turned off the lights when they left. No wonder those deputies can't solve a crime around here, let alone a murder, they're too slow. What's taking them so long? Maybe I should call again."

"No, Mom. No need to do that. They're busy trying to apprehend someone."

"The killer? They found him?"

"Uh, not the killer. A naked man. On Louise Munson's street. We just got done speaking with her. She's in front of her house with a bunch of her neighbors. They're out there in case—"

"I know darned well why they're out there. Louise simply has to be privy to a juicy piece of gossip. A naked man, huh? Did she say who it was? Does she know? Was it one of the neighbors?"

"No, no, and no. And one more thing. It might turn out to be a high school kid on a Halloween prank. You're only a few miles from Canyon Ridge High School."

Marshall was right. My mother had obviously changed out of whatever old housedress she had on prior to our arrival and was now decked out in a classy gray lounger, complete with gold belt and dangling charms. She motioned for Marshall and me to sit down in the living room. "I'll bring us some apple cider. Or do either of you want something else?"

"Apple cider's fine, Harriet," Marshall said. "And thanks. Give me a second and I'll call Deputy Ranston." He turned to me as soon as my mother went into the kitchen. "Those deputies might be playing Keystone Kops all night."

No sooner did Marshall say that when I looked at the front window and saw the familiar blue and red lights in between the shutter flaps. "You can forget the call. They're pulling up now in their 1925 Ford Model T."

"Shh. Try to be serious."

"Mom!" I shouted. "The sheriff's deputies have arrived."

Only it wasn't the deputies. It was two men from the volunteer posse. They explained they couldn't check the Galbraiths' residence unless an MCSO officer was with them and that it had been a particularly trying night for the deputies on duty.

"We should've just called Ranston and gotten it over with," I whispered to Marshall while my mother stood in the doorway demanding to know "when one of those Maricopa County sheriff's officers would be getting off their duffs to respond."

"It shouldn't be much longer," one of the posse volunteers said. "We'll drive around the corner and wait in front of the Galbraiths' residence."

Marshall got up from the couch and walked to the door. He reached in his pocket and showed the posse volunteers his card. "I'm Marshall Gregory with Williams Investigations and we're working with the sheriff's office on a related case. At the same address. If you don't mind, my associate and I will meet you over there."

The men muttered something inaudible and my mother closed the door behind them.

"An associate of yours?" I asked. "An associate?"

Marshall clenched his teeth and shrugged. "It wouldn't have sounded professional if I had said 'girlfriend.' Honest. Besides, you *are* an associate."

"Aargh." I had to admit he was right. And if the truth be known, I had let lots of people believe I was an investigator and not the office bookkeeper/accountant on more than one occasion. "Okay. You're off the hook. Let's get going."

"I need to grab a jacket," my mother said. "It's chilly out there."

Marshall immediately tapped my mother on the shoulder and spoke softly. "If all of us leave, it might really upset the dog. I mean, the flashing lights, the noises, the—"

"Oy, you're right. I wasn't even thinking of my poor Streetman. I'll keep an eye out from the patio door and wait until you get back here. I'm locking this place tighter than Fort Knox. And, Phee, you stay in the car!"

"Um, sure." *Like I'm about to go into the Galbraiths' unarmed. And taking the car is a given. No way we're going to walk across the yards in the dark. Too many river rocks and small cacti.*

We got into Marshall's sedan and drove around the block. West Sentinel Drive was like a ghost town. Other than the streetlights and the backlit house numbers, the place looked like something out of *The Twilight Zone*.

The posse volunteers had pulled up in front of the house and Marshall parked directly behind them, leaving enough room for another deputy car on the other side of the driveway.

"Think they're right?" I asked. "About the deputies arriving soon."

"Your guess is as good as mine, hon."

He turned on his iPhone and looked down. "Ranston might've messaged me."

"Hey, a car's pulling up. No flashers."

I had caught sight of the headlights from the side-view mirror and turned my head. Herb Garrett got out of the car and was running toward us. I rolled the window down.

"Is he here? The naked guy? Bill Saunders from my pinochle group called me a few minutes ago. He lives five or six houses down from that bird woman in your mother's book club."

"Louise. Louise Munson."

"Yeah, yeah. Well? Do the deputies have the naked guy cornered behind your mother's house?"

What is it with these people? If they can get all frazzled over a streaker, I can't imagine what they'd do in the case of a real crisis. "No, Herb. This has nothing to do with that."

"Another corpse?"

"No! My mother saw lights on in the Galbraiths' house. That's all."

"Could be a burglary. That's my guess. Why isn't anyone checking? I see a sheriff's car in front of you."

"It's the posse volunteers. They have to wait."

"I'll swing back later. I was on my way over to Bill's street when I saw the lights."

"Uh, um . . ."

I never spit out a sentence. Not to Herb, anyway. He was back at his car before I could even form a syllable. Marshall put down the iPhone and clapped his hands. "Astonishing. That's what it is around here. Astonishing."

All I could do was nod. "Finally," he said. "Blue and red flashers. Might as well get out of the car."

It was Ranston, all right, but instead of his Grizzly Adams sidekick, he was accompanied by a uniformed deputy.

"I should've figured you'd beat me to this house call." Ranston mumbled to Marshall and me. "Dispatch said it was a possible break-in. What a half-cocked night, pardon the expression. They've got Bowman chasing all over the golf courses because a bunch of old ladies are losing their bloomers over some idiot who's running around naked. And now this. Another incident at the infamous Galbraith residence."

At that moment, the two posse volunteers walked over and introduced themselves.

Ranston suddenly spoke up as if he'd recently found his voice. "This is Deputy Lopez. Maricela Lopez. She recently joined our department from Tucson."

Deputy Lopez offered a slight smile and shook our hands. Marshall introduced us and explained that my mother had seen lights on in the Galbraiths' empty house.

The deputies were all facing the street and I was the only one who had a full view of the vacant house. "Um, uh, my mother's not the only one. Look at the decorative window above the front door. The hallway light just went on."

Marshall grabbed me by the wrist and gave it a light squeeze. "Wait in the car, okay? Who knows what this is going to be." He pressed the car keys in my hand and looked at the house.

"Be careful," I muttered.

Ranston started barking orders before I got the car door open.

"Lopez, you take the back with one of the posse men. Stay put and wait. The other posse volunteer follows me. Same for you, Mr. Gregory. Walk directly behind me. You're carrying, aren't you?"

"Yep," Marshall said.

I got into the driver's side and slammed the door shut. Then I started up the car so I could turn the passenger side window down. Ranston had the master key to the front security lockbox, an emergency feature for the residents of Sun City West who wanted the sheriff and fire departments to have access to their homes in case of trouble.

In a matter of seconds, he opened the box and got the Galbraiths' key. I bit my lower lip as I watched him open the security door first and then the front door. Marshall was behind him but off to the side, and the posse volunteer was behind Marshall.

Ranston's voice was loud but garbled, and I had no idea what he was saying. However, I'd seen enough crime shows on TV to figure it out. One by one, the men entered the house, and all I could see were the two open doors.

My mouth went dry and I kept licking my lips and swallowing. No noise. No screams. No nothing. *Please don't let me hear a gunshot.*

Every minute felt like ten, and my hands began to shake. Then I saw another light go on. This time in the front. Either the kitchen or the bedroom, depending upon the floor plan. The front coach light came on, too, but still, no noise.

Next thing I knew, a girl, who couldn't have been older than sixteen or seventeen, given her loose tunic and tight leggings, stepped out of the doorway. Her voice carried in the still night air. "Don't tell my parents. Please don't tell my parents." She began to sob and Deputy Lopez, who was right behind her, was taking it all in.

I figured Ranston must have opened the back door to let Lopez and the posse volunteer inside.

As the girl continued to wail, another teenager was escorted out of the house. A boy, this time, and his captor was Ranston. The kid appeared to be the same age as the now-hysterical girl. "Give it a rest, Cassie!" he shouted. "You didn't kill anyone."

"No, but my parents are going to kill *me*!"

I figured I wasn't going to be caught up in any gunfire or equally dangerous stuff, so I got out of the car and put the keys in my pocket. I leaned against the car door and watched the bizarre scene in front of me. Marshall and the remaining posse volunteer exited the place and were conferring with Ranston.

Deputy Lopez opened the back door of Ranston's vehicle and nudged the girl inside.

I could still hear the sobs. "We didn't steal anything. Honest."

"Lopez!" Ranston shouted. "Have one of these sheriff volunteers go with you and take the girl to the Sun City West Posse Station. I've already called her parents. When you get back, we'll do the same with Romeo over here."

Deputy Lopez drove off without saying a word. Meanwhile, Ranston rubbed the back of his neck and walked toward the boy.

"What's going on?" I asked Marshall, who was now only a few feet from me.

"You're not going to believe this in a million years. Hell! I don't even believe it."

"What? Those two are the thieves who've been burglarizing the vacant homes? Where's their getaway car? There are no vehicles on the street."

Marshall choked back a laugh and shook his head. "I can't even spit it out. It's so, so insane. Insane and a tad ingenious."

"What? What's going on?"

"First of all, nothing at all to do with Cameron Tully. Absolutely nothing."

"Okay. Then what?"

"The Galbraiths' house is listed on Airtnt."

"Air T and T? Like Airbnb?"

"Uh-huh. Same premise, only slightly different. The 'tnt' stands for 'they're not there.' Some entrepreneur came up with the idea of renting out empty houses for a night to high school kids who want to have sex. And, get this, the 'tenant' has to sign a contract saying he or she will not smoke in the house. Unbelievable, huh? Apparently, the mastermind of this operation scopes out the houses and rents them by the night. They use one of those garage door disrupters to get in. No forced entry. Then, the 'tenants' park their car inside the garage so no one will be suspicious."

"You're kidding!"

"Oh, there's more. It gets better. There's even an app for last-minute bookings."

"My God."

My mind immediately jumped to my mother, who would be completely unnerved to learn that someone was using the house behind hers as a brothel. "We can't tell my mother this. Tell her it was a burglar. A petty thief. Anything but this."

"Hon, she's going to find out sooner or later. The sheriff's office is going to notify the Galbraiths and—"

"Oh, hell no! Don't look now, but here comes Herb Garrett."

Chapter 10

Herb parked his car across the street from ours and came rushing over. We could hear him panting from three yards away. "Whew! Looks like I got back in time. Is that the burglar over there? Looks like a kid. Is it a gang? Where are the rest of them?"

"You're looking at the entire scene," I said, "and he's not a burglar."

"Vandalism, huh? What'd the little creep destroy?"

Marshall and I gave each other that "let's come up with something" stare before he finally spoke. "Nothing. Nothing was destroyed. Or stolen. It was a high school Halloween prank. Seeing if he could get inside. He did. He got caught. Story's over."

Herb let out an exasperated sigh. "That makes two for two. The sheriff's deputies never caught up with the naked guy. So much for that. I'm calling it a night. Tell Harriet I'll talk to her tomorrow."

He collapsed into the front seat of his vehicle and paused. A few seconds later he started it up, made a three-point turn, and drove off.

"You might as well get back in the car, too, Phee," Marshall said. "I'm going to have a quick word with Ranston and we'll head back to your mother's."

As I buckled my seat belt, I turned my head to see the kid seated in the back of the posse car, his legs dangling over the side of the seat. Ranston was all but a foot away, his hand resting on his holstered gun.

Dear God. It's not like he apprehended Bonnie and Clyde.

Marshall approached them, but even with the window down, I couldn't hear the conversation. *Terrific. Of all nights to use "indoor voices."*

Ranston nodded once or twice, and Marshall did the same. Then the conversation ended.

"Everything okay?" I asked when Marshall got back in the car.

"Yeah. They'll arrange for a team to sweep the place to make sure nothing was destroyed, but that's about it. At least it didn't turn out to be anything more than a couple of hormone-driven kids."

"I don't think my mother is going to have the same low-keyed reaction as yours."

"We'll brace ourselves," Marshall replied. And then he laughed.

I was right. My mother's eyes were wide open when she got to the front door and she was rubbing her arms as if it was below zero in the house.

"I was at the back patio door. Watching. Couldn't see a darn thing. What was it? Did they catch a burglar? How many?"

"Only high school kids, Mom."

She slapped both sides of her cheeks and let out a groan. "Poor Janet. Those hoodlums probably ransacked the place. Was it a gang initiation? They come up here, you know. From Phoenix."

"You can relax, Harriet," Marshall said. "In fact, why don't we all sit down for a second?"

My mother plopped herself in one of her floral chairs while Marshall and I resumed our original positions on the couch. Streetman walked into the room, yawned, and trotted off to the master bedroom. For the next three or four minutes, Marshall tried to explain, as delicately as possible, what had ensued at the Galbraith residence.

My mother listened intently, putting a hand over her mouth every now and then.

"So, you see, Harriet," Marshall went on, "these were only high school kids trying to—"

"Turn my neighbors' house into Las Vegas. Next thing you know they'll set up a casino in the utility room."

"If it makes you feel any better, Deputy Ranston plans to investigate this online dating app, for lack of a better description, and shut it down. I get the sense the two kids who were caught will do a lot of talking."

"Sure," my mother said. "Now they'll talk. They've already done everything else! And what on earth am I supposed to tell Janet Galbraith?"

I shook my head and put my index finger to my lips. "Don't tell her anything. Let the sheriff's office call her first. I'm sure she'll call you and you can tell her the truth. You phoned in a nine-one-one call because the lights were on. No need to take it any further."

"I suppose you're right. When the details come out, I can act as shocked and surprised as the next person. At least it wasn't another dead body."

"Nope. No corpses tonight. Well, it's really late and we should get home. The sheriff's posse will check over the house and lock it up. You'll be fine," I said.

"I don't know how you can be so glib about this, Phee." She walked us to the front door. "I'm double-locking the security door like always." She shut it before we could utter, "Good night," and we heard her close and bolt the front one.

I could barely keep my eyes open on the way home and was grateful it was Marshall behind the wheel. Unlike me, he had a renewed sense of energy and was wide awake.

"If you don't mind, hon," he said when we got home, "I'm going to watch some mindless TV before I turn in. I'm too wired."

"I have a better idea to help you unwind." I was now fully awake after dozing off in the car. I put my arms around his neck and kissed both of his cheeks.

He returned the favor with a long, moist kiss. "I'm game for whatever channel you want."

The next morning hit us like a freight train. It was the usual scurry to the bathroom, shower, make coffee, and drive ourselves to the office. In addition to the follow-up interviews of customers and staff at Coldwater Seafood, Marshall still had his other cases to contend with—missing siblings, suspected infidelity, and background checks for one reason or another. He spent most of the day out of the office, and when he was here he was meeting with clients.

Nate's schedule wasn't all that different. I caught glimpses of him as he hustled from one project to the next. Augusta and I were the only ones who were anchored to the office, but both of us were swamped with work, too. Paperwork. At midmorning I told her about Airtnt.

She looked up from her desk and shook her head.

"That's the trouble with living in cities. No barns or haylofts."

I went back to my office and busied myself with spreadsheets and numbers.

The next few days were as routine as could be. With one exception. My mother's phone calls. It seemed she always caught me during my morning break to share gossipy tidbits or observations. It was a ruse. She really wanted to know if we'd made any headway on Cameron Tully's murder. Still, I let her ramble on and on about the other two events in her life—Janet Galbraith's mental state and the second Precious Pooches parade. This time the Thanksgiving theme.

Then, early one Tuesday morning in mid-November, she called me at work to inform me that "the Galbraiths are settling out of court."

"I didn't know the Galbraiths were in court," I said.

"They're not. That's the whole idea. The families of those two teenagers are paying the Galbraiths a lofty sum of money to keep their mouths shut about the unfortunate Halloween incident."

"How lofty?"

"Six thousand dollars. Each family is anteing up three."

"Whoa! I didn't think her house was vandalized or anything."

"It wasn't. But Janet Galbraith insisted she'd never be able to look at her solid maple king-size sleigh bed again. And she swore she'd never so much as touch the mattress. Not to mention the linens, the pillows, and her comforter. Oh, and the towels. Let's not forget the towels."

"Of course not. Heaven forbid we forget the towels."

"I'm being serious, Phee. This was very distressing for Janet. In fact, she's putting off coming back here until Christmas. Muttered something about bedbugs."

"Um, speaking of Christmas, Kalese will be flying in like always, but she wondered if she could stay with you instead of with Marshall and me. I feel awful. I don't want my own daughter to be uncomfortable staying with us. And neither does Marshall."

"Kalese wants to give you some privacy, that's all. She's not a little girl. She's a teacher. In her twenties. And I may have had something to do with her decision."

"What do you mean? What did you tell her?"

"That I haven't had a decent night's sleep since we found the dead body."

"That's not true, and you know it."

"But she doesn't. And I would really enjoy her company. I don't get to see my granddaughter often. And Streetman likes the attention."

Of course. The dog always has to enter into this. "She'll have a great time with you."

My mother's "news of the day" wasn't the only thing that caught my attention that morning. The forensic lab in Phoenix released the complete toxicology report on Elaine Meschow and the Maricopa County Sheriff's Office wanted Nate or Marshall to contact them immediately. Augusta had taken the phone call shortly after eleven and marched into my office to let me know.

"My guess is E. coli. Maybe giardia. Had a cat once with giardia. Left a real mess. Easy to pick up that stuff in one of those senior citizen communities. Those old folks are touching everything. Worse than babies."

"Did you let Nate and Marshall know?" I asked.

"Of course. Called both their cell numbers. So, what do you think? E. coli, huh?"

"According to Marshall, the hospital kept Mrs. Meschow

overnight and sent her home, so I doubt it was anything like salmonella or botulism. Those are the only food-borne illnesses I've really heard of."

"All kinds of bacteria and parasites are out there. Ever hear of vibrio? Nasty little illness. Comes from uncooked seafood. That's why you'll never catch me in one of those sushi places. It's a grilled steak for this girl."

"Um, I seriously don't think the sheriff's office would be contacting our office and insisting Nate or Marshall get back to them ASAP if it was simple food poisoning. When Marshall thought Mrs. Meschow had been poisoned, he was thinking something along the lines of—"

"Cyanide? Strychnine?"

"Er, not as Cold Warrish."

"Hemlock?"

"Too ancient. He was thinking it might be the same toxin they found in Cameron Tully's body—the sago palm."

"That's a jump, isn't it?"

"More like an Evel Knievel Snake River jump, if you ask me. But Marshall seems to have some pretty sharp insights when it comes to this stuff. And if it turns out to be true, then we have to ask ourselves what Elaine Meschow and Cameron Tully might have had in common."

"All this talk about food poisoning and plant poisoning is making me question my lunch choices today," Augusta said. "Forget fish. And I hear the chicken might be imported from China. And beef is always questionable. What the heck does that leave?"

"Bacon, lettuce, and tomato."

"Fine. I'll order one for you and one for me from the deli. The men are on their own."

Nate finally walked in a few seconds before his three

o'clock appointment arrived. A young man in his twenties trying to find his birth mother. And while Augusta and I were dying to know what Mrs. Meschow's tox report said, we couldn't very well broach the subject out in the open.

Augusta did her best to improvise. "So, is that a yes on the decorative sago palm for the outer office, Mr. Williams?" she asked as he escorted his client out of there.

"Decorative what? Ask me about it later, okay?"

"Good try, Augusta. Very subtle." I went back to my office and put aside all thoughts about toxins.

If I couldn't add it, subtract it, or balance it, I didn't want any part of it. The next hour and forty minutes were delightful. A quiet office and simple spreadsheets. Nothing to interrupt my thought processes. That was, until my mother called again.

"Mom, we spoke this morning. Nothing's changed."

"Maybe not for you, but for Elaine Meschow it did. I've been on the phone with her for fifteen minutes."

Gee, what did she do to deserve such a short call? "Um, okay."

"Two detectives stopped by her house today. The same two they always send."

"Ranston and Bowman."

"Yes. Them. Anyway, they informed her of the toxicology results. Said she'd be getting more information from her medical provider, but you and I know that could take at least a month. If not more. They're in no rush when you're over sixty-five."

Oh no. Don't tell me we're going to launch into the demise of health care for senior citizens. "What did they tell her? Was it food poisoning?"

"It was the same thing that killed Cameron Tully. Sago palm poisoning. She's lucky to be alive. It wasn't the same dose or quantity or whatever-you-call-it that Cameron had."

"Oh my gosh. Nate's with a client and Marshall's out of the office. I'm sure the sheriff's office emailed them already. It might not be a coincidence. Marshall might have been right all along."

"Elaine is on the verge of a breakdown. She's petrified to eat or drink anything she hasn't scrutinized."

"Well, that's very understandable. I'm sure the detectives will—"

"Will what? Take their own sweet time? They asked her a million questions, you know. Like what she did that day and who she talked with. My God, Phee, that was the Friday before Halloween. Elaine can't remember who she talked to yesterday, let alone two weeks ago. And she's worried about Prince. In case someone tries to poison the dog."

"It's been over two weeks and the dog's okay, right? Maybe Mrs. Meschow inadvertently poisoned herself by touching one of those plants."

"She doesn't own one. Not in her house or in her yard. And she's not the type to go walking over to someone else's house and fiddle with their landscaping."

"Like I started to say, I'm sure the sheriff's office will get to the bottom of this."

"Oh, come on, Phee. Who are you kidding? I don't think so and neither does Elaine. That's why she wants you to investigate."

"What? Oh no. Oh no. We're not doing this again. What did you tell her? You didn't tell her I was an investigator, did you?"

"Not directly. No. I told her you worked for Williams Investigations. I can't help it if people draw their own conclusions."

Aargh. She had me at that. Truth be known, I had relied on innuendo on more than one occasion. But only to get into a crime scene. Not solve it. And what was I supposed to do when there was a dead body hanging from the catwalk at the theater where my mother had a lead role? Or on the bocce court when her friend Myrna Mittleson thought she killed someone with a stray bocce ball? I closed my eyes and rubbed my forehead.

"I suppose you told her to call me, right?"

"More or less. I told her *you'd* call her tonight. Here's the number: six-two-three five-four-six seven-three—"

"I'm not writing this down."

"Elaine isn't going to get anywhere with those two Neanderthals that call themselves detectives. They make her nervous. And I don't have to tell you that when someone's nervous, they can't think."

Oh God, no! Are we going to relive my fifth-grade talent show? "I'm going to tell her the truth, Mom. That I'm an accountant."

"Fine. Tell her anything you want, but call her."

I thought about it for a moment and realized it could be an opportunity. If I could get Mrs. Meschow to relax and remember the events leading up to her collapse at the dog park, I might be able to find a connection between her near-death moment and Cameron's fait accompli.

"You win. Give me that number again."

Chapter 11

My mother was right. Elaine Meschow was a complete basket case and desperate to see me. I called her that evening after Marshall and I had eaten dinner. Leftover arroz con pollo, aka Spanish chicken, from the night before.

"As far as I'm concerned"—he put the last of the dishes in the dishwasher—"you're simply meeting with a lovely lady from the dog club to find out how she fared after her bout with food poisoning."

"Boy, are you a liar!"

"I'm giving you the official party line. Face it, half the time we're able to solve cases because people are more apt to open up with friends than they are with investigators. Hey, it's no different than Nate and me chatting with the folks connected to Coldwater Seafood. In that case, they'd rather face us instead of the authorities."

"Oh my gosh. You and my mother are beginning to sound alike."

"So, when are you going to see her? Mrs. Meschow, I mean."

"Tomorrow. After work. I'll drive over to her house. That is, if you don't mind picking something up for dinner."

"You name it. I can dial one eight hundred carryout as fast as the next guy."

"Sure you're okay with this?"

He wiped his hands on a kitchen towel and placed them behind my neck, pulling me close. Soft little kisses morphed into a lingering kiss, and I tasted the saffron on his tongue for a brief second.

"Um, I guess you answered my question."

"At your service."

"Seriously, I'm not sure what I should be asking her. In addition to her whereabouts, what she ate, what she touched. That sort of thing."

"Those will be the easy questions. What you want to find out is if she had any connection with Cameron Tully."

"She told the sheriff's deputies she didn't."

"That's because, knowing Ranston and Bowman, they asked her directly. You need to take another route."

"I'm not sure I understand."

"It's simple, really. Try to delve into her background and see if you can pull up anything that might possibly connect the two incidents. I don't think it will be that hard. Take your mother's friends for example. They blurt out more information about themselves and their lives without any prompting. Like the time Louise Munson went on and on about having to drive her bird to Fountain Hills so some specialist could clip its beak. After fifteen grueling minutes listening to her, I wanted to clip a beak, too, only not the bird's."

Both of us broke up laughing and we left it at that. I said I'd try and Marshall did his usual bit of magic convincing me I had the right skill set for the job. I went to sleep that night with a renewed sense of confidence. Unfortunately, the feeling didn't last when I rang Mrs. Meschow's doorbell the next evening.

Her house was located a few blocks north of my mother's place. It was one of many small villas that were managed by a homeowners' association. I had learned from my mother that when Mr. Meschow passed away, his wife didn't want to maintain their enormous golf course home on "millionaire's row," so she sold it at a nice profit and downsized into one of the villas.

And while the house was certainly petite, it was also stunning. Its front patio featured a three-tiered Tuscan-designed water fountain surrounded by boxwood beauties and taller agaves. Offset by muted white LED lights, it looked like something only HGTV could create. Her security door was made-to-order as well, with the agave design running through it instead of the usual straight metal lines.

My finger tapped the intricate bronze doorbell and a dog immediately began to bark. Prince. The little Yorkshire Terrier.

"You must be Phee, Harriet's daughter." Mrs. Meschow opened the door and motioned me inside. Prince sniffed my leg and, for a second, I was certain he was going to lift his.

"He wants you to pick him up. He's excited to see you."

Unless he's going to do something weird and unpredictable like Streetman. I bent down and snatched up the little bundle of fur. "I think he remembers me from the Halloween pet parade at the dog park. I was holding him until your daughter found us."

"What a horrible afternoon. I don't recall anything beyond getting tangled up in those cobwebs. What moron thought of stringing those in the trees?"

"I, er . . ."

"It doesn't matter. I'm just glad to be alive. Come on, have a seat in the living room and feel free to put Prince down. Don't worry. He'll jump up next to you on the couch. Or wherever you sit."

I chose the love seat. It offered the grandest view of her house and plenty of room for me and a furry friend. For a small villa, not much bigger than the casita I rented when I first moved out here, Elaine Meschow's place was breathtaking. I was certain she had hired a decorator to see to every detail. The style was overwhelmingly southwestern from her choice in furnishings to the subtle yellow and beige colors she had selected for her walls. A stone veneer media wall with recessed lighting gave the place its "wow factor."

"Can I offer you something to drink? Soda? Coffee? Water?" she asked.

"Thanks. No. I'm fine."

"I want to tell you how much I appreciate your willingness to find out who's trying to kill me."

"Um, two things. First, you do realize I'm not a licensed private investigator, right? I work for Williams Investigations but not in that capacity."

"Titles don't mean anything to me."

"Uh-huh, and the other thing . . . What makes you think someone is trying to kill you? I mean, I know you ingested some poison, but that could've been an accident or a fluke or—"

"I'd believe *that* if it was food poisoning or a prescription overdose, but you've got to admit, who on earth ever heard of sago palm poisoning until that body was found behind your mother's house?"

"From what I've heard, it's pretty common knowledge among veterinarians, since small animals wind up ingesting the seeds or bits of the palm if they're prone to eating grass or dirt."

"Are you saying it could be Prince's vet? Why on earth would Dr. VanSant want to kill me?"

"Wait. What? That's not what I said. I was only clarifying something. So, er, let's start over. Suppose you backtrack and tell me everything that happened starting the day before the pet parade."

Mrs. Meschow took a deep breath, clasped her hands, and leaned forward. She was seated opposite me on a full-size couch and the Boca coffee table that separated us was fairly large. I leaned forward, too.

There was absolutely nothing unusual about her activities. Breakfasts at home, lunches both days at Bagels 'N More, a local hot spot that my mother and her crew favored, and dinner at home. One stop to the library and a grooming appointment for Prince the day of the parade. All very mundane. I asked her to be a bit more specific about the actual day in question.

"I was feeling perfectly fine Friday morning when I dropped Prince off for his grooming. Fine at lunch, too. Then, shortly before I picked him up in the early afternoon, my stomach felt a bit out of sorts. I figured it must've been the lox I ate at lunch. It can do that to you, you know. Very salty and heavy. I took a few Tums and drank some ginger ale. By that time I had to get ready for the parade."

I nodded.

"My stomach was still out of sorts when I got to the

park, and by then I assumed it was one of those nasty gastrointestinal things. Luckily, Prince was number eighteen, so we didn't have long to wait, and, well, you know the rest."

I knew more than I cared to tell her. With sago palm poisoning, the nervous system was often attacked a few days after the initial indigestion and, worse yet, liver failure and death could occur two or three days later if untreated. Cameron Tully must've thought his initial symptoms were some sort of bug, too.

"Mrs. Meschow, who did you eat lunch with that Friday?"

"My neighbor, Inge. We've been eating lunch together on Fridays since I moved into this house."

Guess I can strike Inge, whoever she is, off the list.

Biting my lower lip, I tried to think of what I could ask Mrs. Meschow next. Then it dawned on me. Marshall had told me to get her to talk about her background. Anything that might give us a lead.

"I understand you have a company that manufactures and sells natural dog food. Guess that comes in handy for Prince."

"Oh, I'm not involved with Spellbound Naturals. It was always my late husband Sanford's enterprise. My daughter and my son-in-law run the business now, but it's in both Bethany's and my names. It's still in Chandler, but so much has changed since it was first established. I hardly recognize the products."

"What do you mean?"

"Back in the late eighties, my husband introduced a line of dog food that was virtually unheard of. It didn't have any fillers or by-products. Only top-quality beef from Iowa. Same with the chicken and turkey. Nothing imported. Ten years later he added venison, duck, and lamb for dogs with sensitive stomachs."

"Uh, how did your husband know so much about the dietary needs of canines?"

"He didn't. He spent a lot of time researching. My husband was in the food service industry for a number of years working with restaurants and hotel chains. He always felt that if certain foods can increase human longevity, then those products must have the same effect on dogs and cats."

This isn't going anywhere. Unless . . .

"You said the products changed. What did you mean?"

"I mean, Spellbound Naturals derives most of its profit from fish."

"Fish."

"Yes. Salmon. Cod. Tuna. Ocean whitefish. Who would ever imagine a dog taking a liking to fish, but apparently they do."

"Fish."

"Yes, that's what I said."

"I'm sorry, I'm just trying to process it." *And not jump out of my skin because I might have actually found a link.*

"You wouldn't happen to know the distributor the company uses, would you?"

"Dear me, no. All of that is Bethany's business. Well, hers and her husband's. Mr. I've-got-a-business-degree-from-Wharton-and-you-don't. They run it."

"Oh. I take it her husband might be a bit of a—"

"Snob. And feel free to leave off the *n*. I shouldn't be saying such things about my son-in-law, but Tucker Cabot fits the bill. I can't believe they're going on their twelfth anniversary. I wouldn't have lasted with that man for twelve weeks, let alone years."

For a split second, I wondered if her son-in-law might have wanted his mother-in-law out of the picture. Inheritance and all. Money was one of the three main motives in murder cases, along with love and revenge. But that wouldn't explain how Cameron Tully wound up under a tarp behind my mother's house.

"When was the last time you saw Tucker?"

"Probably a few weeks ago, but Bethany stops by here whenever she has clients in the area. I much prefer visiting with her alone."

"I can understand that. I mean, if Tucker's such a—"

"Oh, he is. Believe me. He is."

Enough to want to commit murder? "Um, getting back to your original fear, you never said why you thought someone might be trying to kill you. Is there anything I should know?"

"Maybe. I had words with that miserable Phyllis Gruber from the dog park. She's the owner of Sir Breckenthall the Third. Some sort of fancy spaniel. That insufferable woman had the gall to tell me Yorkshire Terriers, like my little Prince, were as commonplace as weeds around here. Said I shouldn't bother entering him in the contest. Was very adamant about that. So I told her where she could stuff it. And I wasn't the least bit polite about it."

Sir Breckenthall the Third. It's a darn good thing he's a dog and not a child or every kid on the playground would be lining up to fight him. "Mrs. Meschow, I honestly don't think Phyllis Gruber tried to poison you. It would be a stretch. Even if she is as nasty as all that. Anyway, my office will keep working on the case. In the meantime, I'd suggest you only eat packaged foods or foods from places you trust. And wash your hands a lot." *By God! I've become my mother.* "Oh, and one more thing . . ."

"Yes?"

"Would Bethany mind if we talked with her? She might be aware of something that you're not."

"Bethany? I'm not sure how she can help you, but sure. Hold on and I'll get you her cell number."

Prince jumped off the couch and followed his mistress into the kitchen while I took a deep breath and tried to think of anything I'd forgotten to ask. Of course, the million-dollar question was whether or not Coldwater Seafood was the distributor for Spellbound Naturals and if it was, could that have something to do with Cameron's unfortunate demise?

Patrons of five-star restaurants would be appalled to learn they were sharing the same premium seafood as their pets. If it turned out to be true and Cameron was about to make it public knowledge, it wouldn't surprise me in the least if some restauranteur decided to bump him off. But why on earth would Cameron do a thing like that? Sabotage his own position with the company. None of this was adding up.

"Here's Bethany's number." Mrs. Meschow handed me a floral note card. "I'm sure she'll want to help. She was quite distraught the day of the incident. Fortunately, she was in the area, in Surprise, when the hospital called her. Usually she meets with her West Valley clientele on Tuesdays and Wednesdays. In fact, I don't remember her ever coming up this way on a Friday. Oh well, it doesn't matter. You've got her number. Give her a call."

I thanked Mrs. Meschow, gave Prince a pat on the head, and reassured her once again that Williams Investigations would work diligently to find out who was behind the sago palm poisonings.

"Have your office send me a bill, dear, would you?

I've learned if you don't pay for services, nothing gets done."

"Um, uh, sure. We'll take care of it."

I stepped outside and took a moment to enjoy her gorgeous front patio. In full darkness, the LED lights made the place look magical. Two minutes later I was in my car and headed home to my own enchanted kingdom. Take-out food and all.

Chapter 12

"I'm home!" I called out to Marshall once I got in the door. "Dinner smells fantastic. What'd you pick up?"

He stepped out of the kitchen with a big grin. "I got tired of pizza and subs, so I got us a rotisserie chicken and actually made fingerling potatoes. They're either raw or overdone. You can decide for yourself. Oh, and before I forget, your mother left a phone message while you were meeting with Elaine Meschow."

"Good grief. It's like my mother has extrasensory perception or, worse yet, a bug on my phone line. She probably wants to know what I found out."

Marshall laughed. "It was more of a reminder call than her usual inquisitions."

I tossed my bag on the small entryway table, kicked off my shoes, and walked to the phone. "Might as well get it over with."

I'm not sure why, but my mother and my aunt Ina had a tendency to raise their voices when they were leaving recorded messages. "We're not preparing for a wartime air-raid drill," I once told them, but it fell on deaf ears. Maybe that was it. Their hearing was slowly diminishing.

I pushed the message button and listened.

"Phee! Marshall! You need to write this down. I'll wait." Long pause. "Okay. The Thanksgiving Precious Pooches pet parade is the Friday before Thanksgiving. At the dog park. I think I told you that. Anyway, it's at three. Three o'clock. Are you writing this down? I wanted you to have plenty of advance notice so you can arrange your schedules. Maybe work through lunch or something. I also left a message for Nate, but he always seems to have business out of town."

"I can't believe this." I wasn't sure if my voice could be heard over my mother's. I stopped talking and let the message continue.

"It's very important to Streetman. Okay, fine. I'll catch you later. Bye."

Marshall rubbed the back of his neck and smiled. "I'm sure the dog is counting the days until your mother stuffs him into that glittering acorn. I probably shouldn't say it, but from what you've described, he's going to look like one of those 1970s disco balls."

"Go ahead. Laugh. It's funny."

We looked at each other, and next thing I knew we were doubled over, tears streaming down both of our faces.

Finally, I took a breath. "All I can say is, Streetman better outshine that Sir Breckenthall or that's all we'll be hearing about. Oh my gosh. That reminds me. Elaine Meschow had an issue with that dog's owner, Phyllis Gruber. In fact, Mrs. Meschow thought Phyllis might have been the one who tried to poison her."

"Seriously?"

"Uh-huh. Apparently, Phyllis Gruber insulted Elaine

Meschow's dog and Mrs. Meschow didn't take it lightly. But poisoning? I told her it was really unlikely."

"Good."

"There's something else. It's a long shot, but it might be a link. Elaine Meschow's daughter, Bethany Cabot, and her husband, Tucker, run the family company, Spellbound Naturals. It's right here in Chandler, and they produce health food for dogs. Natural ingredients only. And one of those ingredients happens to be fish. Fish!"

Marshall squinted and motioned for me to continue.

"Like I said. 'Fish.' Look, we know Cameron Tully's company was supplying all those high-end restaurants and supermarket chains with seafood, but what if he was also supplying the dog food manufacturing company? If word got out that La Mar Maravillosa or any of those other fancy places were buying their 'catch of the day' from a dog food distributor, it would make headlines and not in the gourmet section of the papers."

"True. True. But that's motive for *Cameron* to silence the would-be snitch. Not the other way around."

I tapped my teeth for a moment, an annoying habit I hoped Marshall wouldn't notice. "Unless Cameron had every intention of doing so, but the killer found a way to poison him first. So do you think I might be on to something?"

Marshall took a step toward me and, before I could say another word, planted a sweet but short kiss on my lips. "We'll find out soon enough. First thing tomorrow I'll call the Cabots and ask them."

"Uh, it's probably inconsequential, but Elaine Meschow isn't very fond of her son-in-law. Thinks the guy is a bit of a snot. Overbearing, too. He's one of those who have to make all the decisions."

"Yikes. Remind me to stay on your mother's good

side. Listen, my dinner's probably in enough trouble as it is without getting cold. Come on, grab a plate."

I wasted no time tasting the food.

"I'm hiring you as the full-time chef." I dabbed a bit of butter from the corner of my mouth. "I've had fingerling potatoes before but not with herb butter. It's definitely a keeper."

"If you like my potatoes, you'll adore what I can do with Minute Rice. Or any prepackaged meal, for that matter."

I gave him a wink and cleared the table.

"Need a hand with the dishwasher?" he asked.

"Nah. Go relax. You've done more than your share tonight."

"I don't mind. I really enjoy this. It was never fun cooking or eating alone all those years. I'm making up for lost time."

I had to admit, he was right. After Kalese left for college, preparing food had always seemed like such a burden, and eating out got old fast. But with Marshall and me, things seemed to flow. Maybe because we were so new to the relationship. I'd call it the honeymoon phase, but we weren't even engaged. I refused to let myself think any further than that for fear I'd send him packing and flying back to Minnesota. Nope, if anything was going to scare him, let it be my mother and the book club ladies.

We migrated to the couch and turned on the TV to find "Breaking News" instead of the usual lineup. The Tempe police were on the scene at La Mar Maravillosa, where someone in a dark hoodie and scream mask held the owner at gunpoint in the kitchen. It was only when one of the dishwashers was able to get to their alarm system and push the panic button that the person in the scream mask exited the place. No one was injured and nothing was taken. According to the news, the suspect was still "at large."

"That's Jocelyn Amaro's restaurant. Cameron's former girlfriend," Marshall said. "Looks like your dog food company lead will have to wait. I'll have Augusta check my schedule tomorrow and see when I can get over to Tempe to have a word with Jocelyn."

"You think the situation at her restaurant might have something to do with Cameron's murder?"

"I'm not sure. Remember when I said I thought those restaurant owners might be hiding something? Well, maybe this little event at La Mar Maravillosa isn't random. No sense waiting for a police report when Jocelyn may feel compelled to talk with me."

"I hope you're right. It doesn't sound as if Nate is having any better luck uncovering anything where Coldwater Seafood and those supermarket chains are concerned."

"Yeah. Business as usual. According to Nate, none of the supermarket managers had any issues with Cameron. Deliveries were made on time. The product arrived as specified and there are no delinquent accounts."

"I always like to hear those three words."

"'No delinquent accounts'?"

"Uh-huh. Why? What three words were you thinking of?"

"Come on. I'll show you."

"What? And miss the TV lineup?"

"You bet."

The next morning, Augusta tried as best as she could to rearrange Marshall's schedule, but she was only able to shave off an hour at the end of the day. Still, an hour was better than nothing, and an hour was all he needed. He was ecstatic Jocelyn agreed to see him. Then he did something totally unexpected. He made a reservation for the two of us. Exact time to be determined, dependent upon the ending time of his meeting with her. I seriously wondered how the reservation staff wrote it in their book.

"Are you sure this is all right?" I asked him.

Augusta had finally straightened out his schedule and Marshall appeared to be relieved.

"If you're worried about ditching work early, it's business," he said. "If you don't like gourmet seafood, then we're in trouble."

"I love seafood. It's fish I can't stand. Except maybe for tuna or salmon. Or Friday night fish fry if they do it in beer batter."

"Hmm. I think you'll find something on the menu you'll like. But I have another motive other than wanting to spend as much time as I can with you."

"What? What motive?"

"Sleuthing. You're good at it, you know. You do it without even realizing it half the time."

Oh God no! My mother's rubbing off on him. "Uh-huh. What exactly is it you want me to do?"

"Find out if Jocelyn was telling me the truth about her breakup with Cameron."

"And how am I supposed to do that?"

"While Jocelyn and I discuss last night's break-in, you can unobtrusively chat with the bartender or any other employees. See what they're willing to cough up. It's not a pretty business, but people have been known to talk. Especially about their bosses."

"That's it? The breakup?"

"Partially. I'm also curious about their take on Jocelyn

being held at gunpoint last night. Maybe they're aware of something they don't want to share with the police."

"You think they'll tell me?"

"You have a way with people, Phee. Honestly, they feel comfortable around you."

"Let's hope so." I looked down at my charcoal slacks, matching blazer, and top. "Um, I wasn't exactly prepared for a dinner at La Mar Maravillosa. Am I dressed all right for tonight? It's not as if we're going to have time to run home and change."

"You'd look good in a sackcloth, hon. It's a fancy restaurant, but it's not Buckingham Palace."

"I'll keep that in mind."

Nate had a follow-up meeting with one of the supermarket chain managers and, from there, surveillance for another case. He, too, had thought I was pretty good at sleuthing and at one time tried to convince me I might make a decent detective. That was before I found myself face down in a dumpster trying to find a clue for my mother. Nope, bookkeeping and accounting were fine with me. It wasn't as if I craved a high-octane job.

My day was nondescript. The usual paperwork and revelations from Augusta whenever she took a break. At a little before five, Marshall and I left for Tempe. Jocelyn's late-afternoon/early-evening chef would be on duty at six, the time she agreed to see Marshall.

We took the 101 out of Glendale and crawled along with the rest of the rush-hour traffic. The thirty-five-minute drive had turned into fifty and the street traffic in Tempe slowed us down as well.

"We'll make it right on time." Marshall pulled into their parking lot. "Think you'll be okay?"

"As long as no one holds me at gunpoint, sure."

La Mar Maravillosa was located a few blocks from Mill Avenue, Arizona State University's college hub. The restaurant was housed in a spectacular Spanish colonial building that was the focal point of a huge corner lot. A rarity in the Phoenix area. Graceful topiaries lined the colorful tiled path that led to the front entrance.

Once inside, I looked around slowly, trying to take in the expansive lobby. Wrought-iron benches and three strategically placed water features dominated the area. And while bougainvillea and honeysuckle were abundant, no palm trees were visible. And definitely no sago palms.

Off to the left was a separate room with a long bar and more of the same wrought-iron furnishings. This time in the form of barstools and small bistro tables. Again, the bougainvillea. Five or six patrons were at the bar, with a few more people seated at the bistro tables.

Unlike other restaurants, where the host or hostess area consisted of a podium, La Mar Maravillosa's welcoming station was an elaborately carved oak table framed by two large vases on either side, each filled with fragrant flowers. A thin curly-haired woman, who looked to be my daughter's age, greeted us.

"I'll let Miss Amaro know you're here," she said to Marshall, and quickly picked up the phone, one of the few items on her table.

"That's my hint to saunter over to the bar," I whispered.

As I turned from the table, I froze. Standing directly in front of me were my aunt Ina and uncle Louis. While some people could unobtrusively blend into whatever venue they happened to occupy, my aunt and uncle could not.

Louis Melinsky, all five foot two of him, was wearing

a dark suit with a burgundy tie. That, in combination with his pinstriped shirt, made him look like an old-time gangster. Aunt Ina, however, was no gun moll. She was dressed in a long teal sheath that clung to her hips, making them appear twice their usual size. A wild paisley wrap hung dubiously over one shoulder, but it was her hairdo that really caught my eye. Mine and, I imagined, everyone's in a ten-mile radius.

Usually my aunt wore her long braids with tinsel or ribbon encased in them, but tonight, for some reason, she decided to have her hair swept above her head in a French knot that resembled Mont-Saint-Michel.

"Phee! What are you doing here? Don't tell me Harriet's with you. I can't imagine my sister ever leaving that compound in Sun City West."

"Um, Aunt Ina, Uncle Louis. Great to see you. No, it's only Marshall and me."

At the sound of his name, Marshall turned away from the hostess. "Hi! Nice to see you again. Are you just arriving?"

"Oh, heavens no," my aunt said. "Louis and I are on our way to an art exhibit near the university. The reception begins at seven, but I couldn't bear waiting to eat at some ungodly hour. I'm not twenty-one anymore."

"So, uh, how was your meal?" I asked.

"Splendid. Absolutely splendid. Order the Chilean sea bass. You won't be sorry."

"The mahi-mahi with asparagus and almond sauce was good, too. Always a decent choice," Louis said.

Suddenly my brain kicked into gear. "That's right; I forgot you were a food connoisseur as well as a musician."

Louis smiled and moved closer to my aunt. "Food, music, and the love of my life. I have it all. Of course, if anything had gone wrong with that robbery last night, we wouldn't have had the pleasure of dining in one of our favorite restaurants this evening." Then he looked at Marshall. "Say, is that why you're here? To investigate?"

"The Tempe police are investigating last night's incident," Marshall replied. "Attempted robbery, if that's what it was, is for the local jurisdictions. They usually don't call in private investigators."

My uncle motioned Marshall and me closer and spoke softly. "That would depend on what the perpetrator was trying to rob. If you ask me, they should've chosen Taste of the Sea in Scottsdale and absconded with their seafood. The quality has been spiraling downhill for months. And Neptune's Delicacies in Phoenix isn't much better, I'm afraid. What a sad state of affairs. And don't get me started on Aphrodite's Appetite downtown. Their garlic shrimp skewers were more like guppies on a stick. At least La Mar Maravillosa has maintained its standards. When they closed for a week to redo their kitchen, or whatever they were working on, Ina and I had to resort to red meat and an overabundance of chicken. Do you have any idea how boring chicken can be? Anyway, we must be getting along or we won't find a decent parking spot for the art show."

My aunt took a step toward me and gave me a hug, her wrap practically covering my face.

"Take care, Aunt Ina. Uncle Louis, too. See you soon."

Marshall waved good-bye to them and gave my arm a light squeeze. "Coldwater Seafood is the distributor for all three of the restaurants Louis mentioned. A problem with their chefs or with the fish? As I recall, none of those restaurants had any issues with Cameron Tully, unless they weren't being forthright with me. Great. That'll keep gnawing at me all night."

I didn't get a chance to respond because Jocelyn approached us within seconds of my aunt and uncle leaving. Tall and slender, with jet-black hair in a stylish upsweep. Marshall introduced me and told her I'd be waiting at the bar while they talked. I muttered something about it being nice making her acquaintance and she replied with similar small talk.

"Catch you in a bit," I said to Marshall.

Jocelyn held her palm up and smiled. "Hold on a second, will you? Let the bartender know you're my guest. He'll comp your drinks."

"Oh. Thanks. That's nice of you."

"My pleasure." She motioned for Marshall to follow her, and I watched as they walked past the bar to a small alcove that I presumed led to her office.

Marshall whipped his head around and caught my eye. "Wait for me at the bar."

I nodded.

A few more patrons had taken their places at the bar and the bistro tables were filling up fast. I took one of the empty seats at the end, giving me a full view of the room. Within seconds, a robust bartender with a full mustache and goatee greeted me. I explained I was a guest of the owner and he didn't question it.

"What would you like?"

"Tonic water and lime."

"Hang on."

The guy was fast. He placed a small bowl of assorted rice crackers and wasabi peas in front of me and followed it with my tonic water. At the far end of the bar, another bartender was waiting on customers. A woman. Tall, with shoulder-length brown hair that was a shade darker than her skin. Late twenties or early thirties.

"Can I get you anything else?" my bartender asked. "The wait times around here can be long."

"I'm fine, thanks. Probably a whole lot better than your boss. I'm surprised the restaurant opened today. It was all over the news. Her being held at gunpoint and all. That poor woman. I wouldn't blame her if she'd stayed home."

"Jocelyn can't afford to lose a day's business. Yeah, she was shaken up, but not hurt or anything. And nothing was broken or stolen. Probably some jerk who was looking for the cash drawer. Didn't stop to think we're not Quick Stop or the 7-Eleven. These high-end restaurants have safes, not cash drawers."

"Were you working last night? Did you see what happened?"

"Yes and no. Working, yes. But I was here at the bar. From what I know, all the regulars were working last night. That's the strange thing. None of us saw the gunman walk in. It was a busy night. Oh heck. They're all busy nights and the weekends are worse. Real easy for someone to walk in, pull a hoodie over his or her head, and stick a scream mask on. Probably bought it for a discount after Halloween."

"You think they were looking for money, huh?"

"Uh, yeah. I mean, what else would they want? Not many people are going to walk out of the place with a barrel full of fresh fish."

I paused for a second to pull my thoughts together. "I agree with you, you know."

"What do you mean?"

"About the person not realizing there was no cash drawer. Unless that wasn't it at all. Unless they weren't after money. Unless it was personal. Like revenge. Funny, that Jocelyn's ex-boyfriend was found dead under suspicious circumstances."

"Whoa! Hold it right there. How do you know so much? Wait a minute. Wait a minute. . . ."

Damn it, I'm trapped.

"Were you in here the other night with that group of women who sat in the back and kept ordering white wine? I thought you looked familiar. It was Paige, wasn't it? I swear that waitress can't keep her mouth shut. Tough break for Cameron Tully, but Jocelyn wouldn't so much as kill a fly. I've worked here for over six years, and she's not like that."

Geez, I hope I'm not starting a scene. What if this guy has the hots for his boss? "Um, sorry if I hit a nerve. I didn't mean to."

"No worries. Cameron Tully didn't deserve to die like that, but he was a real piece of work. Believe me, I could think of lots of words to describe him, but this is a respectable establishment."

Chapter 13

I took a sip of my drink and rolled the small straw around in my glass. "I don't suppose you have any ideas who might have killed him?"

"It had to be a woman." He grabbed a dishcloth and wiped the bar. "To pull off murdering someone using a sago palm instead of a gun or a knife. Yeah, it was a woman, all right. Someone he jilted before Jocelyn came along. Cameron was always on the prowl for the latest catch of the day, even when he was dating someone as gorgeous as her."

"Were the two of them dating long?"

"He spent more time flirting with her before he actually started dating her. I've worked in other establishments like this before, and I've never known a food distributor to show up so often."

"You think it was personal. His murder, I mean."

"I doubt it was business related. La Mar Maravillosa has never had any problems with Coldwater Seafood. Deliveries are always on time and the chefs never complain about the product. Yep, it has to be a woman out for revenge. Excuse me, will you? I've got a customer a few seats down."

I nursed my drink for a few minutes and watched the steady stream of patrons enter or exit the bar. At one point, I checked the time on my iPhone and scanned for emails. The bartender returned and brought me another drink.

"Thanks. So, deliveries are on time and all that. It sounds as if you're pretty familiar with how this restaurant runs."

"Six years on the job. I should hope so. It's not bad for a retirement gig."

"Retirement? You look too young to be retired."

The guy swaggered as he reached behind to get a glass. "Twenty years as a Phoenix firefighter. Then two years working for Happy Valley Nurseries. Too much digging and planting for me. Tending bar gives me the best of both worlds—some excitement now and then and enough exercise."

I watched as he filled the glass with Kahlúa and rum before handing it to the man seated two stools away from me.

"Um, one more question and I promise to leave you alone."

"Go ahead."

"Do you know why Cameron ended their relationship?"

"Who told you he was the one who ended the relationship? Oh yeah. Probably Paige. Well, this time she got it wrong. Jocelyn dumped him and dropped her account with his company. I think he took it harder than anyone would expect. Came back here to talk to Jocelyn shortly before he was found dead."

My fingers moved the swizzle stick faster in my drink and all I could say was, "Oh."

"Yeah. And of all things, he winds up having a run-in with her brother. Talk about another piece of work. The brother was in the area and stopped by. They got into it back there." He pointed to the far corner of the bar.

"About the breakup?" I asked.

The bartender shook his head. "I think it had more to do with Coldwater Seafood. Cameron was spouting off about fraud and I heard him all the way over here. He said, 'That's nothing to brag about. I've a good mind to notify the authorities.' And then the brother said, 'You won't be able to prove a thing.' They must've been talking about something Jocelyn was doing, but I'd be hard pressed to believe she would put this restaurant at risk."

"Yikes."

"Oh, it gets better. Cameron's feathers must've gotten really ruffled, because next thing I heard him say was, 'One call and your ass is on the line. Think I'm kidding? Try me.'"

"What happened?"

"The brother got up and stormed out. Came back for his jacket and made sure to knock over Cameron's drink."

"Bet that didn't go over too well."

"Not as bad as expected. Cameron was drinking a dark ale we had on tap. Next thing I knew, the brother bought him another one and I brought it to the table. After that, nothing. He left and Cameron stayed till he finished his beer."

Marshall appeared a few minutes later and took the empty seat next to mine. "Hey, good looking, can I buy you a drink?"

"Any more drinks and I'll float out of here. But we really need to leave the bartender a very generous tip."

"Stellar service?"

"Stellar intel. Oh, and we've got to be sure we ask for Paige to be our waitress."

As our luck would have it, Paige was off for the night and our waiter was an older gentleman by the name of Bernard. He was efficient, mild mannered, and tight-lipped. The only thing we got out of him was five-star service and a fabulous meal. Prawn risotto for me and salmon piccata for Marshall.

We were seated at a dimly lit corner table far enough away from the other guests so we didn't have to worry about being overheard.

"Jocelyn lied. Cameron didn't dump her. At least not according to the bartender." I picked up the menu but then put it down. "I don't get it. Usually it's the other way around. You know, the woman telling everyone it was her idea to lose the louse."

"Not if *she* was the one double-timing him. I had a hunch and your sleuthing paid off. Look, I'm no expert on these kinds of things, but when Jocelyn first told me about the breakup, it sounded as if she was giving me a line from a well-rehearsed script. Especially the part about securing another seafood distributor. Nate checked into that and found out it's not as easy as one would think. The market is fickle, and most companies have enough trouble maintaining their inventory for the regular customers."

"So, if the bartender is on the up-and-up, Jocelyn had this in the works long before she said bye-bye to Cameron. Hmm, what if he wasn't willing to move on and she found a more permanent way to get him out of the picture?"

"Not a strong enough motive for murder. Even if the

guy hung on her like a clinging vine or badgered her with calls or threats. It would have annoyed her, not enraged her."

I picked up the menu again and perused the entrées. "What about her encounter with the gun-toting guy in the mask and hoodie? Did she share anything with you that she didn't tell the police?"

"Yep. She didn't think it was a man."

"Whoa. That's pretty major in my book. Why hide that from the Tempe police?"

"She said she was so shaken up all she could do was describe the scream mask and the hoodie."

"Then what made her believe it was a woman?"

"Here's where it gets interesting. Jocelyn told me she'd been trained to be highly discerning when it comes to aromas. A valuable skill in a seafood restaurant. Anyhow, she said she could always detect the scent of a man. Either his deodorant, aftershave, body wash, or frankly, unwashed, unshaved body if it came down to that. She even said men's clothing carries a certain smell."

"And . . . ?"

"The guy who held the gun to her head didn't smell like a man."

"Then why not tell the police?"

"She was convinced they'd think she was a bit 'off' and not take her seriously."

"But she told you."

"I'm not the one filing a police report or doing anything that would give her restaurant unwanted publicity. You know how the media always takes a small tidbit of information and blows it up to an astronomical size."

"Kind of like my mother and the rumor mill. So, did Jocelyn have any idea who that masked woman was? Or what she was after?"

"If she did, I wasn't privy to an answer. She took the safe route. Said it was probably someone looking for some quick cash."

"What was your take on her explanation?"

"I don't think it was money she was after. Like I said, I have this nagging feeling I'm missing something. Anyway, we might as well order and enjoy a good meal before this place succumbs to what your uncle called 'a downhill spiral.'"

"Louis Melinsky happens to be the fussiest eater I've ever encountered. I wouldn't exactly be waving the white flag if I was one of those restaurant owners."

"Yeah, I was kind of surprised about his opinion. All I can verify from my research is that none of those places received a grade less than A+ from the Maricopa County Health Department and none of them owed back taxes or any delinquent debts. But as far as the quality of the seafood? That's way out of my league. Heck, I'm fine with a good tuna melt."

"Hallelujah, that's one meal I can prepare. And speaking of meals . . . Thanksgiving is just around the corner and, well . . ."

"Let me wager a guess. We're invited to your mother's."

I cringed and didn't say a word.

"That's fine, hon. As long as she doesn't seat the dog next to me."

"No, he'll be under the table begging for scraps. Unless, of course, my mother prepares him a plate of his own."

"I take it Shirley and Lucinda will be there?"

"With bells on."

"Good. Besides, I'd be kind of insulted if your mom didn't invite us."

A subtle warmth filled my cheeks and I reached for the

iced water. If I could describe the moment in one word, it would be "comfortable." We continued to discuss Cameron Tully's murder and the frustration everyone was beginning to feel since not a whole lot of progress had been made on the case.

Marshall, on the one hand, planned to revisit the other three restaurants during the week, using the intruder incident at La Mar Maravillosa as an excuse. Nate, on the other hand, was going to conduct his research from his office chair. According to the Maricopa County Sheriff's Office, Jocelyn was a "person of interest." She was the ex-girlfriend and, without any other viable suspects, her name was at the top of the list. That gave the sheriff's office and the Tempe police a good reason to check her phone records.

"What are they looking for?" I asked.

"Repeat numbers and patterns. Especially on the days leading up to Cameron's death."

"Where does Nate fit in?"

"He's the lucky gumshoe who gets to follow up on the information. Unless, of course, one of those numbers belongs to another seafood restaurant. Then, it's all mine."

Our meal ended with coffee and crème brûlée. As I savored the last spoonful of the caramelized sugar and vanilla bean dessert, I realized something. It would be relatively easy to slip a bit of ground sago palm seeds, or nuts as they're referred to, into the mixture undetected. Crème brûlée or any confection, really. The heavy cream and sugar would drown out the toxic ingredient. Marshall insisted a while back that no chef in his or her right mind would jeopardize their restaurant by doing such a thing, but what if the dessert was prepared elsewhere? Or, better yet, what if Jocelyn served it to Cameron at his own place and then removed the evidence? It wasn't like cyanide or even belladonna. Sago palm poisoning could take days to achieve the desired effect.

"You've got to find out why she cut off the relationship with him," I said.

"Huh? What?"

"Jocelyn. Cameron. That nagging feeling you have? It's your gut instinct. I get it, too, only with things like suddenly checking the tire pressure in my car or throwing out a can of food I just opened because I have a bad feeling about it."

Marshall propped his elbows on the table, clasped his hands, and rested his chin. "Sounds like you have a theory of your own."

"'Theory' is not exactly the right word. A theory means there's evidence. No, what I have is conjecture. Pure and simple. I think it has to do with her business. Maybe she needed better prices from Coldwater Seafood and that wasn't about to happen. Even though she was sharing a bed with the guy. Or maybe she noticed the quality of the product was going down. Remember what you said earlier? About her sense of smell?"

"It's not going to be that easy getting her to recant what she told me."

"Then you'll have to resort to the Harriet Plunkett school of information gathering—nag her to death."

"Terrific. I'll be so sick of seafood by the end of this case, we'll be living on hamburgers."

"Does that mean you'll give it a try?"

"I'd never disappoint you, Phee. At least not intentionally."

Yep. Comfortable. I smiled, reached my hand across the table, and gave his wrist a squeeze.

"And while we're on the subject of not disappointing you," he continued, "I'll have to brace myself for the next

Precious Pooches pet parade. That's coming up pretty quick."

"I know. The Friday before Thanksgiving will be here in no time. I don't know who I feel sorry for more, the two of us for telling my mother we'd go or Streetman, who has to wear that Swarovski crystal acorn."

"Streetman. Definitely. Nate got an invite, too, you know, and it scared the daylights out of him."

"Really? Why?"

"Because he's running out of excuses."

Chapter 14

A week had passed since our dinner at La Mar Maravillosa and, while Marshall was able to meet with the owners of the other three seafood restaurants, Jocelyn avoided him. At least it looked that way. She didn't return his calls or emails.

"I'll make an impromptu visit this coming week," he said. "Meanwhile we'd better get going to that 'Precious Pooches Turkey Day Parade' or whatever the heck it is."

"If you ask me," Augusta said as Marshall and I headed for the front door of the office, "it's a darn good excuse to get out of work early."

Marshall spun around and grinned. "You're welcome to join us, you know. We'll find a way to make it look like business."

Augusta shuffled some papers around on her desk and laughed. "Not on your life. With Nate out on that fraud case in Peoria, someone has to give the appearance that our office is open for business."

"Okay, but if you change your mind . . ."

"Don't worry. That's not happening. Bunch of dogs

running around in costumes. Sheer lunacy, if you ask me. Back in Wisconsin we stuck to cattle and livestock judging. Heifers, swine, horses, and chickens. My late husband would've had a canary bird if he was asked to deck out our milk cow. Next thing you know they'll be adding cats to that shindig in Sun City West."

"I don't think they can afford the insurance." I opened the door. "But I'll put it in their suggestion box. Have a good evening."

"I'll guarantee one thing. It'll be less stressful than yours. Don't say I didn't warn you."

I gave her a quick wave as the door closed behind us.

"Flip a coin to see whose car we take?" Marshall asked.

"It doesn't matter to me."

"Okay, I'll drive and we'll pick your car up on the way home."

It was two thirty-five. Plenty of time to get to the dog park before the parade's start time of three. With the shorter days, the parade schedule was moved up from the Halloween one. Thankfully we made good time, arriving just before the event started.

"Same deal as before?" Marshall parked the car in the large recreation center lot.

"Not quite." My mother explained it to me this morning, but I was laughing so hard and holding my hand over the phone, I wasn't sure I caught everything.

"It can't possibly be any worse than last time."

"Oh, yes, it is. Much worse. Instead of having an individual dog and their owner walk around the circle when their number is called, the entire entourage will be circling the knoll while that 1963 song by Little Eva 'Let's Turkey Trot' is being played in the background."

Marshall turned off the car's ignition and buried his

face in his hands. All I could hear was sputtering sounds as he tried to muffle his laughter. "My mother played that song when she cleaned the house. I still remember singing, 'Gobbididily gobbididily,' or something like that. You're serious, aren't you?"

"Uh-huh."

"Augusta was right. This really is a nightmare. Please tell me you're exaggerating."

"I'm not. Each dog owner will be carrying a sign with their number on it. That's how the judges will know one dog from another."

"It's surreal. Absolutely surreal. All the contestants march round and round the knoll while the judges render their decision?"

"You've got it. At some point, when their choices are made, the entire parade will be directed to march back into the dog park and wait for the announcer to read off the names of the winners."

"Guess we can't hide in the car any longer. Might as well trot on over to the knoll."

"Nice word choice."

The dog park was a frenzy of activity and yet, amid all the chaos, Marshall and I were able to spot my mother. Apparently, Streetman wasn't the only one decked out in hand-cut crystals. My mother was wearing a dark fedora trimmed with sparkling jewels, instead of the usual leather or ribbon band. I put a hand over my mouth so I wouldn't gasp. "I can't believe what I'm seeing."

Marshall studied the dog park the way some people studied maps. "What part can't you believe?"

"My mother. She looks like Lady Gaga. Say, isn't that Elaine Meschow talking to her? It *is*. It *is* Elaine. I didn't think she was going to enter Prince in this contest after what happened last month. Not the poisoning. That had nothing to do with it. The tree decorations. Those awful cobwebs."

"Looks like the trees have been left unscathed. But get a load of that giant blow-up turkey. It must be over ten feet tall. Should scare the crap out of most of the little ankle biters, and the big dogs might sink their teeth into it. Who comes up with these ideas?"

"Um, the dog park committee, I think."

We walked over to the park and gave my mother a shout. She immediately picked up Streetman and met us at the fence.

"Hurry up and get a good place in front of the knoll. I think Shirley and Lucinda are somewhere up front. Myrna's standing with the bocce club crew, and I'm not sure where Cecilia and Louise are."

"Is Aunt Ina coming?" I asked.

"Are you kidding? She says she's allergic to all of the pet dander, but if you ask me, she's probably having a facial or a hot stone massage in preparation for a night out with Louis. Don't worry about your aunt. Get a good spot in front of the knoll. And doesn't my little man look perfect?"

The dog was squirming to get out of my mother's arms, and she finally relented. "We're number fourteen this time. Not that you need a number to recognize us. Meet me back here after the contest."

Marshall leaned over the fence and shook my mother's hand. "Good luck, Harriet. You, too, Streetman." Then he took my arm and ushered me toward a spot at the edge of the knoll in full view of the giant balloon turkey. "Want to wager a bet on how long that thing remains vertical?"

"Hopefully long enough to see this fiasco through."

No sooner did I finish speaking than the turkey trot

music came on and the announcer welcomed everyone to the second event in the Precious Pooches Holiday Extravaganza. He thanked committee members, rec center members, and anyone apparently who'd set foot in the community during the last decade. It was worse than the Academy Awards. Finally, the music got louder and the contest began.

Marshall and I held our breath as the dogs and their owners paraded around the circular knoll to Little Eva's rendition of "Let's Turkey Trot." I had to turn away at least four or five times because I was laughing so much and Marshall wasn't much better.

"Do you think they'll bring Little Eva back next month for 'The Locomotion'?"

"Shh. You're making me laugh."

And while Marshall and I were practically in hysterics, my mother and Streetman were taking the event seriously. The little dog pranced to the music and held his head up for two laps around the knoll. The sun was slowly setting and three pillars of giant stage lights that had been brought in for the occasion illuminated Streetman's costume. It was dazzling. Well, blinding, actually.

I saw Elaine Meschow with Prince, who was dressed up to look like a cornucopia. And I couldn't help but notice Sir Breckenthall the Third as Miles Standish. At least I thought it was Miles Standish. The costume looked as if it had been hand-tailored, and I had no doubt it was. The other contestants were decked out as turkeys, Pilgrims, and Native Americans.

With one lap to go, as per the announcer, I bit my lower lip and prayed Streetman wouldn't do anything to jeopardize this event for my mother. I glanced at Marshall and saw that he, too, was just as concerned. "I hope the little bugger makes it for the last spin around the hill."

"You and me both," I said.

"Amazing, but none of those dogs bothered the big balloon turkey. I thought that would be the first thing to go."

Just then, the announcer directed all of the contestants to finish circling the knoll and walk back to the dog park to await the results.

"He did it," I said. "Streetman behaved like a perfect gentleman. I wonder if my mother slipped him anything before the parade."

"I don't know about the dog, but after watching this, I could sure use something."

Myrna and Louise spotted us and waved. They were farther down in front, but it was impossible to reach them. Finally, the announcer spoke.

"Ladies and gentlemen, we have the results for the second event in the Precious Pooches Holiday Extravaganza. In third place, dog number twenty, Prince. Owner, Elaine Meschow. Please exit the dog park and walk directly to the judges' table in front of the circle."

"That's wonderful, Marshall, isn't it? It makes up for last month."

He winced and shrugged. "I wouldn't go that far."

Prince was awarded a twenty-five-dollar gift certificate from Gracie's Groomers and a basket of grooming supplies and toys.

"If Streetman doesn't at least place second, my mother will be devastated."

"And now, ladies and gentlemen," the announcer went on, "in second place, Sir Breckenthall the Third, owner Phyllis Gruber. Please exit the dog park and walk directly to the judges' table in front of the circle."

Phyllis Gruber didn't walk. She stormed over to the judges' table to collect her prize with poor Sir Breckenthall the Third in tow. The little spaniel was awarded a fifty-dollar gift certificate from Cascade Kennels, a basket of goodies from Dapper Doggies, and a free grooming from LuLu's Lovelies.

Marshall rubbed his chin and shook his head. "That woman looks as if Santa left her a stocking full of coal instead of all the neat gifts."

"She didn't take first place," I said. "That's what it's all about for her."

"Ladies and gentlemen," the voice cut in. "And now for our first-place winner. Today's winner will walk home with a full year of grooming from The Stylish Pet, a basket of treats from Furry Friends Boutique, and a seventy-five-dollar prepaid Visa card from one of our local banks. Please congratulate Streetman and his owner, Harriet Plunkett."

The applause was thunderous, and I swore I heard Myrna and Louise shrieking.

"I don't believe it! He took first place! He took first place! There's my mother now, walking over to the judges' table."

I couldn't see what was going on at the judges' table, but Shirley and Lucinda walked over to carry the basket of goodies for my mom. That was the last sane thing I remembered before "the incident."

The crowd had started to disperse and the owner of a large white poodle made his way to the giant turkey balloon, presumably to wait it out with his dog. The man had removed most of the dog's costume, but a ring of colored felt feathers was still visible on the dog's neck.

My mother was at the opposite end of the circle, and she headed back to the dog park where she'd told us to meet her. Then, for no apparent reason known to humans, Streetman picked up his chin, sniffed the air, and bolted across the knoll to the white poodle, leash and all.

"Oh my God, Marshall. This isn't good. Streetman's not a fighter. That means only one thing. The poodle is a female and that neurotic Chiweenie is about to make more than a casual acquaintance with her."

My mother started yelling at the top of her lungs. All sorts of words. Words like, "Streetman, no!," "Streetman, stop it!," "Streetman, come back here!," and finally, "No! No! No!"

Marshall took off after the dog, with my mother a good five or six yards behind. I whipped my head around to where the poodle was standing, only to see Streetman taking a giant leap onto the poodle's back. That sudden leap forced the poodle to stand on her hind legs and press her front legs against the giant blow-up turkey. From that point on, Streetman was unstoppable.

"Bad boy! Bad, bad boy!" My mother's voice echoed past the dog park all the way to the bocce courts. Meanwhile, the poodle's owner was shouting as well.

"Princess Leia, get away from that dog! Come over here!"

I moved as quickly as I could, but it was impossible. The crowd had heard the commotion and decided to watch this new source of entertainment. I had to elbow my way down the sidewalk by the knoll in order to reach Marshall and my mother. I got there just in time to see Marshall pull Streetman off of Princess Leia. And just in time to watch the giant Thanksgiving balloon deflate. First the head, then the neck, then the fat body.

"Oh my gosh. What happened?"

Marshall handed the dog over to my mother and took a breath. "Streetman gave Princess Leia a nip on the neck and she panicked. Bit right into the blow-up balloon."

"This is going to cost us." My mother nuzzled the dog and then looped her hand through the end of his leash.

I took in the entire scene from Princess Leia's octogenarian owner checking over his pet to the rubber puddle of what was once a blow-up turkey, now lying on the ground like an oil spill.

"Us? What do you mean 'us'?" I asked.

Before my mother could answer, Princess Leia's owner spoke. "She's okay. He didn't break the skin. Just gave her a good scare. She's fifteen. She's like me. She doesn't see much action."

"I'm so sorry," my mother said. "Is there anything I can do?"

"Nah. We'll be fine. Might want to have your dog neutered, though."

"He *is* neutered," I blurted out. "Neutered and nuts!"

The man chuckled, leashed his dog, and headed across the parking lot.

"I suppose I'll be getting a bill for the blow-up turkey," my mother said. "They've got my name and address."

Marshall gave her a pat on the shoulder and glanced back at the spot where the balloon had been standing. "I doubt that. These kinds of venues take those things into account. If it wasn't Streetman initiating the disaster, it would've been some other dog. Come on, Harriet. Looks like the book club ladies are waiting for you over there."

He pointed to the side gate of the dog park, where Cecilia, Shirley, Lucinda, Myrna, and Louise were standing. Shirley was still holding the basket of goodies Streetman had won.

"Might as well relish your accomplishment, Mom. No sense getting aggravated over what happened with that poodle. Heck, Streetman probably put a twinkle in her eye she hadn't seen in years."

"Sophie Vera Kimball, shame on you for talking about such things."

The three of us ambled over to the dog park, where my mother was regaled with compliments and hugs.

"Shirley deserves all of the credit," Mom said. "Designing a costume that's fit for a Paris runway."

While my mother and the other women were chatting, Shirley grabbed me by the arm and motioned for Marshall to join us. "You're not going to believe what happened a few minutes before you got here. That terrible Phyllis Gruber came over to me and told me, in no uncertain terms, that if Streetman wins the final contest, that will be the last thing he or your mother ever win."

My hand flew to my mouth and I froze for a second. "Oh my gosh. She did something similar with Elaine Meschow and her dog. Not an actual threat but a veiled one. Whatever you do, Shirley, you can't tell my mother about this. Not yet. She won't simply call the dog park committee. Oh no. Harriet Plunkett will be all over the sheriff's office and Homeland Security. She's got those numbers on speed dial and she'll—"

Marshall looked directly at me and gave my hand a pat. "I think I'll be the one looking into this Phyllis Gruber. Maybe Elaine Meschow wasn't overreacting when she told you she thought Phyllis might have been the one to poison her. For all we know, Sir Wrecking Ball may not be the only prize that woman owns."

"What do you mean?" I asked.

"Lots of these wealthy retirees are the beneficiaries of their late husbands' businesses. We'll just have to see if hers had anything to do with seafood."

Chapter 15

My mother walked over to where we were standing and invited Marshall and me to join her and the ladies at the Homey Hut. "We have to hurry because the early-bird dinner specials end in forty minutes. I'll drop my little man off at home and head right over there." She bent down to remove the dog's costume, but for some inexplicable reason, he wasn't cooperating.

"Shirley or Phee, will one of you please hold him so I can pull the Velcro apart?"

Marshall picked up the dog and released the jeweled acorn before Streetman even knew what was happening.

"Quick," my mom said, "give me the thing before he decides to tug on it."

Marshall handed her the prized costume. "I have no idea how to remove the hat."

Shirley immediately stepped in. "That's the easy part. It'll unsnap from the collar. My own design."

The dog was au naturel within seconds and rolling on the grass. While my mother yelled at him, I seized the opportunity to whisper to Marshall. "You really don't want to get stuck on a Friday night at the Homey Hut, do you?"

He must have seen the look of fear in my eyes and took a step toward my mother. "Thanks so much, Harriet and everyone, but I've got an early-morning appointment with the sheriff's deputies on the Tully case. Can't afford to miss it. Maybe another time."

"You still have to eat, don't you?" she asked.

I immediately chirped up. "We have leftovers and don't want them to go bad."

My mother glanced at her watch. "Okay. Okay. Another time."

Marshall and I tried to say good-bye to the group, but everyone was talking at once.

"Come on, this is our golden opportunity to hightail it out of here." He put his arm around my waist and hustled me out of the dog park. "Leftovers, huh? How about we get your car, pick up a pizza or wings, and head home?"

"Done. Was that the truth about your meeting tomorrow? On a Saturday?"

"Unfortunately, yes. I didn't get a chance to have a decent conversation with you today. Nate and I are meeting the deputies at ten. Their office. Right now, all we're doing is spinning theories. I know these things take time, but if we could only catch one little break, it might open up the whole case for us. Of course, there's still the Cabot connection. *If* it turns out they're using Coldwater Seafood as their distributor. Believe it or not, I haven't had a chance to check. And Nate's up to his neck finalizing the info on those supermarket chains. Boy, when did I become such a whiner?"

"You're not whining. You're unwinding."

We were less than a yard from his car when he stopped and kissed me. "Thanks for going easy on me."

* * *

I couldn't get Phyllis Gruber's stinging remark out of my mind the next morning. Marshall had left ten minutes ago at a little past nine. He was going to grab some coffee and meet up with Nate at the sheriff's station in Sun City West. I took the last bite of my chalky fiber bar and looked around our house. No laundry to do, no pets to walk, and no visible signs of dust. Plenty of time for me to conduct a bit of my own sleuthing. If it wasn't for the fact that Phyllis's threat hit home, I would've dismissed the entire thing as the ranting of a jealous and self-centered woman. But if she had far more sinister intentions, who knew what she could do.

As much as I detested snooping around the dog park, I knew it was Sun City West's best source of information—real or imaginary. Too bad it was after seven, because that meant Cindy Dolton wouldn't be there. Still, I was bound to run into someone who knew about the infamous Sir Breckenthall the Third and his owner.

Slipping on my jeans and a sweatshirt, I paused to catch a glimpse of myself in the bedroom mirror. Crow's-feet under control and no new laugh lines, thank God. I dabbed on some tinted sunblock and lip gloss, gave my hair a quick brush, and walked back to the kitchen for my keys and bag. A half hour later, I opened the fence to the dog park and stepped inside. Unlike the first time I visited the park, no one shouted, "Hey, lady! Did you forget your dog?"

They were all too busy chatting it up on the benches. At least four or five women and three or four men. Small bundles of white fur ran all over the place, while one slightly overweight beagle sat under a tree licking himself.

I didn't recognize anyone, but that didn't stop me from

taking a seat on one of the benches. A grayish poodle mix immediately jumped into my lap and began licking my face.

"You'll have to excuse him," a buxom woman with reddish hair said. "Brodie likes everyone. A bit too much at times."

"That's all right. If I could handle the hubbub at the pet parade last night, I can certainly deal with a cuddly pup."

"Oh, were you there? Which dog is yours?"

She started to look around, and I shook my head. "I was there with my mother. Her dog. He was in the event. In fact, he was the winner."

"The acorn! The jeweled acorn. I don't think Catherine the Great wore anything that dazzling. Do you know who made the costume?"

"Um, a friend of my mother's, I think." *Shirley Johnson has enough on her plate without having to sew more designer dog costumes.*

"Next year I'll enter Brodie in the event. Right now, he's too young. Only five months and way too rambunctious. I left him home so I could enjoy the event. Didn't see the awards presentation, though. I wanted to beat the crowd."

Thank goodness. That means she didn't witness Streetman's debacle with the poodle and the blow-up balloon. "Oh, you didn't miss much."

"I heard the second-place winner was really bent out of shape her dog didn't take first place. Someone said she planned to get even. They overheard her talking to whoever would listen. Anyway, it doesn't involve me."

The tall man sitting on the other side of her leaned forward and laughed. "Count your lucky stars. That woman happens to be my next-door neighbor. Real pain in the butt, and I don't mind saying it out loud. Complains that my palm trees, which have been on the property for years, are too close to her yard and the fronds might fall in her pool if it gets windy."

"Yikes," I said.

The guy chuckled and grinned. "Oh, that's not the best part. Want to hear the best part? My wife and I have two decorative sago palms on either side of our driveway. Phyllis—that's the neighbor's name—cut off the leaves on the plant closest to her house. Can you believe it? She took a scissors and cut them off. Just like that. Didn't bother to ask our permission. Told us the leaves hung over onto her property and she didn't like it. Ridiculous, huh? Now one of those palms looks absolutely anemic. And it wasn't even that close to her driveway. I would've contacted the property owners' association, but it wasn't worth the time or trouble."

I gave Brodie a quick pat and nudged him off my lap. "Sago palms? Is that what you said?"

"Uh-huh. Gorgeous sago palms. Of course, they're toxic if you ingest them. In fact, wasn't there a murder around here not too long ago where the guy was poisoned that way? Yes, I'm sure there was. I read it in the papers. Too bad he didn't share the meal with my neighbor."

The woman who owned Brodie looked at him as if he'd suggested nuking the nearest mall.

"I'm only kidding. Relax. It's bad enough we have one nutcase living on Thornhill Drive."

"Thornhill Drive. Where's that?" I asked.

The man pointed directly behind him. "On the same street as the country club. Only Thornhill Drive is really a cul-de-sac. Only six houses. And *she* has to live in one of them. Yeesh."

At that point, he got up, said it was nice talking to us, and shouted for his dog. As both of them approached the fence, my jaw tightened and I clenched my teeth. My mother was on the other side of the gate with Streetman. It was impossible to run, duck, or hide. She spotted me like a hawk going after a field mouse. Only hawks weren't loud.

"Phee! What are you doing here?"

"That's the little acorn without his jewels," I whispered to Brodie's owner. "I'd better head over to my mother. It was a pleasure meeting you."

Streetman flew past me and ran around the park. My mother shrugged, holding both palms up. "Well, what are you doing here? What's going on? Did something happen?"

Yes. I wanted to do some sleuthing without conducting damage control for Streetman.

"No." I had to think fast. Not my strong suit. "Um, er, I came back here because I left my sunglasses on one of the benches last night. It was getting dark, so I took them off. Then this morning I couldn't find them and that's when I remembered where I had last seen them."

As long as they don't bring out the lie detector machine, I'll be all right.

"You could've called me. You didn't have to make a special trip. I would've picked them up for you. Then again, had you called, you could have taken Streetman."

Naturally. "Um, guess I wasn't thinking. It was only a quick errand. Marshall and Nate are meeting with the deputies and I have the morning to myself."

Oh hell. What did I just say?

"Oh, it's too bad this isn't one of our book club brunches at Bagels 'N More. That's next Saturday. Today Shirley and I are driving to Holiday World in Scottsdale to check out costume ideas for the final extravaganza.

I'm thinking of having Streetman go as one of the characters from *The Nutcracker Suite*."

"Yeah, uh, about that . . . um, do you really have to have him compete in the third contest? I mean, why not have him quit while he's ahead?"

"What?? And have us miss out on the possibility of a spa weekend at the JW Marriott? Are you crazy? Streetman and I need a spa weekend."

Oh, you'll get more than that if Phyllis Gruber has her way. "Can't you just take him to the groomers and call it a day?"

"Don't be ridiculous. Look at him, will you? If he's not a prizewinner, I don't know who is."

"Your prizewinner seems to be leaving you one."

"Harrumph. I'd better get over there before someone starts yelling. Say, if you don't have plans, you're certainly welcome to join Shirley and me."

"Thanks, but I really have more unpacking and sorting to do. The big items are all in place, but the little stuff is endless."

"All right. I'll give you a buzz and let you know how we make out at Holiday World."

"Sounds good. See you later."

While my mother went off to tackle the dog's business, I decided to expand my Phyllis Gruber snooping and cruise down Thornhill Drive. I knew exactly where the country club and elegant cul-de-sac were located. I'd passed them numerous times driving around with my mother. If what the man in the dog park told me was true, Phyllis's house would be easy to spot. All I had to find was a lopsided sago palm at the foot of a driveway.

A lineup of cars waiting to turn into the parking lot told me I had timed my dog park excursion well. I made a right-hand turn out of the rec center area and headed directly for Phyllis's residence. Not that I had any plan in mind. Or any idea of what I expected to find, but still, I was curious.

The guy in the park had been right. There were only six houses on that cul-de-sac, and I drove too fast to eyeball the bushes and palms that bordered their driveways. Wasn't the first time in my life I needed a "do-over." I drove a few yards past the cul-de-sac and executed a three-point turn on the street. Unlike my first attempt, with absolutely no traffic in sight, I was now directly behind a light blue Lexus with a commercial van in front of it. The Lexus signaled and pulled into the first house in the cul-de-sac. I studied its driveway carefully. No bushes. No palms. Instead, decorative agaves and rock bordered it.

Cross that one off the list.

The commercial van pulled into the third driveway, adjacent to the one with the droopy-looking sago palm. Phyllis had arranged for either dog-grooming services, housecleaning services, or a repair. I couldn't see the vehicle's signage clearly, so I pulled off to the side of the street, rolled down my windows, and put the car in park. With it obscured by the van, no one in her house would be able to see my car, but I would have a decent view of whoever was parked in her driveway.

A food delivery van. And not fast food or pizza. Schwan's and Meals on Wheels were the two main fixtures in Sun City West, but that didn't mean there weren't competitors. The van I was staring at was painted teal and white and sported a logo I thought I had seen somewhere before—a strange cloverleaf that seemed to morph into a fish if you stared at it long enough. Above the logo were the words "The Bountiful Life." I'd never heard of them.

Suddenly a car door slammed and a man walked behind

the delivery truck. Youngish, light hair, medium build. I immediately took out my cell phone and pretended to be using it. He opened the back door, pulled out a handcart, and loaded a few large boxes on it. Again, the same logo on the boxes.

Whatever strange diet Phyllis Gruber was on was no concern of mine. Nothing about her really was, except for the fact that she had made a veiled threat against my mother and who-knew-what regarding Elaine Meschow. At this juncture in time, I didn't even know if the woman was married, divorced, widowed, or a lifelong spinster.

I was about to drive off when I heard the delivery guy. "Good morning, Mrs. Gruber. Do you want these in the same place in your garage?"

"Yes. Hold on. I'll open it for you."

"Sorry I'm late. Snowbirds are back. Got a zillion deliveries."

"By the way, thanks for cleaning up those plant cuttings on the driveway last time. What a mess. I noticed it after you had left. That was nice of you."

The garage door went up, the voices got muffled, and I figured I'd better get the heck out of there while she was preoccupied. Just then, the delivery guy ran back to the van and grabbed another box. A smaller one.

"Almost forgot this baby!" he yelled out. "Follow the precautions on the labels. Oh, and don't forget to soak the salmon roe before you freeze it. Unless you want me to do it!"

Precautions? Labels? We're talking food here, aren't we?

Again, the voices were muted and there was no way I could make sense of what they were saying. No reason to risk being seen. I signaled left, pulled out, and headed down the block. Once out of sight, I pulled over again. This time to do some genuine research.

My curiosity was piqued and, like an itch that begged to be scratched, I couldn't wait. I pulled my iPhone from my bag and immediately googled "The Bountiful Life." I expected the usual cadre of pre-prepared meals, mixes, and health food drinks. What I saw instead made me look twice.

It was food, all right, but that was where the similarity ended. Past the testimonials and usual hype about life-extending products, The Bountiful Life boosted brain-enhancing nutrition based on seafood. Freeze-dried seafood that was converted into all sorts of meals. And while they sounded like the kinds of things I'd put on my dinner plate, they weren't.

The meatloaf and gravy was a seasoned fish pâté with a kelp-based au jus. The lasagna and cheese was derived from reconstituted salmon roe and pollock. And the chicken casserole was concocted out of reconstituted whitefish and dried vegetables. All meals with a ten-year shelf life.

Maybe that explained why Phyllis Gruber had a perpetual scowl on her face. Nothing a Big Mac wouldn't cure. And while the first page of menu items was certainly an eye-opener, the second page was the real shocker—the price list. Those menu items didn't come cheaply. I supposed that would be the case for "organically sourced seafood."

I scrolled to the next page and scanned a never-ending list of health food supplements and vitamins. Also with big price tags. And most probably with precautions. No wonder the delivery guy made mention of reading the labels. I exited the website and shut the phone, pausing for a second to think about the vulnerable senior citizen population and how they were likely to be scammed by companies like his. At least I didn't have to worry about my mother or the book club ladies. If they couldn't shmear it with cream cheese, dip it in greasy sauce, or fry it in a pan, they wouldn't eat it.

The teal and white van pulled past me and continued down the block as I continued to wonder how many elderly suckers were on his route.

Chapter 16

Nate and Marshall weren't able to glean too much information from Ranston and Bowman when they met Saturday morning. No new insights regarding Cameron Tully's connections and nothing that would link Elaine Meschow to him, other than the fact that they both ingested toxins from the sago palm. What *was* certain was that the sheriff's deputies, along with Williams Investigations, had all but exhausted all contacts related to both victims.

Marshall puzzled over the entire matter most of the weekend when he wasn't conferring with Nate on the phone.

"I can't believe Thanksgiving is this Thursday and we still haven't gotten anywhere," he said as we folded a batch of laundry on Sunday night. "I couldn't even enjoy spreading out on the couch and watching the football game today."

A washcloth dropped on the floor and I picked it up. "You made a good stab at it."

"Yeah, well, a guy's got to try something. Oh geez, I completely forgot to tell you—I called Bethany Cabot to ask about their distributor. Got to speak with her husband. Tucker, right?"

"Uh-huh."

"Anyway, it wasn't Coldwater Seafood. We can scratch that off our list. Spellbound Naturals has used the same distributor for the past five years. Not a familiar name, but then again, I'm not up on dog food suppliers."

"Was Tucker as obnoxious as Elaine Meschow says he is?"

"Not really. Not on the phone anyway. I told him what was going on and why we thought there might be a motive for Cameron's murder if the same distributor was used for dog food as well as gourmet seafood."

"What was his reaction?"

"Believe it or not, he laughed. Said the food they source is natural, all right, but nothing humans would consume. Gave me the lowdown on Asian carp. Did you know those fish were gradually introduced into our lakes and waterways with an unexpected outcome?"

"Um, no."

Marshall stopped rolling his socks into neat tubes and let out a breath. "The Asian carp are really aggressive fish. Aggressive and very adaptable. Apparently, those little stinkers outcompete the native fish for food and habitat. And those carp keep growing in size. It wouldn't pose a problem if they were edible, but those things are boney as hell."

"Ugh. Sounds horrid."

"It is. The exploding carp population correlates to a decreasing supply of other freshwater fish and that's not all."

"You mean there's more?"

"Oh yeah. Those fish have no natural predators. And they breed faster than rabbits. Although I think the actual word is 'spawn.' Tucker gave me the complete run-down."

"Why?"

"Because that's what's in the dog food—Asian carp. Not to say the food doesn't contain salmon, tuna, or other fish, but the carp make up a large percentage of the product."

"Isn't that illegal or something?"

"Nope. The ingredients are listed on the packaging, according to content, and the labels are rather generic. They use words like 'ultra formula,' 'premium formula,' 'natural formula,' and my personal favorite, 'healthy formula.' Everything's on the up-and-up. Anyway, Tucker had a good chuckle when I told him we thought there might be a connection."

"So, the dogs eat that canned food, huh? Fish bones and all. Pretty dangerous, if you ask me."

"Not canned. Kibble. The carp, bone and all, are crushed. Pulverized. Then processed. It's what they do at the plant in Chandler. Like I said, all on the up-and-up."

I tossed a T-shirt to him and he promptly folded it. "So much for that theory. Now what?"

"We keep at it."

For the next three days, up until Thanksgiving, that was exactly what Nate and Marshall did. More interviews. More timelines. And more disappointments. Ranston called to let them know he finally located the men who delivered the Galbraiths' grill. They were employees for the big-box store where the grill was purchased. Employees with spotless records, no priors, and no reason whatsoever to dump a body behind the house where they had made a delivery.

"Let's all enjoy the long weekend, shall we?" Nate said as we left the office Wednesday night. "Maybe Monday morning will be more promising. At least it will be quieter. I've got to drive Mr. Fluffypants down to Sierra Vista for Thanksgiving, and he'll be squawking the entire time. Oddly, my aunt misses him. Too bad the assisted-living place refuses to let him stay. Anyway, see you all on Monday."

Augusta put the key in the lock and gave the door an extra tug. "Yep, see all of you on Monday." Then she patted Marshall on the arm. "I'd take some Pepto capsules with me tomorrow if I were you. While your stomach's trying to digest the food, your brain's likely to be spinning."

"It'll be fine," I said. "It's only my mom, Shirley, and Lucinda. Oh, and maybe Herb. She usually invites Herb."

"Like I said, can't go wrong with some Pepto in your pocket."

Marshall gave my hand a squeeze as we walked to our cars. "As long as there's not another naked person running around or another teenage hookup at the neighbors' place, we should be fine."

Our contribution to the Thanksgiving meal, in addition to the rolls I bought, was an amazing dill dip Marshall had prepared. He even got up extra early to buy two fresh rye breads for the dip and cut out the round openings on top.

"What time do we have to be there?" he asked when he got back from the store.

"Around two. Harriet Plunkett time. That means anytime between one thirty and two thirty."

"Great. That red dust is getting to me. I'm going to hose down our cars and sprawl out on the couch when I'm done. Someone's bound to be playing football somewhere. Or soccer. I'm not particular. What about you?"

"I'm going to give Lyndy a call about getting together

sometime this weekend. She and her aunt are going to be dining out for Thanksgiving. They've had reservations for months. Then I intend to tidy up and check out the Black Friday deals."

"Oh no. Don't tell me you want to get up at some ungodly hour tomorrow and wait in a long line with a bunch of—"

"Equally crazy nutcases? No. I'm looking at online deals. There's nothing I absolutely have to have that would compel me to fight those crowds. Last year alone, three fights broke out in Walmart's and Target's areas."

"Good. Because you had me scared for a minute."

Marshall and I arrived at my mother's house at a little past two. Shirley's maroon Buick was parked out in front and we pulled up behind it.

"She probably picked up Lucinda," I said. "They usually drive together."

While Marshall juggled the rolls, bread, and dip, I rang the doorbell. "I'm warning you again. This isn't going to be like any Thanksgiving you've ever had."

"Good. Mine include the cousins overeating and barricading themselves in the bathroom while my uncles relive their army days."

The door flung open and my mother ushered us inside. "Hurry up. Come on in. We need your opinion."

With that, she turned her back and walked into the kitchen.

I gave Marshall a shrug. "Guess you can put the dip in the fridge and the bread on the counter."

The usual platters of nuts, crackers, cheeses, and spreads took up the coffee table and the end tables in the living room. Shirley and Lucinda were seated on the couch, but that wasn't what caught my eye the minute I set foot in the room.

Giant poster boards featuring assorted costumes for Tchaikovsky's Mouse King were all over the place. On the sideboard table, against the walls, and on one of the floral chairs.

I gasped. "What on earth . . . ?"

"Which one do you like?" Shirley asked. "And please don't tell me it's the one with the heavy metal chains and grizzly fur. That design is *way* too extreme. Even for me."

"I, I, um . . ."

My mother set another platter of canapés on the coffee table and motioned for Marshall and me to take a seat. "Just move the big poster. There's plenty of room. Well? What do you think? And before you say a word, you'll never guess where these posters came from."

"Um, Holiday World in Scottsdale?"

My mother sighed. "Don't be silly. They specialize in holiday attire for people and their pets, not theatrical costume posters."

"Okay, fine. I give up. Where? Where did these come from? And why are they so . . . so . . . strange?"

"They're not strange," my mother said. "They're historical. And they happen to come from your aunt Ina."

Marshall all but spit out the cheese and cracker he had popped into his mouth. "*This* I have got to hear."

I jabbed him in the elbow and mouthed the words, *No you don't*, but it was too late.

My mother puffed up her chest as if she was about to deliver a soliloquy. "When my sister found out we had chosen the *Nutcracker* theme for Streetman, she told Louis. He, naturally, had a friend who once worked for the Bolshoi Theatre in Moscow and just so happened to have a collection of posters depicting some of the costumes for the Mouse King. These posters are on loan.

They arrived yesterday. Special delivery from Toronto. That's where Louis's friend lives."

I was speechless. Literally speechless. I opened my mouth, but nothing came out. Not even small guttural sounds. Luckily, no one noticed and my mother kept talking.

"We have to return the posters next week. That's why it's paramount we decide on Streetman's costume."

I looked around. "Um, speaking of the little rat, where is he?"

"In your mother's bedroom with a rawhide chewy," Lucinda said. "It was our Thanksgiving treat for him."

"Well?" my mother asked. "Which design do you like best?"

I glanced at Shirley, who looked as if she was resigned to anything at that point. "Gee, I don't know, Mom. They're all kind of complicated and weird. Except maybe for the one hanging on the bathroom door."

My mother jumped. "That's not a Mouse King costume. It's a painting I bought at the craft sale. And if you look closely, it's not a rat, it's a cute little mouse with daisies."

Yep. And this is why I'll never volunteer to judge any kind of contest.

"I like the sassy-looking one, Harriet," Marshall said. "The rat with the blue velvet jacket and those big teeth." Then he turned to Shirley. "How would you do the teeth?"

"Oh, easy enough. The teeth would be part of a mask that would hang over the dog's nose. Kind of like a muzzle. Of course, with Streetman being so fussy about anything on his face and head, I think I'm better off working it from the collar."

Too bad. A muzzle on that dog is beginning to sound

good to me. Especially the way he behaves around other canines.

My mother shook her head and looked at the posters again. "Those dark tailored suits with the gray faux fur look stunning, but I'm afraid it would be too heavy for Streetman. Yes, I suppose Marshall's right. The blue velvet is rather regal looking and, with a gold crown and large rodent ears, Streetman will be breathtaking."

If he doesn't lose the ears and stomp on the crown.

Just then the doorbell rang and we heard Herb's voice. "It's me. Herb. Hurry up. My arms are getting tired."

"What's he bringing?" I asked.

Lucinda rolled her eyes. "Probably the same thing he did last year. Two six-packs."

Marshall quickly got out of his seat. "Sounds good to me."

Herb said hello and headed straight for the refrigerator. "Don't need these babies to sit out in room temperature. Good. No one started eating without me."

"The kitchen table's all set," my mother said. "I'll start warming up the turkey and stuffing. Phee, you can microwave the yams and the squash while Shirley and Lucinda bring out the salads." Then she looked at Herb and Marshall. "All right. I suppose you two can grab a beer and wait it out in the living room."

Herb winked at my mother. "That's what I like about you, Harriet. You get right to the point."

Twenty minutes later we were all seated around the kitchen table, with Streetman directly under it.

"At least you won't have to vacuum the kitchen," I said to my mother. "Your Hoover is fast at work."

I looked around and realized Streetman wasn't the only one indulging in the Thanksgiving meal. All I could hear were chewing and chomping noises accompanied by

Herb's continual requests for someone to pass something. Casserole. Turkey. Cranberry sauce. Buttered yams. It didn't matter. Our arms got as much of a workout as our stomachs.

At some point in the meal, I thought about that delivery to Phyllis's house. "Hey, have any of you heard of The Bountiful Life? It's a company that makes health food from fish. I saw their delivery van on Saturday."

"The teal and white van with that large picture of a mermaid chasing her own tail?" Lucinda asked. "I thought it was a cleaning service that specialized in backyard water features. You know. Like a pool service only for decorative ponds. That thing's all over Sun City West. Was that where you saw it?"

"Um, yeah. I left my sunglasses at the dog park and had to drive over." *Okay, it's a teeny little lie.*

"I've seen that van, too," Shirley said. "But I thought it was one of those duct-cleaning services. Hidden dust and all that hoopla. Why worry about hidden dust in your house when there's more than enough of the regular stuff?"

Herb gnawed a large chunk of his dinner roll and grimaced. "Health food from fish? Sounds absolutely sickening. What do they do? Freeze it and reconstitute it?"

"As a matter of fact, they do," I said. "I was curious, so I checked out their website. And by the way, I think the design is a fish-themed cloverleaf."

My mother's head was bent under the table so she could feed the dog little tidbits of food. Her voice sounded muffled. "Where did you see the van? Which one of our neighbors is eating that junk this time?"

I lifted the tablecloth and leaned down. "What do you mean 'this time'?"

The dog was still nibbling from her hand.

"Remember Gloria Wong who used to live in this neighborhood? She had a contract with those Bountiful Life people. Until they upped the prices on her. Now she's back to shopping at Costco and checking out the health food stores."

"Will both of you please have a conversation at the table?" Lucinda said. "I don't want to miss anything."

We bolted upright as if it was a drill, and my mother continued. "Gloria told me the prices for reconstituted seafood had skyrocketed because some yuppie-duppy natural dog food company was buying up most of the product."

"Ew!" Shirley blurted out. "When I was back in South Carolina, people told tales about old folks who were so poor they were eating cans of cat food. I never really believed it. Now it turns out, some of us are apparently eating dog food and paying a fortune for it."

Marshall, who was absently moving his fork across the plate, stopped and pushed his head back. "Spellbound Naturals. The company Elaine Meschow and her daughter own. Even though Elaine is a silent partner. And, she refers to it as her daughter's company. Anyway, they use freeze-dried seafood. I wonder if—"

"It tastes like crap?" Herb answered before Marshall could finish his thought. "Yep. Probably tastes like hell. Enough to gag a maggot."

Marshall pushed his plate toward the center of the table. "Well, on that note, I think I've had more than enough. The meal was wonderful, Harriet. And the casseroles were scrumptious."

Lucinda and Shirley both stood up and immediately started clearing the plates from the table.

"We'll stack them by the dishwasher," Shirley said. "In case you have a special way of loading it."

I stood up, too. “I’ll wrap the leftovers and get them into the fridge.”

“What about dessert?” my mother asked. “Do you want it now or should we wait a little while?”

I looked at the crew and tried to read the expressions on their faces. “I vote for waiting.”

No sooner did I say that when a chorus of “let’s wait,” “I’m full,” and “hold off until later” followed.

Suddenly Streetman got out from under the table, ran to the Arizona room, and began barking and growling at the patio doors.

“Now what?” I asked. “Does he have to go out?”

My mother shrugged. “He runs to the front door for that. I’d better see what’s going on.”

“Maybe it’s another body dump,” Herb said. “I’d better look, too.”

Shirley shot him a look that would kill. “Hush. Probably some quail out there making noises.”

Marshall was the first one to make it to the patio doors. Streetman was on his hind legs, pawing at the glass and growling.

“It’s okay. Nothing to worry about. Three coyotes are milling around your yard and the Galbraiths’ place. No big deal. Nothing to get concerned—Oh no!”

“What?” my mother shouted. “What are they doing? Someone get me my Screamer. It’s on a key chain somewhere. No, wait. That will only scare poor Streetman and he’ll pee on the floor.”

“Relax, Harriet,” Marshall said. “They’ve gone already, but they left a calling card on your back patio. Got a shovel in your garage? I’ll take care of it.”

Dessert followed the coyote incident and the rest of the visit went smoothly. I thanked my lucky stars.

Chapter 17

Marshall slid the driver's side seat back from the steering wheel. "I have to say, that was one incredible Thanksgiving dinner. I don't think I'll be able to look at food until Monday."

"You will. Around nine tonight. We'll be ravenous by then."

"Yeah, but at least your mom sent us home with goody bags."

"It was that or she'd invite us back tomorrow. So, uh, what did you make about that whole business with Spellbound Naturals and The Bountiful Life?"

"Under ordinary circumstances I wouldn't give it a thought. I mean, we don't even know if Bethany and her mother's company is the one responsible for the decrease in product at The Bountiful Life. Although Tucker did tell me business was booming. Really booming. Dog owners consider their canines family, not pets. And they want those four-legged relatives to eat nutritious, healthy foods. Not by-products or worse."

"I wouldn't give it a thought, either. Except for one thing."

"Elaine Meschow?" he asked.

"More like Elaine Meschow's near-death-but-not-quite sago palm poisoning. All of them, Elaine, Bethany, Tucker, Jocelyn, and, well, Cameron, are, or, in his case, *were*, somehow linked in this fish business. Two of them ingested the same toxin and two of them were dating. Maybe there's more to this situation."

We were well past Sun City West and only a few minutes from our house. As if someone turned on a switch, colorful house lights illuminated the night. Reds, greens, blues, and whites. It must have caught Marshall's eye, too, because he suddenly changed the subject. "Geez, I don't think I've ever decorated my house for the holidays. Usually I buy a poinsettia and call it a day."

"Are you saying you want to decorate our place?"

"Uh, well, yeah. But only if you want to. And simple. Really simple. Not *National Lampoon* style."

"No, I think my aunt Ina and uncle Louis will have that covered. And my mother won't be far behind. She'll have menorahs on the counter, lots of holiday tchotchkes, and a small Christmas tree on the patio. Growing up with mixed family traditions, we celebrated everything. And I did the same when Kalese was growing up."

He reached over and gave my hand a squeeze. "Sounds like a terrific tradition."

As we drove onto our block, the first thing we noticed was the house across the street. Marshall stopped the car and we both stared.

"I was kidding," he said, "when I mentioned *National Lampoon*. Yikes. Who on earth lives there? Clark Griswold?"

"My God. They must've spent the entire day decorating. So much for Thanksgiving."

"Good thing our bedroom is in back. Those lights are blinding. And the twinkling strobe snowflakes would push me over the edge. So, what were you thinking for our place?"

I looked at the monstrosity across the street and sighed. "I don't know. Maybe a nice wreath or swag on the door and a few little lights on our cacti."

"Phew! That's easy to handle. A heck of a lot easier than that tangled fishnet of a murder case we've got." He pulled the car into our garage and shut off the engine. "Now, if Cameron had been the distributor who serviced The Bountiful Life, I could see someone in that enterprise doing away with him. Especially if the guy was shifting the inventory to the Meschows' little empire. But Cameron's company deals in high-priced seafood. Not invasive bottom-feeders, which leaves our investigation right where we started—unable to determine if it was business or something personal."

We got out of the car and walked into the kitchen, each of us carrying a small bag of leftovers.

I glanced at the answering machine and saw the familiar flashing red light. "I already spoke to Kalese this morning. Who else could be calling us?"

Hearing the voice on the machine was like having a cold gust of wind blow through the house. "Marshall. It's Ranston. I already spoke to Nate. Call me. Hope *you're* not too far away from Sun City West."

"My God," I said. "Who leaves a message like that on Thanksgiving?"

Marshall closed the refrigerator door and took out his cell phone. I couldn't read anything on his face and stood there waiting for him to place the call. I knew he had Ranston's and Bowman's numbers on speed dial since Williams Investigations shared cases with the county sheriff's office often.

I bit my lower lip and leaned against the counter. It seemed to take forever until Marshall's call went through. His side of the conversation was enough for me to get a general sense of what was going on, but it was like reaching for something in the closet with the lights out. He motioned for me to move closer to the phone, but I still couldn't hear Ranston, only Marshall's responses.

"Uh-huh." Pause. "Was anyone home?" Pause. "Yeah, I agree. That *is* odd."

He put his hand over the speaker and mouthed, *Break-in*, before continuing his conversation with Deputy Ranston. After what seemed like minutes, instead of seconds, he put the phone down. "Elaine Meschow was at her daughter's for Thanksgiving. While she was gone, someone broke into her house. Normally the deputies wouldn't bother me with this, but since Elaine and Cameron were both subjected to the same toxin . . ."

"I know. I know. His death and her poisoning might be connected somehow."

"Yep. Ranston's at the scene and asked if I'd stop by. I'll understand if you're pooped and want to pass on this one."

"No way. The food's in the fridge. What are we waiting for?"

I was glad Marshall had gassed up his car earlier in the day, because the back-and-forth trips were adding up. Luckily, traffic was really light and we arrived at Elaine's place in less than a half hour. Unlike the last time I was there, the soft LED lighting that accented her water fountain and agaves was replaced by the harsh red and blue strobe lights from Ranston's vehicle.

As we approached the security door, I grabbed Marshall's wrist. "The dog. Prince. Her little Yorkie. I forgot to ask—"

"He's okay. He went with her to the daughter's house. He wasn't home during the break-in."

The muscles that had tightened in my body suddenly relaxed, but only for a split second. Ranston must have heard us, because he opened the front door and motioned us inside. Elaine was seated on her love seat with Prince in her lap. She looked as if she had aged overnight. Puffy eyes, red nose, and hair that looked as if she had run her hands through it one time too many.

"The locksmith should be here any time now." Her voice was monotone and low. "At least they didn't break any windows. So much for the security alarm. Whoever broke in had time enough to scavenge through the place before the sheriff's office could respond."

I walked over to her and sat down in one of the small chairs next to the love seat. At least this time the large Boca coffee table didn't separate us. Marshall and Ranston were conferring with each other near the kitchen, so I was the one who tried to console Elaine. "I'm sorry, Mrs. Meschow. I can't imagine how upset you must be."

"It had to be that awful Phyllis Gruber. Who else would do something like this to me?"

The living room was far from what anyone would call ransacked, and the kitchen looked intact as well. However, off to the side of the living room, where her small study was located, it appeared as if every piece of paper that had been on her desk was now strewn all over the floor.

Her computer screen displayed a backdrop of some butterflies, and I wasn't sure if she had left it that way or if her intruder had been the last one to use it. Marshall had walked over to that room and was now surveying the damage.

I was about to say something when Ranston strode over to us and spoke. "I'll say this much. Whoever broke in here knew how to jimmy a lock. Could have been a lot worse. A forensic crew is on its way to dust for fingerprints, so don't touch anything."

He stared directly at me when he made that last comment. I opened my mouth to speak, but he cut me off and turned to Elaine. "Not telling you what to do, Mrs. Meschow, but if I were you, I'd dump everything in my refrigerator in case that intruder poisoned it."

With that, Elaine gasped and started to cry.

"It's okay," I said. "It'll be okay. I'll help you toss out any foods that aren't sealed."

"Before you do that," Ranston said, "look for anything that might've been tampered with. I'll have those items taken back to the lab."

"There's not much in my refrigerator. Only some fruits and cottage cheese. Oh, and a ton of leftover turkey and fixings my daughter sent me home with. Those should be fine."

Elaine stood up, forcing Prince to jump off her lap.

"With the forensic crew coming," I said, "maybe we should lock him in a bedroom where he'll be safe."

"That's a good idea. His little dog bed is in my room. I'll put him in there." She scooped up the small dog and left the room.

I used that opportunity to walk into her study to have a quick look. "Is anyone canvassing the neighborhood to see if any of her neighbors saw anyone or heard anything?" I asked Ranston as I got closer to the study.

"Of course. Deputy Lopez is going door-to-door, but I doubt we'll have much luck. Mrs. Meschow told us her neighbors on either side of her villa are out of town. We're not sure about the folks who live across the street, but we'll check."

I mumbled something and nodded. Marshall was trying to make sense of the few papers on her desk, as well as the Post-its hanging from her monitor.

"Not a whole lot to go on," he said. "Unless anyone cares that the dog has a grooming next Thursday and her mahjong game's been postponed till the first week in December."

Ranston made small annoying guttural sounds as he looked around. "What do you think they were after? Her jewelry hasn't been touched and no one went near the fire safe she keeps in her back closet. None of her personal items appear to have been stolen, and no money was taken."

"It had to be something else," Marshall said. "She's still an owner and a silent partner for that natural dog food company, even though her daughter and son-in-law are running it. Maybe it had to do with the business."

Ranston gave a nod. "So you don't think this Phyllis Gruber woman is a concern? Elaine Meschow did."

"With what motive? Yeah, Phyllis made some offhanded and insensitive remarks about the Meschow dog, but I hardly equate that to a real threat. Although she did say something a bit more sinister to the woman who's sewing costumes for Phee's mother's dog."

Ranston's jaw all but dropped to the floor and small smile lines appeared around the corners of his mouth. No matter how hard he tried to prevent it, he burst out laughing. "Costumes for your girlfriend's mother's dog?"

"It's a long story," I said. "My mother, along with a zillion other fanatical dog owners in Sun City West, entered her dog in their first annual Precious Pooches Holiday Extravaganza. So did Phyllis Gruber and Elaine Meschow."

The deputy clasped his hands together into tight fists and pressed them against his chest. "Please don't tell me someone would be looney enough to commit a crime over a dog contest."

"I, uh, um . . ."

Marshall shook his head. "It might explain the Meschow poisoning and this break-in, but it doesn't even come near Cameron Tully's death. You know, I *was* going to have a little chat with Phyllis, but I kept putting it off. Too far-fetched. Still, it wouldn't hurt to get inside her house and see if there was any possible, albeit unlikely, connection between her and our recently deceased Mr. Tully."

"That's the first good idea I've heard today." Ranston studied the Post-its on the computer monitor. "Who uses these anymore? Put it on an app reminder."

He walked out of the study and looked out the window. "Forensic team's pulling up. Lopez is back, too. I see her near the driveway. Better let Mrs. Meschow know they're here."

"I'll do that," I offered. "She's probably getting the dog settled in her room."

I knocked on her bedroom door and waited for her to give me the okay. "Are you all right, Mrs. Meschow?" I asked. No answer. I knocked again. This time harder. When I didn't get a response, I slid the door open a crack and peered in. The dog was lying in his bed adjacent to her queen-size canopy one and she was just stepping out of the bathroom.

"Forgive me," she said. "I had to wash my face and run a comb through my hair. I must look a fright."

"It's understandable. Mrs. Meschow . . . Elaine. Look, I know how miserable Phyllis Gruber has been, but, other than her, is there anyone, anyone at all, who would have a reason to break into your house? Whoever it was, they weren't interested in your jewelry or collectibles, but they *were* rummaging through your little office area. Do you have any idea why?"

"Not really. No. The only thing I use the computer for is online shopping, bill paying, and solitaire. Oh, and my emails. I don't even belong to those face-chat-in-your-face sites or those single-dating sites. Too dangerous. Lots of lunatics out there."

"What about when Mr. Meschow was alive? Did he use it for anything?"

"Hmm, now that's a good question. I honestly don't know. There are lots of files on there, but I ignore them. I doubt he used it for the business, though. They have their own computers at Spellbound Naturals. More modern ones. At least that's what he always told me. You don't think the break-in had anything to do with the business, do you? Oh my. I really need to call Bethany. I didn't want to worry her, but now . . ."

Now I've managed to push worrying up the Richter scale. "It may not be that at all; it may just be a fluke."

Oh, who am I kidding? Even she knows it was no fluke someone deliberately jimmied the locks to her doors.

Elaine sat on her bed near her landline phone. "Give me a few minutes. I really do need to call my daughter."

"Okay. I'll be right outside if you need me."

When I stepped back into the living room, Deputy Lopez was speaking quietly with her counterpart and Marshall. She brushed her long bangs off to the side of her face and grimaced.

"Like I said, only three people on the block were home around the time of the break-in, and no one heard or saw anything. Two homeowners have hearing aids. Even with them turned up, they could barely make out what I was saying. And I was standing right in front of them. The other homeowner was busy cooking for friends and listening to talk radio all day. So much for that."

"Um, excuse me for a moment. I'd like a word with Marshall," I said.

He gave me a nod and we walked into the kitchen. "What's up?"

I kept my voice low. Really low. "Elaine told me her late husband had files on the computer, but she hasn't opened any of them. To be honest, I don't think she knows how. Or wants to, for that matter. She's kind of like my mother in that respect. Using the computer for card games and email." I rolled my eyes. "Maybe there really was only one distributor for Spellbound Naturals and The Bountiful Life. One distributor who dealt with flash-frozen fish. And suppose some sort of shady deal was brokered between the dog food company and the distributor that resulted in diminished inventory for The Bountiful Life. That would give those Bountiful people a motive to break into Elaine's house to find out the truth. It makes sense, doesn't it?"

Marshall rubbed his chin and made some sort of weird grimace. "Last thing we need is to jump to conclusions, but yeah, it does make sense. Nothing else in this place was disturbed. Only the papers on Elaine's desk. And with the alarm going off, the intruder might've been scared away before he or she had time to turn on the computer and open the files."

"*They* might not have had time, but *we* do. If I'm not mistaken, since Elaine hasn't committed any crimes, the sheriff's office can't take her computer to see what's on it. But maybe we can convince her to have us take a look. You know, for her own safety or something like that."

Marshall gave me the strangest look. "You keep amazing me more and more each day. Are you sure you majored in accounting and not criminal justice?"

"Very funny. So, what do you think?"

"Pretty darn clever, but without a flash drive, we're out of luck."

"Who says we're without a flash drive? I have a thumb drive in my bag with this week's spreadsheets. I wanted to double-check my accounting at home since I've kind of been preoccupied at work. Once we download Elaine's files onto the drive, we can read them back at our place. That is, after we scan the thing for viruses and malware. Last thing I need to do is contaminate my own computer or, worse yet, merge her files with my own. Let's hope what we're about to download is business related."

"The forensic team will dust for prints."

"No problem. I'm Harriet Plunkett's daughter and she'd kill me if I left home without a pair of food-prep gloves in my bag just in case."

Marshall shook his head and chuckled. "So, what do you propose? Waiting it out while the forensic team takes its time in here? That could be hours."

"Not if we get them to start in the kitchen while we wait out here. Ranston said he was leaving once those forensic guys arrive. Give me five minutes with Elaine. Stall. Tell Ranston I needed to have a few more minutes with Elaine because she was so upset. I'll get her okay and then we can download those files once Ranston and his partner are out of here."

Marshall pressed his lips together and paused. "You do realize this isn't *MacGyver* or *NCIS*. Downloading files only takes two to three seconds when it's happening on a TV show or in a movie."

"I know. I know. But if the files are strictly text, they'll go pretty fast. The crime tech guys will still be in her kitchen. Especially if you bombard them with questions."

"Did I say 'clever'? I'm changing the word to 'diabolical.'"

I leaned closer and gave him a quick peck on his cheek before turning toward the living room.

"I'm going to check on Mrs. Meschow," I announced as I walked past the deputies.

Neither of them said a word.

I gave her bedroom door a quick knock and stuck my head inside. Elaine's back was to me, and I wasn't sure if she was still talking with her daughter.

"Is it all right if I come in? Are you on the phone?"

"Come in. Come on in. Bethany and Tucker are driving over from Chandler. They should be here in an hour and a half, depending on traffic. Lots of people heading home after Thanksgiving dinners. Ugh. This was the last thing I wanted to do. Make my daughter drive all the way over here at night."

I moved closer to where she was sitting on the bed. "I'm sure she wouldn't be coming if she wasn't worried about you. I know I'd be doing the same thing if it was my mother."

Doing the same thing? Hell! I took a flight from Mankato to Phoenix two years ago because my mother thought she was threatened by a book curse!

Chapter 18

Prince was in his dog bed, adjacent to Elaine's, licking his front paws.

"My mother's dog does that, too," I said, "before he goes to sleep. Must be some sort of dog ritual."

"He's been doing that ever since I got him. Thank goodness he's with me. I don't know what I'd do without him."

I reached down and gave the little Yorkie a pat on the head. "I know the forensic team will be dusting for fingerprints and the sheriff's office will be looking at all sorts of clues, along with my boss's agency. Since you're the victim, they can't remove your computer."

"Why on earth would they do that?"

"Um, well, to see if there's anything on it that might give some nefarious individual a reason to—"

Elaine froze. "Kill me?"

"No. No! That wasn't what I was going to say. I meant a reason to break in. You know, to find some information. Maybe from your late husband's business."

"My husband did bring work home from time to time, but I always thought all the business records were at the plant. In Chandler."

"Listen, would you mind very much if I were to make a copy of those files? The ones you haven't opened. If there's something on them that might pose a threat to your safety, we'd know immediately."

She narrowed her eyes and furrowed her brow. "Wouldn't the deputies be doing that?"

Yes. Wouldn't the deputies be doing that? Yeesh. I need to think fast. "True. True. But they'd have to go through all sorts of protocol. And that takes time. Lots of time. Marshall Gregory, the investigator from Williams Investigations, who's with me tonight, can review those files right away. If anything appears to be a concern, we'd contact you immediately. And, of course, the sheriff's office."

I continued to pet the dog while I waited for her response.

Finally, she spoke. "Oh, I don't suppose there's any harm to it. Go ahead. Did you bring one of those little round disks with you?"

"Um, actually, I have this and I can download the information right away." I showed Elaine my thumb drive as I stood up. "When the forensic team arrives, we'll ask them to start in the kitchen. You can wait here with Prince or come back to the living room."

"I think I'm going to stay put right here. This whole thing is making me terribly nervous. On second thought, I'm glad Bethany is on her way."

"Me, too. Oh, before I forget, does your computer have a password?"

"Yes. My name. Elaine Meschow."

I forced my mouth closed and didn't say a word. Her

name. Her password was her name. Same thing with my mother. What was it with these people? They might as well put a sign on their computers that reads: "Open for Business."

"Okay. Thanks."

I stepped back into the living room just as the forensic team arrived. Two men who looked as if they were in high school. Ranston didn't bother to introduce them by name, only by title—forensic examiners. He spoke with them briefly, then motioned for Deputy Lopez to head out the door with him.

"I'm going to have another word with Mrs. Meschow before we take off," Marshall said to Ranston. "I'll give your office a call in the morning."

"If this break-in turns out to be a result of that dog costume contest," Ranston grumbled, "I'll pull what little hair I have right out of my head!"

"What contest?" Deputy Lopez asked.

"I'll tell you on the way back to the station."

The two of them closed the door behind them and I laughed. "I'd better tell Elaine the forensic team is in her house taking pictures of the crime scene."

"While you're doing that, I'll usher them into the kitchen and you can play James Bond with her computer. Or should I say Agent 99 in keeping with gender?"

"Very funny. You've been watching too many *Get Smart* reruns."

Once the tech guys had moved to the kitchen and Marshall blocked the arched doorway that led to the living room, I rushed into the small study and immediately went to the office files Elaine told me about. Either Elaine had been on the computer and didn't shut it down or someone else had gotten on. Yep, so much for password protection.

The files, at least by title, looked fairly innocuous. Golf

tips for sand traps. Golf tips for wet surfaces. I glossed over those. There were at least six or seven files marked "SN Proposals," which I assumed were Spellbound Naturals, a marketing plan dated November 18, 2014, and a file marked "Correspondence." I downloaded all of them. I also spied three files marked "Taxes" and was about to copy those when I heard Marshall's voice. He wasn't speaking to me directly, but the loudness and tone of his voice to the forensic techs was a dead giveaway for me to hurry up.

"There's an outside door by the kitchen. You shouldn't miss that."

The team had finished dusting for prints in the kitchen and walked toward the study. My ankles began to shake, a quirk that seemed to defy how ordinary people reacted to stress. I tried not to think about it and focused instead on the files. I made sure to copy each one of them before I clicked the little green icon that told me it was safe to remove the thumb drive. I had barely clasped the small thumb drive in my hand and removed the plastic gloves when the two guys entered the study.

I spun around in the chair and pointed to the papers on the floor and all over the desk. "Uh, you might want to start in here. This is the only place where the intruder made a mess. The computer was on when we arrived. Cute background screen, huh?"

The men didn't say a word. Marshall motioned for me to join him in the living room and I immediately left the study.

"All's well that ends well," I whispered.

"Yeah, Shakespeare thought so, too. We'd better let Elaine know we're leaving."

"Think she'll be okay with those two in here?"

"Geez, I hope so. If we can't trust the good guys, who can we trust? Besides, you said her daughter and son-in-law were on their way, right?"

"Uh-huh, but that could take a while."

"I think she'll be fine." Marshall pulled out his iPhone and sighed. "It's nine forty-two already. Good thing we're off work tomorrow. Oh, who the heck am I kidding? We may be off work but not off this case."

"Tell me about it. If I wasn't so tired, I'd boot up the computer at home and see what little gems are on the flash drive."

"Tired my you-know-what. Your imagination is ten steps ahead of you. Promise me you'll wait until tomorrow."

"Um, well . . ."

"I know you. That little thumb drive you're carrying is like a Christmas present staring at you from under the tree."

"Or eight little Hanukkah ones that beg to be opened at once."

"Fine. Fine. I'll make us some coffee when we get home and we can have a sneak peek."

I reached out my arm, tousled his hair, and smiled. "Admit it. You're chomping at the bit, too. Come on. We'd better say good night to Elaine."

The little Yorkie was snoring quietly when we entered the bedroom. Cute little muffled noises, unlike Streetman, who sounded like a furnace in dire need of repair.

"We're taking off now, Mrs. Meschow," Marshall said. "You've got our phone number and Deputy Ranston's if you need anything. The forensic team shouldn't be that much longer. If these files provide us with information that can explain the break-in or the poisoning, we'll let you know right away. In either case, we'll touch base with you the beginning of the week. Try to enjoy the Thanksgiving weekend if you can."

She wiped her eyes with a crumpled tissue and nodded. "Bethany will insist I spend the night with them, but I have no intention of driving all the way back to Chandler or, worse yet, having them do it. If she's that worried, she and Tucker can sleep in the guest room. In fact, I'll insist on it."

"Good idea," I said. "We'll let ourselves out. Make sure the door's locked when the forensic examiners leave. We'll let them know we're on our way out."

I glanced back at the house from the driveway and made sure the thumb drive was still in my pocket. "Think those files will give us our answer tonight? It's the only thing that makes sense. Nothing else was disturbed."

Marshall swung his arm around my shoulder as we walked to the car. "Even if the answer is on those files, I'm not so sure you and I will be able to figure out what it is."

"Like if they're encrypted or something?"

"I wasn't thinking encrypted as much as baffling. You know, entries that make sense to the person who's creating the file, but not to anyone else."

"Hmm, I know what you're saying."

Two hours later we were splashing cold water on our faces and rummaging through the kitchen cabinets for more K-cups.

Marshall leaned over my shoulder as I closed one of the files. "Sorry, hon. I forgot to pick up another box of dark roast. We do have some Lemon Zinger tea, but the only thing that stuff will keep going is our kidneys."

"I'm pretty wired. I can handle another hour or so before I crash. What about you?"

"Same here. The good news is we've been through the

Spellbound Naturals proposals and the only thing of consequence was the one about shifting to fish nutrients by gradually introducing reconstituted carp to the formula. And according to the records, that didn't happen until Bethany and Tucker took over."

I groaned. "Old news. Elaine already told us that. Nothing unusual about their marketing plan, either. The company was just starting to use the internet for paid advertising and word of mouth from social media."

"Too bad the files marked 'Taxes' were the personal taxes for Elaine and her husband and not his company's. They were well-to-do but, by today's standards, they'd hardly qualify as upper echelon."

I tapped my teeth and then bit my lower lip. "Maybe that's the real reason she sold her mega house and moved into a small villa. Okay. So much for those files. Maybe the ones marked 'Correspondence' will give us something meatier to go on."

"Meatier. I can't believe you said the word 'meatier.' It made my stomach growl. Power of suggestion and all that. Anyway, I'm getting hungry. Really hungry. How about I make us a couple of sandwiches, we take a ten-minute break, and then get back to midnight sleuthing?"

"Sounds good."

It was longer than ten minutes. More like an hour and it was *way* past midnight. The digital clock on the microwave read 2:34.

"Are you sure you want to continue this tonight?" Marshall asked. "We're like zombies already."

"If I get into bed, I won't be able to sleep. I'll be lying there wondering what's on those Excel sheets. We can sleep late tomorrow. Let everyone else go crazy Black Friday shopping. I discovered Amazon Prime, and I'm not saying another word."

"Give me a second. I've got to splash my face again."

Marshall and I opened the first of four files marked "Correspondence." It was a letter from Cornell University's College of Veterinary Medicine regarding a study they had conducted on grain-free dog food. That's when my head literally hit the keyboard and Marshall insisted we stop.

"It'll make more sense in the morning. Honest. Give up the ghost and let's call it a night."

I didn't argue. I logged off the computer, made sure the flash drive was safe in the desk drawer, and crept into bed. I didn't wake up until five after eleven, when I heard the front door slam shut. I sat bolt upright and looked around. Sudden noises had a way of clearing up brain fog in a matter of seconds.

"Is that you?" I shouted, reaching for a T-shirt.

"Depends on who you were expecting. But if I were you, I'd go for the guy who brought coffee and donuts."

The tightness in my muscles seemed to let go, and I slipped on my jeans. "Be there in a second." I raced to brush my teeth and wash up.

"I missed the early-morning madhouse at Dunkin' Donuts. They had a lineup of customers at five a.m. Heck, if we kept at it last night, we could've been one of them. Of course, I'd be useless by now, but—"

"Useless is the last thing you are." I threw my arms around Marshall's neck and planted a warm, slow kiss on his lips.

"I'm going to make these coffee runs more often. Look, I know you want to get right to it, but I really need to stretch out and let my body know I don't intend to torture it humped over a computer for hours."

"Me, too. We've got all day. All weekend, really. Even if it's cold outside, the water temperature in the pool is always between eighty-six and eighty-seven. How about if I grab a quick swim after coffee and you work out at the fitness center? We can pick up on the files in the afternoon. And we don't even need to go out for lunch or make something. My mother sent us home with enough stuff to ensure we don't wither away."

"Sold!"

One swim, one workout, and two large turkey and cranberry sandwiches later, we were back at it. There were four correspondence files and the first three were from veterinary schools about canine dietary needs and recent research. Marshall pulled his chair closer to mine, and I turned the monitor slightly so he didn't have to lean in order to read the screen.

"This is getting us nowhere," I moaned. "Elaine already told me her husband did scads of research on healthier products for dogs. That's why the food sources include venison, lamb, duck, and, ugh, rabbit."

"Yep. All before the fish products shoved them out of the limelight. I'm still not sure if it was Tucker's idea or Bethany's."

"She didn't say."

I opened the last of the correspondence files. Unlike the others, this one consisted of one letter, and it was marked "Draft."

Marshall grabbed my wrist and shook it. "Holy Cow! Am I reading that right? I am, aren't I? Looks like we hit pay dirt, hon."

I swallowed what little moisture was in my mouth and leaned closer to the screen.

One of these days I'll really need bifocals, but not today.

The letter was addressed to Tucker Cabot, and it was a job offer dated September 16, 2005. The start date was left blank, along with the entry-level salary. A single sentence caught my eye as well as Marshall's. It read: "The glowing recommendation you received from the CEO at Coldwater Seafood leaves little doubt in my mind you would indeed be our candidate of choice for the product developer position at Spellbound Naturals." It went on to say his degree from Wharton, coupled with his business acumen, would seem a perfect fit.

I placed both hands on my desk and shoved my chair back. "My God. Tucker worked for Coldwater Seafood long before he took over the Meschows' company. He must've known Cameron Tully, right? Maybe they were friends. And when did Tucker marry Bethany? Did he know her before or after he was hired by her father? Oh my gosh. Is it possible Bethany knew Cameron?"

"Slow down. Slow down. One thing at a time or we'll be spinning webs all day. The only thing I know for certain, according to Ranston and Bowman's research, is that Cameron Tully's been with Coldwater Seafood for well over two decades."

"Then it really *is* possible. A Bethany and Cameron connection with Tucker in the middle. I don't know how you can be so calm about this. We may have stumbled on Cameron's killer."

"'Stumble' is a good word because it may also imply 'fall on our faces.' Listen, hon, I'm more than overjoyed with this discovery. It gives us the first viable connection to Cameron and Elaine, other than the toxin they both ingested. However, that's all it gives us right now. We need to tackle this carefully and systematically."

He was right. I'd been around my mother, the book club ladies, and my aunt Ina for so long, I'd forgotten how to do anything systematically other than the accounting and payroll for Williams Investigations.

"Okay. Where do you want to start?"

"Lucky for us, I kept my rough notes on a small pad. Hold on; I'll get them."

I tapped on the desk as I read Sanford Meschow's letter again. Then I stood up, stretched, and moved to the couch. No need to be hunched over the computer.

Marshall came back from the kitchen, waved the pad in the air, and plopped down next to me. "Who says longhand is out of style?"

I didn't say a word as he flipped through the pages.

A few "hmms," "huhs," and "ah-hahs" later, he put the pad down and grinned. "Based on the conversation I had with Tucker, he's been with Spellbound Naturals for over fifteen years."

"And Elaine told me Bethany and Tucker had been married for twelve. What about those three years in-between? If Tucker was friends with Cameron, it's conceivable Bethany knew him, too. I wonder why neither of them mentioned that juicy tidbit to you or the sheriff's investigators."

"Only one way to find out. And it'll have to wait until Monday. When their plant opens again and I can pay them a visit."

"Um, not necessarily. I'm probably going to regret this, but what if I got my mother to call Elaine and arrange for a playdate with Streetman and Prince?"

"A what? A playdate? Isn't that something people arrange for their toddlers?"

"In Sun City West, the dogs *are* their toddlers."

"You want to dial the number or should I?"

Chapter 19

My mother picked up on the second ring. "Why do I have to hear everything from Herb first? I could barely get my packages in the house when he came charging up the driveway. He found out someone broke into Elaine's house and now the daughter's staying with her for a few days. What's going on? Is Elaine on someone's hit list? Why can't all of you solve this case?"

"We're working on it, believe me. That's why I called. We need your help."

The minute I said the word "help," everything changed. My mother was ready to call out the nearest militia if it meant getting any closer to finding out who dumped a body behind her house and tried to murder a neighbor of hers. "Just tell me what you need."

I couldn't go into all the details, but when I explained it was imperative I speak privately with Bethany, my mother had the same idea I did. The dog park. *Heaven help me. I've inherited the Plunkett genes and there's no turning back.*

"Don't worry. I'll give Elaine a call and get back to

you. Tomorrow's Saturday. The book club ladies are eating brunch at Bagels 'N More. You can meet us there and then pick up Streetman. How does that sound?"

Like sheer torture. "Um, fine with me. Except . . . well, how do you know Bethany will meet me at the dog park?"

"Simple. I'll tell Elaine you're following up on the investigation and need to speak privately with her daughter. And what better place than the dog park? Everyone's too busy with their own pets to worry about you and yours."

"You sure it'll work?"

"I'm sure. Oh, and before I forget, if you get there and see a red and white French Bulldog, it's probably Ruby. Keep Streetman away from her."

"Oh no. I don't want to deal with a dogfight."

"A fight? He doesn't want to fight with her. He wants to romance her. Ever since the first pet parade, he's been crazy about Bulldogs."

"Yeesh."

Sure enough, my mother called me back. "Noon. Bethany will meet you at noon. It'll work out perfectly. Meet us at ten thirty for brunch. You know, Marshall's always welcome to join us."

I couldn't use the excuse about him having to work that morning, so I invented a new one. The first thing that came into my mind after watching a TV commercial. "He has to get the car tires rotated."

Technically, I wasn't telling a fib. He *did* have to get his car tires rotated. Only it wasn't going to be tomorrow. Or any day soon.

It looked as if the entire Booked 4 Murder book club had commandeered the large table in the middle of Bagels

'N More. With a green ostrich hat perched above those braids of hers, my aunt Ina reminded me of an early-twentieth-century fan dancer. Lucinda looked as if the nearest hurricane had blown her in, and Cecilia was still wearing black. With the exception of Shirley, who was sporting a beige and black ensemble, everyone else, including my mother, was decked out in holiday garb. Mainly sweatshirts with embroidered Santas, reindeer, or holiday ornaments. I took a seat next to Shirley in time for the waitress to fill my coffee cup. It sounded as if ten different conversations were going on at once, but everything came to an abrupt halt as soon as my mother said the word "snow."

"That's what I'm telling all of you. Snow! I got an email from the dog club and they're going to truck in loads and loads of snow from up north for the final event in the Precious Pooches Holiday Extravaganza. They're going to spread it all over the knoll."

Myrna adjusted her magenta scarf and gave the knot a tug. "North-north or Arizona-north?"

"What difference does it make?" Lucinda asked. "Those dogs are going to pee on it whether it came from Flagstaff or Billings, Montana."

"She's right," Louise added. "The City of Surprise always trucks in that stuff for their holiday events, and an hour later it's an ungodly mess. Of course, it's all gone by the next day, so no big deal."

Like a Ping-Pong ball, my gaze darted across the table as I tried to keep up with the conversation. Finally, when I had reached the moment when I thought I'd fling silverware across the room, I cleared my throat. "It's nice to see everyone again. I hope you all had a wonderful Thanksgiving."

Suddenly the conversation shifted to what I ate, what I

should have eaten, and what everyone else ate. I wondered if I had made a mistake by sidetracking the original discussion. It didn't matter. The waitress arrived with our food, and I got to enjoy three or four minutes of blissful silence.

Until my mother opened her mouth. "Phee is investigating those poisonings. It's very hush-hush."

If it's so hush-hush, why is she announcing it at gossip's epicenter? "I, um, uh . . ."

"That's right," she went on. "It shouldn't be too much longer."

Says who? "Er, what my mother's trying to say is that Williams Investigations and the sheriff's office have some substantial leads."

Myrna stabbed the small pickle on the side of her plate and held it momentarily. "If you ask me, Phyllis Gruber is behind all of this. I don't know *how* exactly, but she is. Take my word on it. And it has nothing to do with that dog of hers. Sir What-do-you-call-it. The bad blood between her and Elaine Meschow goes way back."

What? Bad blood? What the heck? What did I miss? "What do you mean?" My question sounded more like a high-pitched whine. "What bad blood?"

Myrna took a bite of the pickle, propped her arm on the table, and leaned forward. "It happened a few years ago. The only reason I know about it is because I was using the same hairdresser as Phyllis back then. Gladys Briston. Poor thing got arthritis so bad she had to retire."

Fine. Fine. Arthritis. Who doesn't have arthritis around here? "Know about what? What was going on between Phyllis and Elaine?" By now I was getting really antsy, and apparently I wasn't the only one.

"Dish the dirt, Myrna," Louise said, "while most of us still have our hearing."

"All right. All right. It was really idiotic, if you ask me. Phyllis and Elaine both belonged to the same health food home delivery service. Freeze-dried fish for the brain or something like that."

"It has to be The Bountiful Life," Shirley said. "We were just talking about it the other day at Harriet's. It *has* to be them. I mean, how many of those places are out there?"

Myrna shrugged her shoulders. "To get to the point, Phyllis always received her deliveries first. Then, for some reason, the driver started going to Elaine's house first and wound up giving her the last order of salmon croquettes. I remember Gladys at the beauty parlor telling me specifically it was salmon croquettes."

My God! I am literally going to crawl out of my skin. "Uh-huh, then what?"

"Phyllis pitched a fit. A really hissy fit. Accused Elaine of plotting to get the last croquette order. Seemed Phyllis had been planning on having it for dinner that night with her husband."

I slapped the palms of my hands on my cheeks and took a breath. "That was it? That was the big hoopla? Phyllis didn't get her order of salmon croquettes?"

"More or less. She accused Elaine of arranging for her delivery first and it went from bad to worse. I'm telling you, I wouldn't put anything past Phyllis. She's probably been boiling over this for years and finally figured out a way to poison Elaine. Of course, that doesn't explain the dead body across from your mother's patio."

"That's, uh, very interesting, Myrna. Very interesting. Unfortunately, there's nothing in a timeline that would connect Phyllis with Elaine before the parade. Not like she had her over for lunch or something and decided to mix in some sago palm greens with the salad."

"She probably found another way," Lucinda blurted out. "Keep working on it, Phee You'll figure it out."

Frankly, I wasn't too sure. I pulled out my iPhone and checked the time. "I hate to rush off, but, believe it or not, I'm taking Streetman to the dog park for a playdate with another dog." Then I turned to my mother. "We really should get going."

"I knew it!" Shirley exclaimed. "You were right, Harriet. Phee is really becoming attached to that Chiweenie of yours."

Bethany was standing at the dog park gate holding Prince. A few fluffy white poodle types were milling about a few yards away, their owners sitting on the benches. Other than that, it was a very quiet afternoon.

As soon as we walked inside the park I unleashed Streetman and smiled at Bethany. "Thanks so much for meeting with me. I think it's safe for you to put Prince down. He'll be okay."

The little dog scampered over to Streetman, who was busy marking his territory on a tree.

"Come on," I said to Bethany. "There's a bench at the far end of the park. No one's in hearing distance."

"My mother's been a wreck since the break-in. I don't know what the investigators told her because she won't say, but she's convinced her life is in danger. Frankly, I'm beginning to agree with her. First the food poisoning and now this. What do they want? She doesn't have that much money."

"Um, I don't think any of this is about money. Well, not directly anyway." I paused for a second to make sure the bench was clean and then sat down. "Phyllis Gruber's name has been bantered about. I'm sure you've heard all about that."

"Oh yeah."

"I'm also aware there was some long-standing issue over a food delivery that resulted in some nasty accusations a few years ago."

"Really? I thought it was about that ridiculous doggie costume contest and the parades."

"That's part of it. Grudges are like snowballs going downhill. They pick up whatever's in their path. Look, I'm not saying your mother's suspicions are without merit, but when it comes to murder and attempted murder, I think the motive's got to be stronger."

Bethany glanced at Prince and Streetman, who seemed to be having some sort of bizarre territorial marking thing going on. "I don't know how I can help you. I don't have any information."

This was the part of the conversation that made me the most uncomfortable. I didn't want to accuse her of anything, but I did need to find out how Cameron Tully fit into her life. *If* he fit into her life. Nate and Marshall were trained in this sort of questioning. All I had going for me was my mother's belief that deep down I was meant to be a detective. Boy, was she wrong.

"Please don't take this the wrong way." *And storm out of here. People will think Streetman did something awful and my mother will get another letter from the rec center.* "Um, it appears as if there's a link between Cameron Tully, whose body was found under the grill on Sentinel Drive, and your husband."

Bethany started to say something, but I was so intent on spitting out what I had rehearsed in my mind that I kept on going. "Tucker used to work for the same company Cameron did. Coldwater Seafood. It was their recommendation that got your husband the position at your family's business, Spellbound Naturals. What I need to know, well, what the investigators need to know, is if they knew each other. If they were friends. If—"

"If I knew Cameron? I was afraid something like this would come out the minute his body was identified. And when my mother was diagnosed with sago palm poisoning, I told Tucker to let those sheriff's deputies know he and Cameron used to work together. But Tucker said it would only muddy the waters. That it didn't matter. Because he hadn't spoken to the guy in years."

Up close, I could see she had been biting her fingernails. They were chipped and broken. Maybe she was hiding something.

I took a breath and swallowed. "What about you? Did you know Cameron?"

"I met him once or twice. When Tucker and I started dating."

I don't know what on earth possessed me, but the words jumped out of my mouth. "You were seeing him, weren't you?"

She squeezed her hands together and looked down. "It's not what you think."

Why do people always say that? I don't even know what I think at this point. "Then tell me."

"About a year ago, out of nowhere, Cameron called me at the plant. Said it was urgent I speak with him. We met for coffee on my day off. A day Tucker was working."

"And?"

"He told me he had reason to believe my husband was cheating on me. When I asked him for specifics, all he would tell me was it was with one of his Coldwater Seafood clients and that I should ask my husband."

"Did you?"

"No. I never did. I thought Cameron was making the whole thing up. Why? I have no idea. Tucker never gave me any indication he was unhappy in our marriage, and the last thing I needed to do was create a problem when one never existed. Besides, if Cameron was genuinely concerned, he would've told me who the woman was. Don't you think?"

She had a point. I tried to gauge her expression, but she turned away for a second. Then something occurred to me. When people told a lie, they usually told it with enough truth wrapped in so it appeared genuine. Was Bethany doing the same? Maybe she did have that encounter with Cameron, but instead of ignoring him, she confronted her husband. That would give Tucker a motive for killing the guy.

"Thanks," I said. "For being so honest. I know it couldn't've been easy. And I can't imagine how uncomfortable that conversation with Cameron was."

"Like I told you, it was a long time ago. I doubt any of that had to do with the man's murder or my mother's situation."

I was about to stand and yell for Streetman when I realized something. A year wasn't that long ago. Not really. Not when it came to business matters. Maybe Cameron had revealed other information to Bethany that she dismissed.

"Um, before we head out, there's one more thing. When you met with Cameron, did he simply blurt out his suspicions about Tucker or did you talk about other things as well?"

"Now that you mention it, we did. Small talk really. About the seafood distribution business. I wasn't really that interested, but when I walked into the coffee shop, he looked up from his iPhone and said, 'Next thing you know they'll be offering a dollar menu like McDonald's.' When I asked him what he meant by that, he told me some of his clients were shying away from their usual requests and asking for more moderately priced seafood."

"Was that a problem?"

"Not a problem, per se, but it could result in profit loss. The more expensive the cut, the more the distributor makes. It's the same thing with our flash-frozen dog food products. Only we're not substituting our domestic Asian carp for the cheaper foreign imports. The fish are too small, and that means too many bones in the product."

"Did Cameron say anything else?"

"No. We ordered coffee and that's when he told me the reason he asked to see me."

The conversation had come full circle. I thanked her again and called for Streetman. As Bethany and I approached the gate, one of the ladies on the benches shouted, "Is that Harriet Plunkett's dog?"

Before I could answer, she continued, "I loved his Thanksgiving costume. Tell her to give us the name of his clothing designer."

Chapter 20

Streetman sank down in the front seat and closed his eyes as I drove him back to my mother's. I reached over and petted him behind the ears. "Did that little Yorkie wear you out?" He bumped my hand as he lifted his head.

"So, what do you think, Streetman? Was Bethany telling me the truth? That she hadn't confronted her husband? Hard to believe, huh? At least that bit about the seafood sounded credible. And familiar. Where did I hear that before? Where? My mind is getting way too cluttered."

The dog shifted in his seat at the same moment I remembered where I had heard about inferior seafood. From my uncle Louis when Marshall and I ran into him and Aunt Ina at La Mar Maravillosa. Louis complained that the other three gourmet seafood restaurants in the valley were going downhill. Maybe Cameron was on to something and that was what got him killed. It would be awfully hard to prove, though. Not as easy as a jealous husband or a grudge-carrying neighbor.

"Well? What did you find out? Did Bethany know

Cameron?" my mother asked as soon as I stepped in the door. "More important, did Streetman behave himself?"

"Yes and yes. Streetman was fine and Bethany did know Cameron."

"Ah-hah! Give me a minute. I want to hand the dog a treat; then we'll talk."

"Um, actually, there isn't a whole lot for me to tell you." *Because it would circulate around that book club in record time.* "She said they met, but that's about it."

"Do you think she could've been having an affair with him? Those things are quite common, you know."

My body jolted slightly as soon as she said the word "affair." She might've been right about that, but it wasn't Bethany and Cameron. *More like her husband and some restaurant bimbo he met.* "I didn't get that impression, but Nate and Marshall can take it from here. Anyhow, I should get going. I'll talk to you this week, okay?"

"Okay. Phone me because—Oh my goodness. I forgot to tell you. Janet Galbraith called me while you were at the dog park. They're coming in this week. They couldn't put it off too much longer or it would be impossible for them to make the drive from all the way up north."

"Has she calmed down?"

"She sounded better. They'll be staying at the Hampton Inn for a few days while she gets the house cleaned again and sets up the new furniture once it arrives."

"Cleaned again?"

"The poor woman still can't get over the fact her bedroom was used as a brothel. I think that bothered her more than the dead body. By the way, we got to talking and she mentioned starting up a home food delivery service again. I told her I didn't know she belonged to one and then she told me they used to belong to The Bountiful

Life. What is it with these people and all their health food obsessions? I told her when I want fish, I order lox on my bagels. Phee, are you listening to me?"

"Huh? Yes. Bagels. Lox. Fish. Health food. The Bountiful Life."

That company's name kept cropping up, and I wondered just how people in this community were suckered into using it.

"Anyway, don't forget to give me a call this week. And let me know if Nate or Marshall gets any closer on this case."

"Don't worry. I will."

Monday morning came out of nowhere, and Marshall and I were back to our usual routines. Separate cars. Same arrival time. Augusta regaled us with a description of her canasta club's Thanksgiving dinner as soon as we walked into the office. Short of shooting and plucking the turkey themselves, those women were really into what my mother would call a pioneer meal, with everything homegrown or close to it. One of the women even churned the butter for their feast.

"Nope," Augusta said. "None of those preservatives or artificial anything for us. The women I play cards with all grew up on Midwestern farms. We have our traditions."

Marshall gave her a quick wink and walked toward Nate's door. "I'm sure you do. I take it Nate's fast at work already."

"That Deputy Bowman called here first thing. I was still turning the key in the lock. Maybe they caught a break in that murder case."

"We should be so lucky," I said. "Usually the breaks come from us."

I opened the door to my office and stepped inside. "My work awaits me. Let me know if anything exciting happens."

Nothing did. Bowman had called my boss to let him know the forensic team had completed their thorough investigation of Cameron Tully's residence The lab analyses were complete, too. They studied every bit of food in his refrigerator and pantry, looking for any indication of where that sago palm toxin had originated. They also combed through his bathroom and even tested the toothpaste and mouthwash the guy used. Not even a single suspicious germ, let alone a dangerous poison. I wondered if they had been as thorough at Elaine's house, but I doubted it. Her bout with the toxin didn't classify as a homicide. Thank goodness.

It was midmorning and I was at the Keurig taking my coffee break. The phone rang for the umpteenth time, and Augusta picked up. She held her hand over the receiver and mouthed, *Not the murder.* A few seconds later, I heard her say, "Yes, I'll be sure Mr. Williams gets your message." Then she hung up.

"It's a boring case," she told me. "Family ancestry. Why is it whenever the holidays roll around, everyone decides it's time to find out if they have any rich relatives?"

I laughed. "It's not the relatives they should be concerned about; it's the will." As soon as I said that, I froze.

"What's the matter? You look like Death did a dance on your shoulder."

"I had the strangest thought, Augusta. Oh my gosh. Are Nate and Marshall still in?"

"Mr. Williams left a few minutes ago. Said he wouldn't be long, and Mr. Gregory is still in his office."

"Thanks," I said.

"Aren't you going to tell me what this is about?"

"Only if I'm right."

Marshall's door was slightly ajar and I peered in. "Are you busy? I had a revelation. Well, not exactly a revelation, but close enough."

"Whoa. Wouldn't want to miss that. What's up?"

I leaned against the tall file cabinet in his office and smiled. "Cameron Tully's will. He must've had a will. Did anyone look into it? There are lots of beneficiaries who never know they've got money coming because the insurance companies don't notify them. It was a big scandal a few years back. On *Sixty Minutes*. Or was it *Frontline*? Oh well, it doesn't matter. What matters is whether or not the guy had a will and if someone killed him in order to collect on it."

Marshall had this strange sheepish look on his face. "Nate and I discussed that with Ranston and Bowman when we joined the investigation, but it never went any further. We got so busy with the other tentacles in this case, we kind of dropped the ball. Good thing you've got your wits about you. I'll make some calls."

"Okay. Catch you later."

"Hey, before you go, thought you'd like to know we've been busy this morning looking into the Coldwater Seafood clients of Cameron's who could've been having an affair with Tucker. I'm surprised Bethany was so upfront. Jealousy's certainly a motive for murder. Let's hope she didn't inadvertently shoot herself in the foot."

"She said she never asked her husband. But then again—"

Marshall tapped his fingers on the desk. "I know. I know. People lie and we get stuck sorting things out."

"Is that what Nate's doing right now? Sorting things out?"

"Uh-huh. He's checking with some of those other clients. According to what he told me, only two of those supermarket chains had female managers. He's paying both of them another visit."

"Do you think Tucker came in contact with those women when he worked for Coldwater Seafood?" I asked.

"That's the only way I can figure. Short of coincidence. Like meeting someone at a laundromat or in line at the motor vehicle department. Which reminds me, I need to do my homework, too. That means revisiting those fancy seafood places."

"Yeah. About that. Remember when my uncle Louis complained about the quality of the seafood at three of those spots? Maybe Coldwater Seafood was pulling a switch on them. Giving them an inferior product but charging them as if it were premium. Those restaurants would gradually lose their reputations and their business. If Cameron was responsible, it would be another motive for murder."

"Criminy! We've got more motives than we can count on one hand."

"True. But look at it this way. One of them is bound to be the real deal."

"Thanks, Sherlock. I'd better have Augusta set up some return visits for me this week to those restaurants. I'll be so sick of seafood I won't even want to open a can of tuna. Hey, I can always chat with the owners in the evening. Unlike other businesses, restaurant owners are usually around for the night crowd. Any of those establishments sound enticing to you?"

"Not according to what Louis says. But I wouldn't mind a return visit to La Mar Maravillosa. I never did get to try the Chilean sea bass. You can check out the other places on your own."

"Fine. By the end of the week, the mercury level in my body will have skyrocketed. I'll have Augusta start with Taste of the Sea in Scottsdale and go from there. Nothing like walking into a restaurant with two thoughts on my mind—was the owner screwing Tucker Cabot or was Cameron Tully screwing the owner? Sorry, hon, for the vulgarities."

"I've heard worse from Herb's pinochle guys. Remember? More expletives were shouted from the catwalk at the Stardust Theater than anything you or I could come up with."

Marshall shook his head and chuckled. "How true."

By Wednesday afternoon, Marshall and Nate had completed yet another round of revisiting possible suspects on the guise of information gathering. Unfortunately, all of their efforts resulted in one big fat zero. It was getting depressing. As for me, I got to drive over to my mother's house the day before to "catch a first glimpse of Streetman's *Nutcracker Suite* costume." Shirley was still making adjustments because her measurements weren't as accurate as she would've liked. Mainly because the dog was so squirmy.

As I entered Sun City West, I could see the residents had wasted no time tossing out their dried-up pumpkins and cornstalk figures and replacing them with anything that glittered, glowed, or sparkled. On our block in Vistancia, the house next door had swapped its giant Halloween spider and plastic turkey in exchange for an enormous Santa balloon that dropped its pants, revealing red and white polka-dotted boxers.

The contrast between the two neighborhoods was astonishing. On my mother's block, most of the cacti had small holiday lights wrapped around them and the palm trees featured dazzling white lights, sometimes offset with greens, reds, or blues. It was the same on other streets as well with some exceptions. The ceramic pig was now dressed as Mrs. Claus, complete with wire-rimmed glasses. According to my mother, the Iowans who own the pig dress it up seasonally. Don't ask. In our neck of the woods, it was all blow-up reindeer balloons, and snowmen.

I rang her doorbell and she greeted me immediately. "Good. You're here. This will only take a second. I want you to see how cute he looks. We'll remeasure him tomorrow. I bought some string cheese so I can bribe him to stand still."

What I saw took my breath away. Shirley must've been working nonstop all weekend to produce the masterpiece in front of me. My mother held up a deep blue velvet jacket with tiny seed pearls sewn around the edges. Painstaking work. The buttons were made of pearls as well, and a faux mink stole graced the collar.

"It's a double-layered costume," she explained. "Shirley used a lovely shade of gray suede to create the Mouse King. She stuffed it with pillow batting and is working on the tail. She's considering sewing the jacket right onto the rest of the costume so everything stays in place."

"Holy Cow! It looks like—"

"It is! It's one of the designs from the Bolshoi Theatre. Don't you want to see how it looks on Streetman?"

I looked across the room at the small dog who was curled into a ball on the couch. *What I don't want to see is the process involved in getting him to wear it.* "No! I mean, no. I want to be surprised at the parade. I'll wait and be dazzled like everyone else."

"If you insist."

I insisted all right, all the way to the front door. That

was when my mother took me by the arm and let out one of her famous long-drawn-out sighs. "I honestly don't know how much longer I can stand this."

"The anticipation?"

"No! That unsolved murder. Every time I look out at the back patio, all I think about is that corpse."

"The Galbraiths will be back any day now. They'll decorate the place and you can think about something else."

"Until your boyfriend, your boss, and that deputy duo figure it out, the only thing I'll be thinking about is how this could've happened in the first place."

"The murder?"

"Not the murder. The location. Why did they have to pick my backyard neighbors?"

"Everyone investigating thinks it was random."

"But you don't, do you?"

"I, um, er . . ."

"That's what I thought. You need to do what you've done before, Phee. Put all those little notes of yours together and come up with a solution. Hanukkah and Christmas are weeks away. I want to enjoy myself with my granddaughter. I don't need this nightmare hanging over my head."

Granted, she was going a bit overboard with the drama, but she was right about one thing. While I was doing little bits of sleuthing and a whole lot of sharing and telling with my boyfriend and my boss, I wasn't actively putting things together. Maybe it was time to get out of the back seat.

That opportunity came the following day, on that dog-tired Thursday afternoon. Marshall had already talked a second time with the owners and managers at the two Phoenix establishments and the one in Scottsdale. He waited until he had completed his last visit before opening up with Nate and me. I was taking a late-afternoon break and Nate was conferring with Augusta about something.

Marshall walked out of his office, popped a K-cup into the Keurig, and groaned. "Unless Tucker's gay, and there's absolutely no indication of that, there's no way he was carrying on with any of the owners or managers at the restaurants I visited this week. And that includes today. Most of them are happily married, divorced and intending to keep it that way, or at least twenty years his senior."

"So, that leaves Jocelyn at La Mar Maravillosa," I said. "Hmm, that would be a tight little circle. I mean, she dated Cameron, now an affair with Tucker . . ."

Nate swiveled his head away from Augusta's desk. "Unless the Tucker affair was first."

I stepped closer to where Nate was standing. "Or the Tucker affair was the reason Jocelyn and Cameron broke up. And we've got two different versions of how that went down."

Augusta slapped a hand on her desk. "Do all of you plan on standing here playing 'who's got the better rumor' or are you going to confront that little hussy?"

"We don't know she's a hussy, yet," I said.

Augusta grinned. "You will tonight. I called La Mar Maravillosa and told them one of our investigators needed a few more minutes with Ms. Jocelyn Amaro."

Marshall looked at me, his face flushed. "Uh-oh. I forgot to tell you. I asked Augusta to set up that meeting this evening. I thought we'd get dinner there. I meant to say something this morning, but it completely slipped my mind."

"Chilean sea bass it is!" I exclaimed. "Along with a side order of hussy."

At that point, we all laughed.

Surprisingly, the traffic into Tempe was light. I expected long delays, especially since it was the week after Thanksgiving and lots of shoppers would be on the road, not to mention tourists and commuters. We arrived at La Mar Maravillosa a little before seven. In addition to informing them that Marshall needed to speak with Jocelyn, Augusta had also made us a reservation for seven thirty.

The road traffic might've been light, but the restaurant was packed. Marshall checked in with the hostess, the same thin curly-haired woman who had greeted us the last time. She suggested we relax at the bar and waved her hand in that direction.

The bartender whom I'd met the last time wasn't there. Maybe it was his night off. Marshall and I sat at one of the bistro tables toward the rear of the bar and perused the place. A spiky-haired girl with freckles and screaming red lipstick bounced over to us with more energy than most toddlers. "Hi! I'm Paige. What can I get you?"

Paige. The blabbermouth waitress. You can get us information and lots of it. I jabbed Marshall in the ankle and mouthed, *Paige.*

"I know," he whispered, but Paige heard him. "Good! I'm glad you both know what you want." She stared at me and smiled.

I had to think fast and the only thing that came to mind was a holiday commercial I watched the night before. One in which everyone was at a wine tasting. "Um, I'll have a semi-dry Riesling and . . ."

"Samuel Adams," Marshall said. This time considerably louder.

She nodded and sped off.

I sighed. "That was awkward. I hope I like semi-dry Riesling. We'd better figure out how we're going to approach her when she comes back with our drinks."

"Ha! I wondered where that order of yours came from. Listen, hon, I'm so tired and wired I'm going for the jugular. I've still got Jocelyn to deal with, too."

As soon as Paige returned to our table and set the small cocktail napkins down, Marshall cleared his throat. "I hope there haven't been more encounters like the one your boss had a while back with that burglar. We're hoping for a quiet meal and not a robbery."

Paige leaned over the table as she put Marshall's drink down. "I wouldn't worry if I were you. I'm pretty sure it wasn't the money that guy was after."

"Really?" I sounded more like Pollyanna than Stephanie Plum.

"Uh-huh. Something's going on, that's for sure, but like I said, it was more of a personal nature."

She started to turn away, but Marshall called her back. "The ex-boyfriend, right? The one who was found dead in Sun City West."

"How did you—"

"It's been all over the news. No surprises there. Look, we happen to work for Williams Investigations in Glendale and we're trying to gather information without calling too much attention to ourselves."

With that, he took out his card and his license. *Yep. No time wasted here. Going right for the jugular.*

"All I know is Jocelyn and Cameron had a whooping-big fight about a week before he turned up dead. It was over the seafood. Of all things. I mean, sure, the guy was her distributor and all that, but usually when people are sharing a bed, the fights they have don't involve seafood.

Know what I'm saying? Especially since it was no secret Jocelyn was getting it on with another guy. And get this, I served those men at the bar a few days later. Talk about weird."

Marshall and I bobbed our heads and he motioned for her to continue.

"Anyway, the night Jocelyn and Cameron got into it, I was in the pantry, getting ready to set the dinner tables, when I heard them. They didn't know I was in there. Cameron told Jocelyn he knew something shady was going on and that it didn't take a rocket scientist to figure out they were swapping the high-priced seafood like tuna for cheaper imitations but charging the patrons as if it was the real deal."

Marshall put his hand on my knee and gave it a squeeze as Paige went on.

"I wasn't sure if he was talking about her or if he meant the other restaurants he serviced. It didn't matter because Jocelyn went ballistic. Told him where he could stick his fins, and next thing I knew he stormed out of there."

"So, their breakup was kind of mutual?" I asked.

"Duh," was all she said before looking around again and rushing off.

"So, if what she said was true, it wasn't Coldwater Seafood pulling the switch, it was the restaurants. Boy, my uncle Louis's palate had it right all along."

"We don't exactly know that, yet," Marshall said, "but we're getting closer."

We finished our drinks and were notified by the hostess that our table was ready. The bar filled up to capacity and it was impossible to catch Paige again. Marshall explained to the hostess that his secretary had arranged for him to have a brief chat with the owner once we were done eating. He handed her his card and she nodded.

"I'll let Miss Amaro know. Right now, she's in her office. Her brother stopped by and, from the sound of things, they might be in there longer than anticipated."

Her brother? What brother? "Did you know she has a brother?" I asked Marshall.

"She said she had family, but no one was in the restaurant business with her."

Once the hostess seated us, our waiter arrived. The same one as last time. Tight-lipped, professional Bernard. I ordered the Chilean sea bass and Marshall selected the creamy pesto shrimp over linguini.

"I know a shrimp when I see one," Marshall chided. "It would be tough to substitute them for anything else."

"Do you really think Jocelyn's doing that? Engaging in fish fraud?"

"I was kidding, but obviously Cameron hit a nerve with her. At least, according to Paige. There's one way to find out—compare the menu with the stock order from Coldwater Seafood. Shouldn't be too hard to do. I'll call the company tomorrow. Seems like they're not the ones who have something to hide."

"I'll be right back," I said. "Might as well use this time for a quick stop in the ladies' room."

Marshall stood and pulled my chair back. It was a small gesture, but all those little things reiterated what I already knew. I was head over heels for the guy and glad it was mutual.

I was told the restrooms were located in a small alcove near the ornate welcoming station. The hostess must have stepped away from her spot, because I was the only one standing in the lobby. I took a step toward the arched entrance when I realized I was standing in front of a door with a bronze sign that read: "Office."

Drat! Must be another alcove. This place has more alcoves and columns than a hypostyle prayer hall.

No one was there to see my mistake and I spun around. That's when I heard the argument behind the office doors. Someone had forgotten to close them all the way. I lingered for a second. Long enough to hear the conversation between Jocelyn and her brother.

It was none of my business, and I should've left except for one thing—I was suspicious of anyone and everyone who came in contact with my mother's backyard corpse. And Jocelyn was high on the list. I stood by the door like a statue, trying to glean every word. I didn't have to try too hard. Her brother was practically explosive.

"Who died and put you in charge of my life? And so what if I bought new wheels. Maybe my business is picking up."

Then Jocelyn spoke. "What business? Making deliveries? That's not a business. It's a grunt job. You've got a degree. Why are you wasting it?"

"Who says I'm wasting it? It just so happens I have a lucrative side job that more than pays the rent."

"Oh my God! Are you dealing drugs?"

"What? Are you insane? I figured out a way to put more cash in my pocket, and I'm doing it while I can. Don't knock it. If it wasn't for my menial delivery job, you'd be in a hell of a mess, and you know it. And while we're talking about messes, don't stand there and tell me you haven't monkeyed around with the books, either."

"If you're insinuating I've engaged in fraud like some of those other places, you can get the hell out of here right now."

"That's the best thing you've said so far."

My God! He's going to walk out that door and trip over me.

I had every intention of spinning around and charging toward the ladies' room, but I panicked and my feet froze. Too late to make a dash to the other side of the lobby, I did the next best thing. I tossed my bag on the floor and bent down to retrieve it just as the office door opened and the guy charged out, nearly crashing into me.

"Whoa! I'm sorry," he said. "I wasn't looking down."

As I stood up, my jaw all but dropped. I recognized him. "It's okay. My purse slipped from my hand on the way to the restroom."

He pointed across the lobby. "It's over there. Everyone makes that mistake. They really need to put up bigger signs."

"Um, yeah. Bigger signs."

Forcing a smile, I nodded and charged straight ahead to the restroom. My heart was literally palpitating and I couldn't wait to tell Marshall who Jocelyn's brother was.

"Long line in there?" he asked as soon as I got back.

"No. But I might've done some of my best sleuthing across the hall."

He gave me a quizzical look, and I went on to explain. When I was all finished, he clasped his hands together and leaned across the table. "The delivery guy, huh? From that health food company? The one with the flash-frozen fish products? Are you sure?"

"Absolutely. Light hair, young, and medium build, wearing a shirt with that The Bountiful Life logo on the front. Not a single doubt in my mind."

"You know, this is getting more than coincidental. That company keeps cropping up like a bad penny. Even though they're in the seafood business, their product doesn't even come close to the gourmet stuff Coldwater Seafood handles. Still, I'm going to run some background checks when I get back to the office tomorrow."

"What do you think the guy's sideline is? Jocelyn sounded just a wee bit alarmed."

"Heck. It could be anything. Gambling. Uber driving. Pet sitting . . ."

"Yeah, I suppose his sister was ticked because he was wasting his life. Well, according to her, anyway. And speaking of ticked, boy, did he hit a nerve with that accusation about falsifying the seafood products."

"Guess I'll have to approach that matter gingerly and diplomatically. If she went off the handle with her own brother, who knows how she'll respond to a private investigator a second time. Ugh. One saving grace about this evening, the food's bound to be decent."

Marshall was right about that. The Chilean sea bass was exquisite, just as my aunt Ina said it would be. And Marshall savored every bit of his pesto shrimp.

"Well, it's show time." He handed Bernard a Visa card and gave me a wink. "I'll try to keep the conversation with Jocelyn short and sweet this time."

"No worries. I'll linger at the bar. Who knows what else I might overhear tonight."

Chapter 21

As stray conversations went, I didn't hear much of anything at the bar. The patrons were quiet and Paige was nowhere in sight. Probably on a break. At least she clarified one thing—Cameron wasn't the one making unauthorized seafood exchanges. In my mind, that meant it couldn't have been one of the restaurant owners who murdered him, but Marshall busted that bubble right away on the way home.

"Suppose Cameron confronted one or more of those owners and told them he had enough evidence to prove they were fleecing their customers?" he asked. "It would be enough ammo to put a place out of business and a darn good reason for one of them to knock him off."

"But why would he do such a thing? He'd be cutting his own throat." *Or in this case, choking on his own poison.*

"There are still some boy scouts left in this world, hon. Maybe our victim was one of them."

"What did Jocelyn say when you asked her about it? Did she hit the roof like she did with her brother?"

"No, not at all. Of course, I kept it very businesslike

and spoke in generalities. I figured I'd get the information I needed layer by layer. Believe it or not, she was more than familiar with fraud in her industry. Said the sushi places were the worst, but that was small potatoes. Then she went on to explain how some fish can easily be substituted for others, especially if a master chef was the one preparing the meal."

"Wouldn't it be easy to recognize things like cheap artificial crabmeat instead of the real stuff?"

"In that case, yes. But we're talking fillets. With seasonings, crusts, and sauces, it would be virtually impossible to detect a difference. Unless, of course, your name happens to be Louis Melinsky. The average Joe wouldn't know a cheap tilapia from a red snapper or escolar from tuna. Those were only a few she mentioned. She gave me an entire list."

"Hmm. Doesn't sound as if her restaurant is engaging in nefarious practices, does it? What about the other issue? The one that doesn't involve fish."

"Tucker?"

"Uh-huh. Was she seeing him? Sleeping with him? Maybe Bethany didn't have to ask Tucker because she already knew. Like the lipstick on the collar thing. Although that's a really ancient cliché, isn't it?"

"Turns out Jocelyn did have a thing going with Tucker."

"Oh no!"

"Huh? Why are you so upset about this?"

"Think about it. Every time there's a murder, the first thing my mother does is tell me it's got to be some sort of affair gone bad. She practically drills it into my head. Forget every other conceivable reason in the world why someone would commit murder. Oh no. It's all about tempestuous love affairs and raging jealousy as far as Harriet Plunkett is concerned. We'll never hear the end of this if it turns out the motive for Cameron's death was jealousy on the part of Tucker."

"I think you're getting ahead of yourself."

"I've got another scenario, too. What if Bethany found out and meant to murder Jocelyn with that sago palm toxin? Along comes Cameron and he ingests it instead. Oh my gosh. It gets better! Bethany might've inadvertently served her own mother some of that poison but not enough to kill her."

"I'll give you the motive part of the equation. And the means is easy enough. Those palms are everywhere. However, you forgot one thing—opportunity."

"As in timeline?"

"Uh-huh. Jocelyn told me it was only innocent flirtation when she first met Tucker. That's when he was working for Coldwater Seafood. Things changed and their relationship heated up."

"As in full-blown affair?" I asked.

"Yep. A full-blown affair that reached its apex and fizzled out. Then Jocelyn started seeing Cameron."

"And?"

"Oh, it gets better. Tucker came back into the picture to warn her about Cameron's womanizing and then—"

"Don't tell me! She was seeing both of them?" *This is better than the stuff the book club ladies dish out.*

"She wasn't proud of it."

"Yikes. I can't believe she told you all of this."

"Jocelyn's no dummy. She's aware that her relationship with both men put her in a questionable position as far as Cameron's murder goes. She said she wanted to be up-front and honest with me because the sooner we track down the guy's killer, the sooner she'll be off the hook.

Said she hasn't slept nights for fear someone will show up at her door with a warrant for her arrest. Apparently, she's a big fan of Telemundo, along with your mother."

"My gosh. That's a whole lot to digest in one night."

"First thing tomorrow I intend to scrutinize the timelines again. See if Nate and I overlooked anything regarding Cameron's whereabouts leading up to the minute Streetman sniffed that tarp."

"And Elaine Meschow's whereabouts, too?"

"I'm afraid so. Looks like tomorrow's going to be a long day. So much for the expression 'Fun Friday.'"

Marshall wasn't kidding when he said "long day." Only he meant me. It was Friday morning and I had just completed the monthly billing at a little before noon when Nate rapped on my doorframe.

"Hey, kiddo. How's it going? Got a favor to ask."

"I, uh . . ."

"Any minute now you'll be getting an email from Deputy Ranston. Or Bowman. Or someone from their office. Doesn't matter. The attachments do. They're Excel spreadsheets from Coldwater Seafood listing the last six months of purchases from the four gourmet seafood houses."

"I know where this is going. You want me to do a type and quantity comparison between what the restaurants ordered from their distributor and what they actually listed on their menus, right?"

Nate nodded. "Augusta did a little handiwork for us, too. She pulled up all of the menus going back six months."

I grimaced. "Remind me to thank her."

"Well, I'd better get going. If it's any consolation, lunch

is on me. I told Augusta the same thing. Order out. Knock yourself out. I'll catch up later. Marshall's downtown at Coldwater Seafood, and I'm about to pay Elaine Meschow a visit."

"Um, sure. See you later."

Ten minutes later Augusta came into my office and plopped a stack of restaurant menus on my desk. "I printed these out for you, Phee. I also called those restaurants to see if their menus changed in the last six months. With the exception of special holiday meals, all of them have kept the same menus. Have fun. And while we're on the topic of food, our choices are on the value-priced side. Well, what'll it be? Deli? Pizza? Tacos? All three?"

"Chocolate. I don't care if I have to take it intravenously."

"Okay. Tacos. I'm in the mood for tacos. I'll see if they sell any chocolate churros."

She darted out of my office the very second I received Ranston's email. Guess he was the lucky one who had to deal with Coldwater Seafood. I emailed him back and thanked him.

Marshall had made me a copy of the notes he took last night when Jocelyn told him which fish were commonly swapped. I unfolded the letter-size paper and flattened it on my desk before turning my attention to the seafood menus. I wanted to get a general sense of the types of fish these restaurants were featuring. Then I pulled up the first of Ranston's spreadsheets and searched for those fish orders for the distributor.

With the exception of tilapia, none of the names I expected, like tuna or red snapper, appeared. Instead, I was looking at words such as "escolar," "pollock," "yellowtail," and "dory." I went back three months and it was the same. Then five months. A few orders for tuna, red snapper, cod, and orange roughy were listed. The month before that was similar with the addition of mahi-mahi.

The aroma of Tabasco sauce and fried peppers wafted into my office. Augusta was back from the Mexican restaurant around the corner. "No chocolate churros, but I bought you a Hershey's bar."

I devoured my all-beef supreme taco with extra cheese and washed it down with a Coke. Then I was back to the spreadsheet comparisons. It was grueling. I heard Augusta fielding phone calls in the front office and knew her day wasn't exactly a walk in the park, either.

By quarter to four I had managed to analyze the information from the two Phoenix restaurants, Neptune's Delicacies and Aphrodite's Appetite. No wonder my uncle Louis said they were spiraling downward. More like trawling for garbage fish. I shoved my chair back from my desk and stretched. I needed coffee and lots of it. The caffeine in my Coke only went so far.

"I can't believe it." I closed the lid on the K-cup and pushed the flashing blue button. "Two of those restaurants have engaged in downright fraud. Wouldn't the food inspectors have caught it?"

Augusta looked up from her desk. "Nope. They don't care what the food is, as long as it's cooked right. Now if those restaurants had lied about refrigerator temperatures or falsified expiration dates on stuff . . . well, that would be a different matter. I watch the 'Filthy Dining' segment on KPHO all the time. You'd be amazed at what goes on in those kitchens. Rodent droppings, roaches, employees who don't wash their hands . . ."

"Ugh. I think Cameron was on to them and that's what got him killed. Now there's real evidence. Then again, Nate, Marshall, and those sheriff deputies have talked with everyone in those establishments and couldn't verify anything as far as timeline was concerned. You can't kill someone if you don't come in contact with them."

"Don't tell that to anyone who believes in the paranormal."

"You're not saying—"

"Of course not. That stuff is a bunch of poppycock, but it doesn't mean those restaurants should get off scot-free. Once those deputies get your analysis, I'll wager they issue warrants for consumer fraud."

"I've got one more place to check out—Taste of the Sea in Scottsdale. Did Nate or Marshall say when they'd be back?"

"No. But I'm figuring it'll be within the hour."

"I feel as if I'm on some sort of archeological dig and I don't want to stop. Looks like I'll be working overtime tonight."

"Anything I can do?"

"Nah. I've got it."

I went back to my desk and pulled up Taste of the Sea. I scanned their ordering sheets from Coldwater Seafood, expecting to find yellowtail, dory, pollock, and escolar on the list, but instead, I saw the names of quality fish—tuna, cod, snapper, and mahi-mahi. All in very small quantities. I did, however, notice an abundance of orders for tilapia. I was certain they were cheating their customers, too, but doing it gradually so they stayed under the radar.

The phone rang and Augusta shouted for me. "Phee, your mother's on the line!"

Terrific. Now what?

"I hate to bother you at work, Phee"—*since when*—"but you'll never guess what Streetman pulled out from under the bed in the guest room."

"Mom! I'm mired under with work. Can't we talk about this later?"

"No. It might be yours."

"My what?"

"That's what I'm getting at. Streetman has a habit of hiding things way under the beds. Last week it was that imitation pearl necklace of mine that I always wear."

My eyes were rolling around so many times I was getting dizzy. "I give up. What did he find?"

"I'm not exactly sure what you call them, but it's a small metal thing on a broken lanyard. Someone's always using them on TV when they have to get information out of a computer in a hurry."

"A flash drive?"

"I've got it in my hand. It says 'SanDisk.'"

"That's a flash drive or thumb drive and it's not mine. I doubt it's Marshall's. He doesn't carry one around on a lanyard. Maybe Herb or one of the book club ladies left it at your house. You had lots of people in there when we first found Cameron's body and then again on Thanksgiving. Did you call them?"

"Yes. I even called Janet Galbraith because she was here before Halloween—Oh heavens! I forgot to call Herb. I'll call you right back. Bye."

I went back to the spreadsheets and studied Taste of the Sea's information again. When I heard the phone ring a few minutes later, I shouted to Augusta, "It's probably my mother!"

"That was a quick call to Herb," I said to my mother. "Any luck?"

"No. He told me whatever I do I shouldn't put that thing in my computer or I'll wind up with a virus or worse."

"Yeah. He's right. That's kind of a dangerous practice without running a security scan first."

"I'm not doing anything of the sort. I don't know what this is or where the dog could've gotten it. I would've noticed it if he found it in the dog park. The lanyard's a reddish leather and pretty long. Are you sure it's not Marshall's?"

"Trust me. It's not."

"What about Nate?"

I laughed. "A flash drive would be the last thing he'd be carrying around. He's so old school. Are you sure no one else has been inside your house?"

"No one. I had the furnace checked a few weeks ago, but the guy stayed in the garage. If he was the one who dropped it, I would've noticed Streetman bringing it inside."

My eyes were glued to the spreadsheet in front of me, but my mind was doing backflips. All the way back to the day when the dog uncovered Cameron's body beneath the tarp.

"Do me a favor," I said. "Put that thing in a drawer and don't give it to anyone."

"Who am I going to give it to?"

"Aargh. Sorry. Only a matter of speaking. I'll come over tomorrow and get it. I know how to scan it for viruses and malware. Maybe once I open the files we'll know where it came from."

"Come early in the morning. I'm going to the mall with Shirley and Lucinda in the afternoon. The stores are having their holiday sales, and I need to find an outfit that will blend nicely with Streetman's *Nutcracker* costume."

Dear God. Is there anything in her life that doesn't involve that dog? "Okay. Fine. Um, how long do you think that flash drive's been under the bed?"

"Gee, that's hard to say. The dog finds things and hides them. Then he moves them to other hiding places. Under the couch, under my bed . . . Once I found one of those promotional key chains from an insurance company right behind the toilet in the guest bathroom. Of all places. Why?"

"I'm not sure. I was only thinking out loud. Look, I really have to go. I've got tons of work."

"Fine. See you in the morning."

I hung up the phone, but my hand still remained on top of the receiver. It was as if I couldn't let go of a thought I had. My mother was pretty darn observant when it came to that dog of hers. She'd certainly notice if he picked up something outside and brought it into the house. Especially if they were coming back from a walk or from the dog park. My mother would have to be awfully distracted to not see a red leather lanyard in Streetman's mouth. Unless . . . unless . . . Oh my God! I think I know where he found it and when.

I charged out of my office and over to Augusta's desk, spouting and waving my arms. "I think my mother's dog might've found a flash drive that belonged to the murderer!"

She pushed herself away from the computer screen. "Huh? What?"

"Right before Halloween. My mother and I were so distraught when we found the body, we weren't paying attention to the dog."

I went on to explain how the dog might've found the lanyard with the drive on it and how he easily could've raced into the house with it and darted under a bed. His favorite pastime.

"You might be on to something. God knows. No one else is. This case is dragging on longer than a Viagra commercial."

"It'll have to drag on one more day. I promised Nate I'd get these comparisons done and I want to be sure I've been thorough. That means at least another two hours for me, and I can't ask Marshall to go over there. He had to talk with the management at Coldwater Seafood and touch base with a few of his other clients in the area. Oh, who the hell am I kidding? My mother doesn't go to sleep before ten. Do me a favor, Augusta. I don't want to get stuck on the phone."

"You want me to—"

"Uh-huh. Call her and tell her I'll be picking up that flash drive in a few hours."

"Coward!"

Chapter 22

I left Marshall a voice mail and told him I'd see him at home. Our freezer had enough frozen pizza and other choices so we wouldn't starve. Thank goodness the guy wasn't fussy when it came to eating.

Nate returned to the office a few minutes before five. Augusta was packing it in for the day and I was on my second "sweep" of Neptune's Delicacies, having completed Aphrodite's Appetite, when Nate stuck his head in my door. "Looks like I owe you dinner as well. Huh, kiddo?"

I nodded enthusiastically. "As long as it's not at any of these three restaurants. They've been swindling their customers. Buying cheap fish but passing them off as the more expensive ones. Here, see for yourself."

He pulled up a chair and I toggled back and forth between the menus I had scanned onto the computer and the actual ordering sheets from Coldwater Seafood. I pointed to the computer monitor. "That's fraud, isn't it? Outright consumer fraud. Marshall thinks Cameron was on to it, confronted one of the restaurant owners, and that's what got him killed. Tough to prove, huh? Although we may have a really good clue."

I told him about the flash drive Streetman found and the strong possibility it was retrieved from the body-dumping site under the Galbraiths' grill. "I'm driving over there and picking it up as soon as I'm done with these comparisons."

"Don't get your heart set on finding anything groundbreaking. For all you know, it could be someone's tournament schedule for pickleball."

"Or a very valuable clue. No different than these spreadsheets."

Nate rubbed the bottom of his chin. "Now that information is worth taking to the bank. Wait till Ranston and Bowman see it."

"Give me another thirty or forty minutes. I want to be sure I've got everything in order."

"No problem. I've got enough paperwork on my desk to load up a landfill."

"By the way, how did it go with Elaine? Was she able to give you any specifics regarding her whereabouts before she succumbed to that sago palm toxin?"

"Not really. The only thing she remembered in detail was the delivery service from that freeze-dried fish company."

"The Bountiful Life?"

"Yeah. She said she was glad it was Alender something-or-other. The same man who always made the deliveries. He had to wait while she rearranged her freezer."

"Did she describe him?"

"Young."

"Oh brother."

"Said he'd been making the deliveries in Sun City West for a few years and that he was very familiar with the seafood industry because his sister ran a restaurant."

I slammed my hands on the corner of the desk and threw my head back. "That cinches it! That absolutely cinches it! It's the same delivery guy all right. The same one I saw at Phyllis Gruber's house and at La Mar Maravillosa. It's Jocelyn Amaro's brother. So that's his name—Alender. The bartender at La Mar Maravillosa told me Alender and Cameron had a bit of a row a few days before Cameron turned up dead. Said the conversation was about some sort of fraud. Probably the seafood switcheroo these spreadsheets uncovered."

I clasped my hands and leaned over the desk. My typical thinking pose. "Must be Jocelyn's brother has a propensity for getting into it with people. He was yammering about a lucrative side job when he and his sister got into an ugly argument last night when Marshall and I were at the restaurant. I overheard them. Maybe Jocelyn's brother simply knows how to push the wrong buttons."

My heart was thumping and it felt as if my entire body was shaking. "Holy Cow! His lucrative side job has got to be theft. He's probably stealing those old folks blind when he makes their home deliveries. Did Elaine mention anything missing?"

"No. Not at the time of delivery. And there was nothing missing when her house was broken into recently. Maybe theft isn't Alender's sideline."

"Darn. I was so close. I thought I might've been on to something."

"You are. Lots of very interesting theories."

"I'll stick to my accounting. Right now, I need to get Jocelyn's brother out of my mind and Taste of the Sea's spreadsheets on my screen. So, I guess it was a total bust at Elaine's house, huh?"

"Not really. She showed me photos of her dog and some

pictures her daughter posted from a Halloween party she and the husband went to. Honestly, the costumes these days are so grisly. She went as Ghostface and he was Freddy Krueger from *Nightmare on Elm Street.*"

"Yeesh."

Nate stretched, thanked me again, and stood. A lightbulb went off in the back of my mind and the words flew out of my mouth. "Other than that scream mask, what was she wearing?"

"A dark hoodie. Why?"

"Because that's exactly how that person who held Jocelyn at gunpoint in her restaurant was dressed. Ghostface mask and all. And Jocelyn was certain it was a woman. Nate, I think the perpetrator was Bethany, and I'll go as far as to say Jocelyn knew it, too."

Nate sank down on the hard chair and ran his fingers through his hair. "Because?"

"Because Bethany's two-timing husband, Tucker, was having an on-again off-again affair with Jocelyn. Maybe Bethany decided it was time to put a stop to it."

"By trying to kill Jocelyn?"

"Nah. I doubt it. I think she meant to scare her, that's all. Look, before you say a word, consider this: Jocelyn probably wanted to end the affair, so when Bethany showed up like a Wes Craven sniper, it gave Jocelyn all the impetus she needed to quit cold turkey on Tucker. That's why she didn't tell the Tempe police the truth. Bethany probably confronted her and got her to agree to it that Tucker was off-limits." I sat back.

"I hate to admit it, but you're making sense. Nothing was stolen from the restaurant, nothing was vandalized, and the incident was over almost as fast as it began. At least according to witnesses and the police report. Marshall and I were thinking it had to do with Cameron's death, but given the relationship between Jocelyn, Bethany, and Tucker, coupled with those photos Elaine showed me, it's evidence enough to support your line of reasoning."

"How are we going to get Bethany to admit to it?" I asked.

"We're not. Not right now anyway. It would complicate things. Her husband has a damn good motive for killing Cameron. After all, it was Cameron who tipped off Bethany regarding the affair Tucker was having. I don't buy that bit about her not confronting him. Tucker probably went berserk and found a way to kill Cameron discreetly."

"The sago palm poison?" By now I was chomping at the bit.

"Yep. No muss. No fuss. No blood. No bullets. A nice, hard-to-detect poison that's readily available. Unless, of course, it wasn't Tucker. Those swindling restauranteurs have a strong motive as well—saving their asses. If Cameron was about to go to the police or, worse yet, the Federal Trade Commission, those businesses would be underwater, along with the fish they served."

"And the spreadsheets I've been working on—"

"Give us exactly what we need to have Ranston, Bowman, and the police departments they collaborate with put the kind of pressure on those places that would certainly yield results."

I looked at the clock on the lower right-hand corner of my computer screen. "You'll have your analysis in less than an hour."

"What happened to thirty or forty minutes?"

I smiled. "I had to factor time for interruptions. Do you want me to email everything to you or print it out when I'm done?"

"Email a copy to Marshall. He likes all that cyber correspondence. I'll take mine in a big pile of papers. By the way, good job!"

I was finished with the spreadsheets in less than an hour. Fifty-three minutes to be precise. Nate still had work to do, so I locked up and turned the front lights down. Then I headed right over to my mother's house to get that flash drive.

The dog was burrowed at the end of the couch when I walked in. He lifted his head, as if to acknowledge me, then licked one of his paws and went back to sleep.

"I think he's getting better," I said. "He's not hiding under the couch anymore."

My mother walked over to him and patted his head. "Yes, he's becoming quite the brave little man. He'll make the cutest doggie leprechaun once that contest gets underway in March."

It was hard not to groan. *Doggie leprechaun. Geez, we haven't gotten to December's festivities*. "Okay. Mom, tell me more about the flash drive."

"I still can't imagine where it came from or how long it's been under the bed. Not that I don't dust there. I mop up with the Swiffer, but the dog moves his little treasures all over the place."

I turned the flash drive around in my hand and took a closer look at the lanyard. "It could be anything. I'll keep you posted. Well, I should get going."

"Not so quick. Augusta wouldn't tell me why you changed your mind and came over here tonight instead of tomorrow. What are you hiding from me?"

"Nothing."

"You're not fooling me, Phee."

"Fine. But don't get all worked up like it's a fait accompli."

"What is?"

"What I think might be on that disk."

My mother let out a breath and motioned for me to continue.

"Now listen, this is all conjecture on my part, but I think Streetman might've picked up the flash drive when he was poking under the tarp. You and I were so shaken at the sight of a dead body. Oh, wait a minute. I *was* the one who was shaken. You didn't want to look."

"Get to the point already."

"Okay. Okay. You and I were so unnerved we didn't notice what the dog was doing. When you raced back to the house to get your cell phone, the dog could've easily stashed that thumb drive under the bed. There's a possibility it might've belonged to the victim—Cameron Tully. We need to find out what's on it."

"Call me the second you know for sure."

"It'll take a while. It's got to be scanned for viruses first."

"Scan it, debug it, do whatever you have to, but call me the instant you know something."

I gave her my word I'd let her know and made a dash for the door.

"You sure you don't want anything to eat?"

"No thanks. Marshall's got it covered."

"All right. Don't forget—call me!"

It was a real possibility that the flash drive was Cameron's. And it may hold important information about his assassin. If Arizona didn't have such hefty fines for speeding, I would've pressed harder on the gas.

The aroma of lasagna hit my nostrils the second I got

home and opened the door. "Smells great! What restaurant?"

"Trader Joe's frozen foods. It's that porcini mushroom lasagna we decided to try."

"I'm starving, but I'm also dying to find out what's on this flash drive Streetman found."

"I know. I got your voice mail and, believe it or not, a text from Nate. Looks like he's sliding into the twenty-first century after all. Come on, grab the drive, and we'll run that sucker through McAfee while we eat."

That little device took longer than expected to scan. Especially since Marshall and I all but gobbled up our lasagnas like Huns returning from a raid. We were left staring at my computer muttering things like "maybe we need a faster hard drive" and "what the heck could be on it?"

Finally, after I'd washed the dishes and changed into comfy sweats, Marshall announced, "It's a go!" The engineers at NASA probably weren't as excited as he was.

When the program came on with the option of opening the folder to view the files, I held my breath and clicked. Two files appeared. One marked "Names" and the other "Misc." I bit my lower lip and before Marshall could say a word, I clicked "Names" and focused on the computer screen. I was certain I'd be privy to files that belonged to Cameron. Files that might contain a rock-solid reason for someone to murder the guy. Sure, I had connected the dots and found out the restaurant menus differed from the inventory orders his customers placed, but it wasn't enough. I was hoping for some sort of correspondence between Cameron and one of those restauranteurs. What I saw instead dashed all my hopes of us solving the case before the New Year rolled around.

My elbow thudded on the desk and I rested my head in

the palm of my hand. "Hell. This flash drive doesn't belong to Cameron. Nate was right. We're looking at a stupid club list or something. God knows. It doesn't even say what club. It could be anything from the Boomers to the Art Clubs. Look at the names and addresses. All Sun City West. All alphabetical. It's got to be a club."

Marshall leaned over my shoulder, reached for the mouse, and scrolled down. "Abernathy, 45307 Springdale Drive, Austin, 56709 W. Greystone Drive, Bellis, 15150 Morning Dove Drive."

"I have no idea what this is. A church roster? If someone pirated medical information, it would have insurance numbers. All this has are names and addresses."

I watched as he kept scrolling. Then a familiar name appeared and I gasped—Galbraith. On W. Sentinel Drive, no less.

Marshall put his hand on my shoulder. "Relax. They belong to clubs, don't they? Or maybe some volunteer organization? Maybe it's their flash drive. For all we know it could be Janet Galbraith's water aerobics club. Your mother once said the club had over eighty participants and that was seventy too many. Remember? It very well could be one of Janet's clubs."

"It's not. Because it's not Janet's flash drive. My mother called her when she first discovered the flash drive. She figured maybe Janet or her husband dropped it on the patio."

"Okay. Win some. Lose some. Scratch them off the list."

Marshall continued to scroll until we recognized two other names.

"Would you look at that. I'm beginning to think there's more to this list than a club or a house of worship." He let go of the mouse and backed away. "I'll be darned if I know what. Go ahead, open the other file."

"Miscellaneous" could have meant anything, but in this case, the file was an accounting ledger. Something I was more than familiar with. My eyes darted across the usual headings—"Date," "Description," "Reference number," "Debit," "Credit," and "Balance."

"That's odd," I said. "Usually there's a column for transaction type. Check, money order, credit card, PayPal . . . unless they only accepted one kind of payment. Some companies do that, you know. It's very rare, but they do it. And another odd thing . . ."

"What's that?"

"Under 'Description,' all it has are three capital letters. What do you make of that? Say, do you think this ledger and the list of names go hand in hand?"

"No idea. Can you get any other information off of the spreadsheet?"

"Actually, it's spreadsheets. And lots of them in this file. Dating back two years. At least that information's on top. But no, nothing links them to those names. Could be two totally different things."

"This isn't my area of expertise by a long shot, but why do all the reference numbers end with the same two digits? I'm no mathematical whiz, but shouldn't they increase incrementally or something like that?"

My eyes fixated on the numbers and I was stunned. "Yikes. You're right. The thousandths, hundredths, and tenths columns might be the same, but certainly not the ones. What the heck is going on here?"

"Look again. Notice anything even odder?"

I wiped my eyes, blinked, and stared. "Um, the fact that the last two digits are the ending numbers for this year's date? Oh wait. I misspoke. There are a few numbers that end with next year's date."

"Uh-huh. Strange way to keep track of accounts."

"I'll say. Unless something else is going on. Still, I can't see that any of this has to do with Cameron."

"No, not Cameron," Marshall said. "His killer."

Chapter 23

Even though the next day was Saturday and I was technically off, I wasn't about to have Marshall and Nate tackle the mystery of that flash drive without me.

"You guys are going to turn it over to Rolo Barnes, aren't you?" I said as Marshall put his cereal bowl in the dishwasher.

"Well, uh . . ."

"Oh, admit it. You're thinking it's a code or cryptic numeral sequence that might as well be a code. Don't deny it. Did you call Rolo or did Nate?"

Rolo Barnes was Williams Investigations' cyber sleuth. He used to work for the Mankato police department but ventured into his own cyber detective business. So far off the grid as to stymie most intelligence agencies.

The guy always reminded me of a black Jerry Garcia. Only instead of playing the guitar, his fingers flew across numerous computer keyboards and similar devices. Rolo was affable, interesting, energetic, and downright weird. More idiosyncrasies than any psych textbook could document. And he drove me crazy when it came to payroll. I still twitched when I came across an odd-numbered check.

The worst was his preoccupation with dieting. And collecting kitchen gadgets and appliances. Usually to go along with whatever fad diet he was on—grains, vegan, organic vegan, paleo, kinesthetic . . . you name it, Rolo made it his own. Until he got tired of it. Or wanted a new kitchen toy.

"Don't turn it over to Rolo right away!" This time I was even more emphatic. "We can probably figure it out."

It had to be a pride thing. With a degree in accounting and years of experience, how could I not know what was going on with those spreadsheets on that flash drive? Last thing I needed was to appear like the village idiot. "Where'd we stick that flash drive? In the desk drawer?"

"Yeah. Top drawer on the left. Don't do this to yourself, hon. Face it. Those things may look like spreadsheets and even be labeled like them, but it could very well be a clever cryptic tool."

"I'll see about that."

I grabbed my cup of coffee, went back to the computer, and reinserted the flash drive while Marshall headed to the shower. I toggled the two files again, this time focusing on the three capital letters under the column marked "Description." Since I knew the Galbraiths were on the list of names, I searched the spreadsheet to see if I spotted a "GAL." Sure enough, it was there. Not a coincidence in my book. But what?

I knew that one example wasn't enough to bet the entire farm, but I was hard pressed for time and went with my hunch. Unfortunately, it was those ten-digit reference numbers that plagued me like a bad case of poison ivy.

Social Security numbers were nine digits. Phone numbers were seven digits. Ten with the area code. Were these phone numbers? I minimized the screen and flew to www.wikitravel. Nope. Not with zero as the first number. Forget phone numbers.

Applications and all sorts of forms usually required eight-digit codes for birthdates with two for the day, two for the month, and four for the year. I needed ten. Ten was the magic number in order to solve the puzzle, but nothing came to mind. Rats!

I took a large gulp of coffee and stared at the numbers again. Since the last two digits were the current or future year, I chose to ignore them and focus on the first eight numbers, beginning with the line that listed "GAL" under the description. It had to be the Galbraiths'—reference number 05101105 sans the last two digits of this year's date. It made about as much sense as a binary code. Maybe Marshall was right. Maybe we did need Rolo after all.

"I'll be out of the shower in a minute and then it'll be all yours!" Marshall called out from the bathroom.

Great. Nothing like having my very own ticking clock.

If there was one thing I hated, it was admitting defeat. And I wasn't about to do that. Not with my reputation as an accountant on the line. I looked at the Galbraiths' number again. This time in two-digit increments. Zero five. Zero five. What? What could be zero five? And then it hit me. I opened my mouth, probably in astonishment or desperate need of air, and went to the next two numbers—one zero. Month and day. If I wasn't losing my mind, it read May tenth.

If that was true, the last four digits translated to November fifth. I raced to the kitchen to grab the phone and immediately dialed my mother.

"Phee! Was I right? Was I right? That flash point or

whatever you call it belonged to the dead man. To Cameron Tully. Did it explain who might've killed him? Oh my gosh. My little Streetman might've solved the case."

"Hold your horses. Get a grip." *And let me come up with another cliché to get to my point.* "We don't know yet. We're still working on it. That's why I called. I need some information. Do you know when the Galbraiths left for Canada and when they were originally supposed to return?"

"Why? Are they involved?"

"What? No. We just need the information. Do you have it?"

"Of course I do. I wrote it down on my calendar like I do every year so I know when to begin checking the outside of their house. Hang on. I'll look."

"The shower's all yours!" Marshall shouted again.

"Be right there."

My mother was out of breath but louder than usual. "I'm back. They left May tenth and were supposed to return on November fifth. At least they'll be here for Christmas. Now tell me why. Why did you need those dates?"

My heart began beating faster and I took a long, slow breath. "If I tell you, promise you won't get hysterical and concoct some god-awful scenario."

"Concoct a scenario? I don't have to concoct a scenario. A dead man was dumped a few yards from my patio. Now tell me!"

"All right. Calm down. That flash drive had a long list of names and addresses. The Galbraiths were on it. And Elaine Meschow, too. And—"

"Don't you dare tell me my name was on it."

"It wasn't."

"Good."

"So, like I was saying, there was another list. Well, not a list exactly. Spreadsheets with weird numbers and I think those numbers are dates. Dates when people are out of town. But I'm not sure. I only had you check on the Galbraiths. Don't breathe a word of this to anyone. You hear? Not even Shirley. Especially not Shirley. And definitely not Herb."

"Fine. Now what?"

"Nate and Marshall will work with the sheriff's deputies to see if any of those other dates coincide with when people were out of town. It could be a burglary ring."

"You don't have to sugarcoat this on my account. It's not a burglary ring. It's that horrible bordello business that we uncovered. And I'm no detective. Are you sure there was nothing else on that disk?"

"I'm sure." *And I can't believe she, of all people, might've figured this out.* "And don't say anything to anyone, Mom. Promise?"

"Fine. Fine. Tell your boss and your boyfriend to quit fiddling around and find that killer. Good heavens. You're uncovering everything except Nancy Drew's diary!"

I thanked her, hung up the phone, and felt as if someone had just popped my birthday balloon. She was right, after all. Those dates on that flash drive probably belonged to the mastermind who orchestrated that sex scandal hotel business. Airtnt. Very clever. Very lucrative and impossible to track down. Until now.

Streetman might've broken a case, but it wasn't the one we needed. At least Ranston and Bowman would be elated. They'd notify the Surprise police and who knew? Maybe one of them had a cyber sleuth on staff who could uncover more data from that drive.

That god-awful feeling of being a bridesmaid without ever becoming a bride crept up on me. I was uncovering all sorts of handy information, like Bethany being Jocelyn's assailant and now this, but I was as far removed from finding Cameron's killer as I was the day we discovered his body.

Marshall was toweling off his hair when he came back into the living room. He must've dressed quickly. Jeans and a black *Game of Thrones* T-shirt that read: "Winter Is Coming."

"Any luck?" he asked.

I walked over and planted a huge kiss on his mouth. "You won't get that from Rolo Barnes."

"Eek! I hope not. Does this mean you found something?"

"I think so. I'm pretty certain those reference numbers are dates. Dates that indicate when someone is going to be out of town. It makes sense because the start dates seem to begin in April and the end dates in December and January. Those are the snowbird dates. More or less."

"Whoa." He strode past me and pulled the chair closer to the computer screen. "It would appear as if this drive belonged to someone who was keeping track of vacant houses. It has to be that Airtnt thing. Remember? Little Las Vegas in your mother's backyard."

Geez, how come everyone figured it out but me? "Yeah. That's what I thought, too. And take another look. Some reference numbers aren't numbers at all. They're just a series of ten zeros. Those have to be the homes that belong to year-round residents. Check Elaine Meschow's while you're sitting there. She's year-round. What does it read?"

"Zero, zero, zero—"

"I'm right, aren't I?"

"This is unbelievable. This is a real break in that 'rooms for rent' business. The deputy sheriffs weren't able to get anywhere with that case. The kids were no help since they used an app for their transactions and it was impossible to track down. At least you'll make Ranston and Bowman's day."

"Terrific."

"Yeah. I'm as bummed about it as you are. I was really hoping that flash drive belonged to our killer and that he or she lost it when they dumped Cameron's body. So much for that pipe dream."

By late morning, Ranston and Bowman were able to confirm that the list did indeed match up to the dates when a number of Sun City West residents were out of town. Marshall had notified Nate about our findings and he, in turn, contacted the deputies.

Bowman stopped by Williams Investigations at a little past nine to pick up the flash drive. The deputies figured the guy or gal who was running the operation must've dropped it in the back of the Galbraiths' place when they were scoping out the place for future "rentals." *That* or they were wearing the lanyard and it came undone. Either way, the same result. What the deputies couldn't figure out was how the flash drive's owner came upon that information to begin with.

"It could be anything," I said to Marshall when Bowman left our office earlier that morning. I had just made myself a cup of coffee and tossed the used K-cup in the trash. "Utility companies are informed when people are gone for months. Same with cable and satellite dish service. And newspaper deliveries. Don't forget newspaper deliveries."

"Relax, hon. I'm sure those deputies will have it covered. Meanwhile, I feel as if I've been kicked in the shins regarding Cameron's demise. Maybe we're pushing too hard."

Nate, who had been in his office on the phone with a client, announced that he needed a cup of coffee in order to "revive some damn brain cells."

He grabbed the darkest-roast cup we had and put it in the machine. "The best and possibly only working theory we've got so far is revenge. Or silencing. If that can be considered a theory. If you ask me, Cameron was about to rat on one of those restaurants for defrauding the customers. Not to mention cutting back on the profits his own company was making by purchasing a cheaper product. Unfortunately, we don't have a lick of evidence to prove it."

Marshall groaned. "Want to hear the funny thing? La Mar Maravillosa, the one restaurant that wasn't engaged in that scheme, was the only one with a timeline for Cameron's whereabouts shortly before his body was discovered. This makes no sense."

"Then it had to be personal," I said. "That scenario with Tucker and Jocelyn."

Nate took a sip of his coffee and grimaced. "Guess this stuff is better with cream." He tore open a small packet of the fake stuff and poured it into his cup. "Maybe we're approaching this all wrong. We're trying to solve it using traditional methods. That's been our area of expertise—talking with people, double-checking what they say, backtracking, picking up clues—what we should be doing is getting a handle on where that damn sago palm toxin originated from and who had easy access to it."

"Neptune's Delicacies and Aphrodite's Appetite are the only restaurants that have them in their lobbies," Marshall said. "It gives them motive and means, but not opportunity."

Nate took another sip of his coffee and put the cup down. "We can cross out the supermarket chains. None of them sold those plants. At least we're not dealing with a slew of Home Depots or Lowe's. We'd never pass 'Go.' "

"What about Elaine Meschow?" I asked. "What possible motive would anyone have to poison her? Unless it really is that crazy Phyllis Gruber. And she did have motive and means. She hated Elaine over some bizarre mix-up with a frozen food delivery, not to mention the jealousy over that ridiculous dog contest. And, here's the good part: She cut palm fronds off of her neighbors' sago plants. That meant she had the poison right in her little hand."

Marshall and Nate looked at each other for a few seconds before Nate spoke. "Let's toss a coin to see which one of us gets to question the old bat."

Chapter 24

The following week moved at a slug's pace, but it was especially bad for Nate, who lost the bet and had to endure a rather uncomfortable visit with Phyllis Gruber. To make matters worse, the team at Williams Investigations exhausted all possible leads and wasn't making much progress. If that didn't give us cause for misery, the sheriff's deputies had gotten nowhere with the flash drive.

"Damn it," Marshall said. "Hanukkah and Christmas are less than three weeks away and nothing."

It was a Tuesday evening and we stopped by a small Indian restaurant for dinner on the way home from work. That was the neat thing about living near the Peoria-Glendale area—lots of unique eateries. I picked up a slice of naan bread and tore off a piece. "Maybe we should've given that flash drive to Rolo after all."

Marshall grabbed a slice of the hot flatbread as well, but instead of tearing off a piece to eat, he all but ripped the thing apart. "Rolo would've been hard pressed to find out which company or business had that particular list of names. He'd be able to hack in and eliminate the big players, but we can do that as well. Doesn't take a genius to know the snowbirds don't cut off their electricity when they're gone. Water service, maybe, since a leak would cause a ton of damage, but homeowners don't have to notify the company if they're temporarily shutting off the main source."

"Yeah, I know. My mother once explained how easy it is to turn off the water. It's just a small faucet near the front door. Everyone's house in Sun City West is designed that way."

No sooner did I finish speaking when our tandoori chicken and samosas arrived. For a brief moment, Marshall and I forgot about the investigation and dove into our meals.

When our plates were half-empty and the waiter had refilled our drinks, I switched topics entirely. "A week from Friday is the grand finale for that Precious Pooches Holiday Extravaganza."

"Aargh. Thanks for reminding me. Well, I suppose if we managed to get through the first two, this one won't be as bad."

"They're trucking in snow. Remember? Half those dogs have never seen the stuff. It could be really funny or—"

"A disaster?"

"Try not to think about it. My mother's really gone off the deep end on this one. She's bound and determined Streetman takes home the grand prize. All she's been talking about is that spa weekend at the Marriott. God forbid Phyllis's dog wins. We'll never hear the end of it. Streetman and Sir Breckenthall are neck and neck."

"Yeah. This is one nail-biter I'd like to miss. No offense."

"Are you kidding? If I could slip away to the Bahamas for that weekend, I would. Oh, and one more thing I forgot to mention—Elaine Meschow's dog, Prince, is competing in this contest, too. He's going as one of the little soldiers of *The Nutcracker*. Shirley pitched in and did his costume. Nothing as elaborate as Streetman's, mind you, but still pretty impressive, according to my mother."

"Hmm, you think Bethany and Tucker will be there?"

"I wouldn't be surprised. Especially after that Halloween parade incident. Why?"

"I'd like to catch Tucker off guard and see if I can't get him to admit his role in Cameron's death. I was going to pay Spellbound Naturals a visit this week, but I'll hold off. The element of surprise might yield better results."

"So, you're back to thinking it was personal. The affair with Jocelyn. The rivalry . . ."

"It would connect both poisonings. I mean, if Tucker found a way to use sago palm toxin on Cameron, he might've inadvertently poisoned his mother-in-law."

"I'm glad you said 'inadvertently.' I'd hate to think Bethany is married to a full-blown killer."

"That's ironic. Considering we believe she's the one who held the gun to Jocelyn's head."

"*Alleged* gun. Remember? You wanted to put that theory 'on hold' as I recall. Maybe we should use that so-called element of surprise and engage both of them in lively conversations during that pet parade. I'll take Bethany. What do you say?"

"I say it's 'Game On.' We have nothing to lose."

Three days before the grand finale for the Precious Pooches Holiday Extravaganza, Nate got called away to Tucson for a new lead on a case he'd been working on.

"Tell Harriet it's nothing personal. I'm not deliberately avoiding her invitations," he told me that Tuesday morning. He had just dropped some bills on my desk and was leaving my office. "I don't think she's ever forgiven me for missing the opening night of *The Mousetrap*."

"She'll get over it. Marshall and I will be there, along with all her book club ladies and Herb."

My voice must've carried, because the next thing I knew I heard Augusta say, "I have to work late that day."

Nate and I broke out laughing.

"Look at it this way, kiddo—it'll give Marshall another chance to pick up any scuttlebutt regarding Cameron's death. If anyone in Sun City West is remotely involved, the gossip will have reached new heights."

"Let's hope so," I said. "Because nothing else is."

My mother called us at home that night and every night up until the event, to regale us with ongoing descriptions of Streetman in his Mouse King costume. From there, the conversation morphed into "that despicable Phyllis Gruber," miscellaneous gossip the book club ladies heard, and the usual nagging about the case.

"You mean to tell me those sheriff deputies couldn't figure out anything more from that flash thing the dog found? No wonder they haven't solved the murder. They can't even figure out who's running that sex hotel business. I've got news for you—Gibbs from *NCIS* could have it solved in an hour. Less if you don't count commercials."

And I've got news for you—that's a TV show!

Those were the longest three days Marshall and I endured.

It was a balmy fifty-five degrees that final Friday before Christmas and Hanukkah. As planned, truckloads of snow were delivered to the dog park from some place "up north." My mother had gotten up early, along with Herb, and the two of them drove to the dog park to check it out.

"You'd think she'd never seen snow before," Marshall said when my mother called to let us know what was happening. "She lived all of her life in Mankato. I don't get it."

"It's a nostalgia thing. Like looking at a Norman Rockwell painting or watching *It's a Wonderful Life*. But believe me, that's all it is. When the weather gets into the forties, my mother complains as if the Siberian Express has rolled into town."

Down to the only viable answer to Cameron's murder and Jocelyn's "holdup," Marshall and I had worked out a loosely scripted plan for getting Bethany and Tucker to come clean. "Loosely" being the key word. I was going to tell her the Tempe police found security footage of the person in the hoodie and were going to use facial recognition software. I'd go on to explain the mask slipped around on the face long enough for geometric measurements to work. So what if it was a sci-fi fabrication? I could be quite convincing when I needed to be.

The plan for Tucker was more old school. Marshall was going to confront him directly. Tell him he knew about the affair with Jocelyn and had reason to believe Cameron was all but blackmailing him over it. Marshall would use all the tactics he'd learned to get a confession out of the guy. At least that was the plan.

We were leaving work at a little past two, taking both of our cars, "just in case." Augusta would be fine fielding calls and locking up. I think she was genuinely relieved we didn't insist she join us.

"I'll be in tomorrow morning for a couple of hours," Marshall told her, "so if anything needs my attention, leave me a note. If there's an emergency, you've got my cell. And Phee's."

"If there's going to be an emergency, it'll be at that dog park," she said. "A zillion little costumed ankle biters up to their stomachs in snow. If that's not a disaster in the making, I don't know what is."

The parking lot in front of the dog park looked like Costco on Black Friday. Cars everywhere, including the huge vans from the neighboring independent- and assisted-living facilities. The final pet extravaganza was the hottest thing going in the Sun Cities area. It was so popular we were forced to park near the Men's Club building, a hefty walking distance away.

"My God!" Marshall said. "What is it with these people and snow? They move out here to get away from it, then go out of their way to see it."

The knoll in front of the dog park resembled the bunny hill at Mount Kato, the ski resort Kalese and I used to frequent near Mankato. Closely placed cardboard peppermint sticks cordoned off the knoll, leaving the circular walkway open for the dogs. However, no one had bothered to shovel the walkway, and it appeared to be covered in the white stuff, too.

I groaned as we got closer to the park. "Streetman's going to hate this. He doesn't like water. Even lukewarm water. Snow is downright cold. He'll pitch a fit. What if he refuses to walk on the path? Then what? My mother will go bonkers."

Marshall took my arm and gave it a squeeze. "Relax, hon. It'll be all right."

"In whose universe?"

Throngs of people were crowded around the bottom portion of the walkway, in full view of the festivities. The judges' table, which was designed to resemble a chimney, had been moved from the bottom of the knoll near the parking lot to a spot on the top of the hill. The sound system had been moved as well. No giant balloons this time, only colorful ornaments that hung gracefully from the trees.

"I guess they wanted to avoid any mishaps this time," Marshall said as we made our way to the staging area. "Still, I would've expected at least one giant Santa Claus."

"Bite your tongue and take a look at who's approaching the judges' stand—not one, not two, but three Santas. You got your wish after all."

"Come on, let's wish your mother good luck. She's at the far edge of the staging area in the park and, if I'm not mistaken, isn't that your aunt Ina with her?"

"Oh my gosh, you're right. That *is* Aunt Ina. Either that or someone revived nineteen-twenties raccoon coats and added hats to go with them. Shirley and Lucinda are over there, too. And Myrna. Isn't that Myrna?"

Marshall stretched his neck. "Uh-huh. Looks like her."

We maneuvered our way through the crowd and slipped into the dog park without anyone asking us where our dog was.

"Phee!" my mother shouted. "Hurry up. Wish Streetman good luck before the program starts. Thought you'd want to know, it's not like last time. We're in groups of five as we walk around the park. Not as frenetic."

The dog started to rub against Marshall's leg and wouldn't stop. Shirley let out a gasp and immediately went over to readjust the Mouse King costume. "Lordy, last thing I need is for his crown to become dislodged."

Yep. That's the last thing anyone needs.

My aunt, who'd been conversing with the other book club ladies, suddenly turned around and enveloped me in her huge fur coat. "It's wonderful to see you again. Louis couldn't make it, unfortunately. Stomach trouble. I told him not to eat all that pickled herring last night."

Marshall stifled a laugh but wound up choking. "Frog in my throat. Sorry. Good to see you, Ina. Tell Louis I hope he feels better."

"Oh, he'll be fine. Nothing a little Pepto and some crackers won't cure. Too bad he's missing the excitement."

Suddenly Marshall and I found ourselves standing alone. My mother's entourage, including my aunt, had moved a few yards away. Then, before I realized it, Elaine Meschow approached us, holding Prince. His little red soldier outfit with the brass buttons and white trim was irresistible.

"He's bound to take home a prize," I said. "I hope Bethany and her husband are here to cheer him on." *And get interrogated as well.*

"They're on the far side of the knoll, near the bocce courts," Elaine said. "They're holding a sign that says: 'Vote for Prince.' I told them it was an awfully long drive from Chandler, but they insisted on coming. Both of them were concerned about me. Bethany especially. She said if someone was after me, they could easily blend into a large crowd. I told them not to worry, but frankly, I'm terrified." She took a step closer to Marshall and whispered, "Were you able to find anything in my late husband's files that was any help?"

"We're still sifting through it."

Elaine hugged Prince closer. "I haven't said a word to anyone. Not even Bethany. She's very anxious as it is."

Marshall put his hand on her arm. "If we find something, anything at all, we'll let you know."

Without any warning whatsoever, a thunderous "*Ho ho ho!*" blasted out of the loudspeaker, and Elaine quickly put Prince on the ground. "Dear God. The poor little fellow will pee on himself. And he's in the second group. No time to clean up. What's the matter with those people?"

Before I could say anything, the announcer came on. "Ladies and gentlemen, welcome to the Precious Pooches Holiday Extravaganza Grand Finale! Contestants, you all have your numbers and your places; begin lining up now. We start in five minutes."

"We'd better get going," Marshall said, "or we'll never find a good spot in that crowd."

Halfway to the gate I heard someone shout, "Is there a Phyllis Gruber here? Some guy is pitching a fit. Needs to see her right away!" It was a man's voice and it bellowed all over the place.

I stopped dead in my tracks, all but colliding into Marshall. "It might be something related to the case. She was the one who cut those sago palm fronds from the neighbors' yard. Remember? Why don't you try to find Bethany and Tucker and I'll catch up? I'll recognize Phyllis right away."

"Easier said than done. I have no idea what Bethany or Tucker look like. You've met Bethany, but I've only spoken on the phone with Tucker."

"Bethany's my age. Cute and perky looking. Medium build. Ashy blondish hair. Think Meg Ryan or Helen Hunt. I don't know about Tucker. Wait a sec. Elaine said they've got a sign that says: 'Vote for Prince.' Find that sign and you've got them."

"I'll see what I can do."

Marshall left the chaotic dog park just as the first five dogs were lining up for their debut around the snow-filled knoll. Streetman was number twelve this time. There would be two groups ahead of him. Plenty of time for me to catch him in action.

I looked around the dog park, trying to find Sir Breckenthall. I knew he wouldn't be the only Cavalier King Charles Spaniel in the contest, but I was certain of one thing—his costume would be dazzling. If not downright costly. And his owner wouldn't be farther than a foot away from him.

Just then, the holiday music began and the first five dogs were led out of the park to the tune of "A Holly Jolly Christmas." Sir Breckenthall wasn't one of them. I looked around again. This time I spotted him. Apparently, *The Nutcracker Suite* was the flavor of the day, because the poor little thing was decked out to look like a giant nutcracker, complete with a cardboard collar that must've stood two feet high. I kept a low profile as I approached him.

Phyllis was having an animated conversation with a man whose back was turned away from me. They were by the back maintenance gate, and as I got closer I heard every word.

The man sounded desperate. "It'll only take a few minutes. I'm positive I left my cell phone on your kitchen counter. I can't make the rest of my deliveries without it."

Phyllis was waving her hand as if to brush him off. "Then your deliveries will have to wait."

The man was getting agitated. "Can't someone else walk your dog around?"

Before she could respond, the music changed to "Have Yourself a Merry Little Christmas" and the announcer called for the second group of dogs.

"Sir Breckenthall is in this group and I've got to hurry." She yanked the unsuspecting spaniel by the collar and rushed to the gate.

The man turned around and we were face-to-face. It was the delivery guy from The Bountiful Life. And more important, it was Jocelyn's brother, Alender. He was wearing an unzipped dark blue jacket with a white shirt underneath. His ID card from the health food company hung on a lanyard over his neck. The second I laid eyes on it, I froze.

"Hey, haven't we met before?" he asked. "Yeah, now I remember. At La Mar Maravillosa. You were looking for the ladies' room. I never forget a good-looking woman."

I couldn't stop staring at the lanyard. It was identical to the one Streetman found. Hand-braided reddish leather bola cord with wooden beads and silver tubes. Not the run-of-the-mill polyester ones companies give away as promos or the ones businesses use for their employees.

Everything hit me at once. Those names on the flash drive . . . the list of dates . . . the addresses . . . My God! Jocelyn's brother was the brainchild behind that Airtnt sex business! He must've been the one who dropped that lanyard at the Galbraiths' place. On the patio? By Cameron's body? That would've meant—

"You okay?" He looked down as if I'd caught him with his fly opened.

"Yeah, I'm fine."

For a brief second, it all became clear. Alender was the one who disposed of Cameron's body under the Galbraiths' grill. Like a fog that lifted, everything began to make sense. The Galbraiths were customers of The Bountiful Life and Alender knew they wouldn't return from Canada for months. Somehow, the knot in the lanyard came loose and it must have fallen on the ground by the grill. I rubbed my hands together, not sure what to do next.

"You sure?" he asked.

The music got louder and I looked over my shoulder to see Sir Breckenthall prancing through the knoll with the other dogs in his group.

"That lanyard you're wearing. It isn't the only one you have."

Alender's pleasant expression changed to a cold, steely look. "Huh? What are you talking about?"

"Those are custom made."

"Yeah? So? What are you getting at?"

I'd always prided myself in thinking before I spoke, but apparently I got so caught up in my own revelation that it was too late. The words raced out of my mouth like someone who realized they had the final bingo number. It didn't even sink in that I was about to accuse the guy of murder until I swallowed the last syllable of my sentence. "It wasn't about the seafood after all. It never was. Cameron Tully's murder. You killed him. He found out about your little brothel business and threatened to close you down. When you dumped his body, your lanyard with the flash drive came loose. That's why you returned to the scene days later to look for it. It was you with the flashlight that night. And when you couldn't find it, you thought maybe you dropped it at a customer's house. That's why you broke into Elaine Meschow's place. And she probably wasn't the only one."

In a flash, the music changed to "Walking in a Winter Wonderland" and the next group of dogs was summoned to the knoll. Streetman's group. Last thing I needed was for anything to interfere with his "runway" walk. And I knew I would be toast if I missed it. I lifted my head, trying to spot Marshall, but it was useless.

"Screw you, lady. You're nuts!" Alender gave me a shove, totally unexpected, and I lost my balance, colliding into the backs of a few people who were behind me. In the five or six seconds it took me to regain my balance, and my composure, Alender had made it to the gate.

Not on my watch, you sneaky little son of a gun.

That uncalled-for push had turned me into Attila the Hun. I took a deep breath and patted myself on the back for wearing sneakers instead of fancy shoes. I charged after him, sidestepping dogs and elbowing elderly people. Not my best moment. Alender had made it out of the park but couldn't get through the thick crowd that took up a major section of the parking lot. He must've thought there was an exit behind the knoll, because he got on the same path the parading dogs were on in spite of the announcer shouting, "*No people allowed on the walkway except contestants!*"

For the first time in my life, I understood the concept of a "one-track mind." Nothing else mattered. I ran after him until I was close enough to grab his jacket and give it a yank. Unfortunately, I lost my balance on the slippery walkway and fell into the snow, taking a few cardboard peppermint sticks and Cameron's killer with me. Thankfully, my mother's group of dogs was at the other side of the knoll.

The snow was the thick, heavy kind. Heart attack snow back in Minnesota. Alender and I struggled to stand, but he beat me to it. That was when I grabbed his ankle and he tumbled backward. Both our rumps were firmly pressed into the snow.

"No one is allowed on the knoll. You must leave immediately. This is not a play area!"

I couldn't believe what was happening. I leaned to one side, placed all my weight on one knee, and stood up. Alender had managed to stand upright and move a few feet away. I wasted no time screaming, "Get him! Get him!," fully expecting someone from the crowd, preferably Marshall, to rush to my aid. Instead, two of the larger dogs in my mother's group broke free from their owners and raced over to us. A golden retriever dressed as a reindeer and a small black Lab in an elf outfit. The golden immediately jumped on Alender and began to paw him while the Lab started rolling in the snow.

"This man is a killer!" I screamed. "Someone needs to call the sheriff's posse."

Like a yeti straight out of Nepali folklore, Alender thundered through the snow-covered knoll and disappeared into the crowd. In spite of my sopping-wet jeans and snow-filled sneakers, I followed after him. I didn't bother to assess the chaos I left behind. As I exited the knoll, the music changed to Chuck Berry's "Run Rudolph Run," and I took it literally.

Chapter 25

If Marshall *was* trying to make his way toward me, it was impossible. Whoever coined the term "a sea of humanity" must've been at one of these events.

"That man's a killer!" I screamed, but when I looked around it was as if Alender had vanished. I forced myself to stand still and take a breath.

Elaine had mentioned something about Tucker and Bethany holding a sign that said: "Vote for Prince." I figured if I could spot that sign, I'd be able to find Marshall.

I tried everything from craning my neck to standing on my toes. Still no Marshall. Then, without warning, there was an opening in the crowd, giving me a new vantage point and unbelievably good luck—Marshall was standing with outstretched arms between Alender and a man whom I presumed to be Tucker. For an instant, I forgot about that fracas in the snow and hurried over to see what was going on.

"Stay back, Phee," Marshall warned.

Alender was bellowing accusations at Tucker. If Marshall wasn't standing between the two of them, the situation might've turned physical. Mainly because Alender threatened to use Tucker as a punching bag.

"You dirty stinking lowlife!" he said. "I ought to smack you upside the head. Your company's going to put The Bountiful Life out of business. Stop buying up all those Asian carp and leaving us with the dregs. My company can't compete with the volume like yours does. And if we can't compete, we might go out of business."

Tucker raised an eyebrow and shrugged. "What the hell difference does it make to you? You can deliver Meals on Wheels as well as that health food crap."

Oh no. Did I get this wrong? Is it about seafood after all?

"It's his sideline that's paying off," I said to Marshall, loud enough for him to hear me but far enough away to keep a good distance from the two combatants. "He needs the delivery job to run his other business. The high school sex-for-a-night Airtnt. I can prove it. The flash drive we found is his. The lanyard matches the one he's wearing. Cameron must've found out and that's what got him killed. He knew too much."

Alender spit out his words. "You can't prove a thing. Especially Cameron's murder, because I wasn't the one who poisoned him."

The denial didn't stop me from jumping to the next scenario. "But you were the one who dumped his body. Admit it."

"Yeah. Like I'm about to admit that. Look, lady, if you think his murder had anything to do with Airtnt, you're one lousy investigator."

"I'm not a—'Lousy' is a pretty nasty word, don't you think? We've got enough evidence to have you arrested on the spot, so you might as well come clean. It's bad enough I ruined my mother's dog's debut as the Mouse

King while I was chasing after you." I inhaled and pointed to the judges' stand. "If I don't get back there by the time they award the prizes, I might as well take the next flight to Bolivia. So, excuse me while I grab my cell phone and send for two of the orneriest deputies this side of Phoenix!"

"Hold on. Hold on. No sense getting carried away. It was all a big misunderstanding."

Tucker, who'd been pretty quiet up until that moment, spoke up. "A guy I used to work with was murdered. Murdered. That's a hell of a lot more than a misunderstanding. I hope you've got a better excuse for those sheriff's deputies."

Alender lowered his head and stood there. Behind us, the happy holiday music was blaring, but it didn't soften our moods.

Finally, he spoke. "Jocelyn thought Cameron was poisoned in her restaurant. She found him slumped over in a booth after-hours. Blood trickling down his nose. Must be everyone else thought he'd passed out from drinking too much and didn't pay attention. My sister was terrified. His death would mean the loss of her business. Plus, he was her ex-boyfriend. If that's not a smoking gun, what is? She panicked. Called me and asked me to do something. What was I going to say? She's my sister."

Marshall lowered his hands but still remained standing between the two men. He turned his head slightly and looked Alender in the eye. "And you knew a good place to dispose of the body where it wouldn't be found for at least a month or more."

"Yeah. I had that Airtnt list. Plus, I had scoped out that house with the huge grill and tarp. Too bad someone's stupid dog had to ruin everything."

I cringed and bit my lip. *He has no way of knowing it was Streetman.* "And that's when your lanyard came loose and you lost your flash drive."

Alender nodded. "Yeah. Yeah. You got it right. It was me snooping around a few nights later. That's when I realized I was also at the Meschow place that day. Thought maybe I dropped it inside her house. I didn't want her to make any connections, so I broke in. I'm telling you the truth. I have nothing to hide. I didn't murder Cameron and neither did Jocelyn. Like I said, she was terrified she'd lose La Mar Maravillosa. In case you didn't know it, La Mar was the last restaurant around here that wasn't skimming its patrons."

My uncle Louis immediately came to mind. Last time I saw him, he complained about something like that. Oh my gosh. He also mentioned La Mar Maravillosa being closed so they could reorganize the kitchen. A lump formed in my throat and I coughed. "Is that why Jocelyn closed La Mar Maravillosa for a week? To try and find out how Cameron could've been poisoned in her restaurant?"

"She had to sift through everything and throw out all open containers. Not to mention her spices and anything questionable. We were pretty certain Cameron was poisoned the night she found him but didn't know what kind of quick-acting agent it was. She was afraid maybe rat poison or some cleaning solvent got into the food. Jocelyn couldn't take a chance it might happen to a customer. Then, when it came on the news a few days later that it was sago palm poisoning, she realized it couldn't have happened in La Mar Maravillosa. Sago palm toxin takes days to work, not minutes. By then, it was too late to contact the police."

"Not too late to contact them now," Tucker said with an annoying smugness that made me wonder what Bethany and Jocelyn saw in this guy.

I did a mental eye roll. "It still doesn't answer how Cameron and your mother-in-law wound up ingesting that substance. Hmm, now that I think of it, the waitress at La Mar Maravillosa mentioned serving you at the bar a few days before Cameron's body was discovered. It wasn't a secret you were having an affair with Jocelyn, and that must've really struck a nerve with Cameron. You know what I think?" I answered before Tucker could open his mouth. "I think Cameron threatened to tell your wife and you couldn't let that happen. Bethany Cabot, along with her mother, is the owner of Spellbound Naturals, not you. You'd lose everything if she divorced you."

Tucker rubbed the nape of his neck and didn't say a word. Marshall gave me a half nod and a wink. I don't know how long we were standing there, but, all of a sudden, I heard the announcer call out for the final group of dogs. The music changed to "Rockin' Around the Christmas Tree," but the last thing I felt like doing was dancing.

"Good luck trying to prove anything," Tucker said. "And by the way, if I wanted to kill someone, I'd get a gun and aim, not dilly around with poison. Especially a plant-based one like the sago palm. Not on the top ten lists of toxins. It's so . . . so . . . medieval. That's what it is. Only a horticulturist or someone who practices herbal medicines would be aware of it." Then he turned to Alender. "As much as I've enjoyed our chitchat, I've got to find my wife before this damn program ends. And from the looks of things, The Bountiful Life will have to find someone else to make its deliveries."

"Like hell!" Alender spun around and took off running. He wove in and out of the crowd like a quarterback with less than twenty seconds left in the game.

"Aren't you going after him?" I asked Marshall. "He's getting away. He can be arrested on multiple counts."

"Yeah," Tucker added. "And don't forget to add 'threatening to commit violence.' You heard him. He said something about smacking my head. At the very least it's menacing. That's cause for arrest, isn't it? I'd call the sheriff's office right now if I didn't have to find my wife and deal with my mother-in-law."

With that, Tucker took off in the opposite direction, leaving Marshall and me to ferret things out in the parking lot.

"Alender got away. I can't believe you didn't stop him," I said.

"And what? Create a ridiculous scene where someone could've been hurt? We've got all his information. He's not going anywhere." He flashed a big grin. "Besides, don't you agree you'd rather see Ranston and Bowman get the exercise?"

"I suppose."

"Give me a second. I'll place the call."

While Marshall took out his phone, I stood on my toes to see what was going on with the parade. The final group of dogs had exited the knoll and was at the dog park gate. I imagined they'd be announcing the winners any minute now.

"Come on," I said. "Might as well see if my mother's going to win her spa vacation or grouse about this until Groundhog Day."

Marshall took me by the elbow and we walked toward the far end of the knoll. Close enough to see the judges' stand should Streetman actually win. "Sleigh Ride" began to play and I hoped the event would end soon.

Shirley, Lucinda, Myrna, Louise, and Cecilia were all standing in the front, along with my aunt Ina. I scanned the area for Bethany and Tucker but didn't see them. Tucker was probably still steaming about my accusation, but only if he really was guilty. Otherwise, judging from his personality, he'd shrug it off.

"Do you hear that?" Marshall asked.

"The whinnying sound? It's the horses in the song."

"No. Listen carefully. In the distance. Sirens. Geez, how much do you want to bet it's Ranston and Bowman with their siren on?"

"They wouldn't. Would they?"

The siren noise got closer.

"I think they crave the attention. They were right in the neighborhood following up on a theft. Bowman was ecstatic when I told him what was going on. Don't look now, but that's them pulling into the parking lot."

"Pulling in" was one way to put it. The car careened into the far end of the lot and spun to a stop directly in front of the dog park gate. But not before throngs of people raced to get out of the way. I don't think the Red Sea parted as fast for Moses.

In the background, I heard the announcer thanking everyone.

I tugged at Marshall's arm. "We really should get over there to see if Streetman won."

"Yeah. No problem. I gave the deputies a solid description of Alender and—Oh Holy Hell! Do you see that? Alender never made it to his car. That's him, isn't it? Trying to cut through the knoll. Why would he do an idiotic thing like that? I mean, sure, he's taking the path and not the snow-covered hill but still . . ."

"Lots of people who aren't familiar with the park think

that path leads to an exit. It doesn't. It just winds around the little man-made berm. Oh no. I can't believe it. It's Bowman. Charging for Alender. And Ranston's slogging up the hill as well."

A voice bellowed through the air, "*No people allowed on the knoll. This is not a playground!*"

I stared at the catastrophe in front of me. "Ranston and Bowman aren't in uniform. The announcer doesn't realize they're sheriff deputies."

"Detectives," Marshall said. "Don't let them hear you call them plain old deputies."

"Leave the knoll at once. We have to conclude our program!"

Maybe the announcer thought he'd be able to get on with the festivities, but the crowd began to get agitated. People started shouting all sorts of things, including, "Get your butts out of here!" and some expletives I'd rather forget.

Then, out of nowhere, someone's giant elkhound charged into the knoll and knocked Bowman over. As the disgruntled detective started to stand, the dog began humping him and the crowd went nuts. Meanwhile, Alender was halfway to the top when Ranston must've caught a second wind.

The detective who reminded me of a Sonoran Desert Toad had suddenly become the Celebrated Jumping Frog of Calaveras County. I watched, speechless, as Ranston took a giant step in the soggy snow and pounced on top of Alender, causing the slight delivery guy to lose his balance and tumble on the knoll.

Bowman had managed to disengage the elkhound, but now a new target was in sight. The dog thundered over to Alender and began to trounce on him. A woman's shrill voice reverberated across the hill. "Artimus! You stop that right now. Bad, bad boy. Do you hear me, Artimus? Stop that!"

Someone must've said something to the announcer, because the next thing we knew he said, "*This is official posse business. Please remain where you are. We will commence with the prizes in a few minutes.*"

Then the music came on again. "Jingle Bell Rock" this time.

"Wait here," Marshall said. "I'd better give those guys a hand."

I watched, along with the crowd, as my boyfriend and the two detectives escorted Alender off of the knoll and into the sheriff's car that had blocked the entrance to the dog park. Suddenly I felt a tap on my shoulder and I jumped. It was Herb Garrett.

"Hey, cutie! Is this enough excitement for you? Harriet must be beside herself. That dog of hers isn't going to hold still much longer in a costume. Neurotic little thing, isn't he?"

"I, um, er . . ."

"Hang on. Looks like they're about to start. Got to make my way closer to the action. Nice seeing you."

It was only a matter of minutes until the sheriff's car left, along with Ranston and Bowman's "catch of the day," but it felt like hours. Marshall raced toward me, giving me two thumbs-up.

When he was in earshot, he spoke. "Hate to do this to you, but I've got to go over to the posse station. Alender will be making an official confession, but Ranston and Bowman want to make sure our culprit doesn't leave anything out."

"That could take hours. I know how that paperwork goes. Guess I'll see you at home after this shindig is done.

This is one of those times I'm glad we took two cars to work."

I gave him a quick peck on the cheek before focusing my attention on the judges' stand. The three Santas waved papers in front of one another for what seemed like an eternity. Finally, one of them walked over to the announcer, who was a few feet away.

Please, please let my mother's dog win that stupid prize so we can all get on with our lives.

"Prince. Our third-place winner is Prince Meschow."

I heard a shriek and watched as Elaine and Bethany made their way to the stand. In my mind, Shirley Johnson was the real winner for designing and sewing those costumes. Elaine handed the small dog to her daughter so she could carry the basket of treats home, along with a nice gift certificate.

Bethany still wasn't off the hook as far as I was concerned. I was positive she was the one who held Jocelyn at gunpoint. More dramatic than sending a text saying: "Hands off my husband." She and her mother left the knoll. She was jealous, yes. But it was Cameron who was poisoned, not Jocelyn. So there went my motive.

The announcer cleared his throat and it sounded like a car with engine trouble. *"In second place, Sir Breckenthall the Third. Sir Breckenthall Gruber."*

A few people began to cheer, and when I scanned the crowd I could see it was my mother's friends. They were waving their arms all over the place. Except for my aunt Ina, who was busy adjusting her hat.

Myrna, with a voice louder and stronger than a longshoreman, shouted, "This means Streetman has a chance to win the grand prize!"

Phyllis Gruber stormed up to the judges' table like someone who'd returned spoiled goods to customer service at the supermarket. It was impossible to hear what it was she said, but she dragged her poor dog off the knoll as if he had committed a heinous deed.

Then the moment my mother had been waiting for since October. The announcement of the first-place winner and grand prize winner. If Sir Breckenthall took second place and Streetman secured that first spot, the little Chiweenie would have enough points to be the grand champion.

I held my breath and tried not to bite my nails.

The announcement was loud and clear. *"In first place, Streetman Plunkett."*

Cheers could be heard everywhere and my mother made a mad dash up the knoll. She was a few feet from the announcer's podium when one of the Santa judges rushed past her and handed the announcer a note. He paused to read it and then looked as if he had gotten word the stock market crashed or some equally awful news.

The announcer cleared his throat again and spoke. *"May I have your attention please? It seems we've made a slight error in the awarding of the prizes. The second-place prize belongs to Streetman Plunkett and the first-place prize goes to Sir Breckenthall Gruber. This means Sir Breckenthall Gruber is our grand champion and he, along with his owner, will enjoy a full spa vacation. Thank you for your understanding and we wish everyone happy holidays."*

What followed was a series of collective groans from the crowd, but their reaction was mild compared to my mother's. She bent down to cover the dog's ears before letting loose on the announcer. "What do you mean, Streetman isn't in first place? You named him the winner and you need to stick with it."

Phyllis Gruber nudged herself in front of my mother and thrust the basket of second place goodies at her. "Looks like the Pity Train just derailed at the corner of Suck it Up, Harriet, and Quit Your Whining."

Meanwhile, out of the corner of my eye, I saw Bethany, Tucker, and Elaine in the parking lot. Not willing to miss out on possibly the only chance I'd have to speak with Bethany, since the last thing I intended to do was drive an hour and twenty minutes to Chandler, I shouted to my mother, "Let it go!" and took off after Bethany.

Probably not the right choice of words, given the circumstances.

Chapter 26

As I charged toward Bethany, my mother's entourage made a beeline directly for the knoll and the judges' stand. Knowing the Booked 4 Murder crew as well as I did, all three Santas were about to get an earful, but so was Bethany.

I don't remember elbowing people in the parking lot, but I was told by more than one of my mother's neighbors and acquaintances that I did. All I cared about was getting some answers from Bethany. I hailed her down like a New York City cab. "Wait! Hold up! I need to speak with you. It's important."

I was a few yards from her, her husband, and her mother. Bethany turned around when she heard my voice and motioned for the others to keep going. I walked as fast as I could until we were face-to-face.

"Phee. We're on our way out. Isn't this great news? Prince won. And Tucker told me Jocelyn's brother confessed to the break-in at my mother's house, not to mention some other shady business he was in. For all we know, he could've been the one who murdered Cameron. Maybe he'll think it over and confess to that, too."

"Um, not likely. Sure, he was worried Cameron was going to 'out him' for that brothel business he set up in Sun City West, but that wasn't really a strong motive for murder. Not like jealousy."

"What are you taking about?"

I looked around to make sure no one was listening. The crowd had dispersed quickly and there were only a few people near us. "You know what I mean. You *did* find out the truth. Cameron had been right all along. Tucker *was* having an affair with Jocelyn. It was you who tried to poison her, but something went wrong and Cameron wound up ingesting the sago palm toxin."

"That's ludicrous. I'd never kill anyone. Let alone poison them."

"Then why are you wringing your hands? And you're shaking, too. You might as well admit it and save everyone the embarrassment of a search warrant for your house."

Bethany looked down and whispered, "I'm afraid the only thing they'll find is a small pellet gun without any ammunition. Tucker bought it years ago, but it never left the box. Not until recently when I wanted to make sure Jocelyn kept her hands off of my husband."

"So, it was you in the hoodie and scream mask."

"Not my proudest moment, but yeah. I wanted to give her a good scare. Please. Please don't say anything to your boyfriend. No one got hurt. It was a stupid thing to do, and I regret it. If my mother found out, it could destroy her. She's fragile enough."

I wanted to say, "Then you should've thought about that first," but I kept quiet and let her continue.

"Tucker and I worked things out. What he had with

Jocelyn is history. If you don't believe me, ask them. I'm telling you the truth. I didn't poison Jocelyn. I don't know the first thing about plants. Between you and me, Tucker wasn't the only one who fell for her charms. A while back I had lunch at her restaurant and one of the waitresses told me Jocelyn had men swarming all over her. Granted, she's absolutely gorgeous in a Sophia Loren kind of way, but she's demanding and temperamental."

"The waitress said that?"

"Uh-huh. And there's more. Jocelyn was known to have all sorts of dalliances with the men she hired. Maybe one of them killed Cameron."

Paige should quit her waitressing job and start writing steamy romance novels.

"Hey, Bethany!" Tucker called out. "Are you coming or what? The dog's getting antsy."

Bethany looked at me with wide, moist eyes. "I need to go. Are we? I mean, are you . . ."

"I'm the office accountant for Williams Investigations, not law enforcement. I'll leave that up to you. But if you want my advice, maybe you should call Jocelyn, talk it over with her, and ask if she'd be willing to drop any charges should an arrest be made."

Bethany nodded twice and mumbled, "Thanks."

I suppose I should've congratulated myself for figuring out who the masked intruder was, but it didn't feel like much of a victory. Cameron's killer was still out there, and if he or she wasn't the same person who poisoned Elaine, then two very dangerous individuals were at large.

My mother and her friends had left the knoll and were now standing in a clump near the dog park. Streetman was still in costume, sans the crown. I imagined the women were trying to console my mother, and as much as it was one conversation I didn't feel like joining, I had no choice but to walk over there.

"Can you believe it?" Myrna asked. "I can't believe those judges pulled a stunt like that."

Lucinda pulled out a floral kerchief from her pocket and put it on her head. "They should be ashamed. That's what. Totally unprofessional."

"I'll be fine," my mother said as if she had been told of an impending flood or famine. "Streetman will be fine, too."

Streetman doesn't know what the heck is happening except that he's in an uncomfortable outfit and probably wants to roll around on the grass.

As if my mother could read my mind, she bent down and undid the Velcro that held the outfit together. "No sense in getting this dirty. It's too priceless." Then she looked at me. "The ladies and I are going back to my place for coffee and desserts. Why don't you join us?"

"Oh, I'd love to, but I've got to get home. Marshall will be there soon. He's at the posse station. We took two cars. While you were talking with the judges, the sheriff's deputies arrived to make an arrest. Marshall got a confession out of the man who broke into Elaine's place. It was also the same man you saw that night behind the house. You know, the flashlight."

"I thought someone fell in the parking lot and that's why we heard sirens. An arrest? Who? Who? And why were they in Elaine's house?"

"I'm not at liberty to reveal any names, but we have reason to believe it was the same person who was running that sex-for-rental business in the snowbird homes. Actually, the flash drive Streetman found belonged to the alleged perpetrator."

Suddenly my mother stood up straight and beamed.

"My Streetman solved the case. My Streetman is a little hero. Is that sex-for-rental man the one who killed Cameron Tully and hid his body at the Galbraiths'?"

"Um, no. That part of the investigation is still underway."

A long-drawn-out sigh emanated from my mother's mouth. "Well, you can't expect the dog to solve all of these crimes."

"I, um, er . . ."

"Call me later."

I said good-bye to the women and thanked Shirley again for her amazing costumes. Then I headed home, but not before stopping at Kentucky Fried Chicken for take-out.

Marshall had a similar idea to mine, only he stopped for Italian subs. We had enough food to last the next day and possibly for a snack on Sunday. I told him about Bethany's admission of guilt and he wasn't about to rat her out. We both thought she'd do the right thing.

"So," I asked, "how'd it go with Alender?"

"It went well. I mean, as well as a confession can go. I gave Nate a call and he had the same reaction I did—glad that part of the mystery is solved but stymied over the murder. It's like putting Band-Aids on a bunch of little cuts but ignoring the giant flesh wound."

"Ugh. That's getting too graphic for me. At least the murder wasn't a gory one. Not as if we're dealing with blood and all that."

"Believe it or not, the 'all that' makes it easier for forensics. Poisonings are tough. Especially when it's a substance that can take days to kill. That's why we're better off looking at motive."

"Bethany said something that got me thinking. Tucker and Cameron weren't the only men in Jocelyn's world. My gosh, I'm sounding like a fourth-grade tattletale."

"Tattle away. I'm listening."

"All of this comes secondhand from Paige. Figured I'd better make that clear first. Anyhow, Jocelyn was rumored to have had relationships with the men she hired at La Mar Maravillosa."

"We talked to all of the employees and didn't get a sense of anything personal."

"I did. I didn't catch it at first. It wasn't *what* was said. It was *how*."

"Go on."

"That bartender I spoke with seemed to have a thing for her. A romanticized crush of sorts. Tucker wouldn't pose a threat because he was reeled back in by his wife. But Cameron . . . That's a different story. Suppose the bartender wanted to get Cameron out of the picture for good?"

"By poisoning him?"

"Uh-huh."

Marshall crossed his arms in front and took a breath. "It would take some knowledge of plants to know how to do it. To know what parts of the sago palm were the most toxic and how to get the victim to ingest them."

"The bartender would have that information. He used to work for Happy Valley Nurseries. Motive and means right there. He could've easily ground up some of the crushed leaves or the seeds and put them in one of Cameron's drinks."

"When? When was the opportunity?"

"Up until today, I didn't even realize there was an opportunity. Then I remembered the conversation I had with the bartender. He told me Cameron was in the restaurant a few days before his body was found. He was having a tête-à-tête with Alender. Long story, but the bartender had to bring Cameron another drink—dark ale from the tap. Real easy to add some crushed seeds to the mix. Especially if they were in one of those small plastic pill packets people carry. The bartender must've planned this all along and needed the right moment."

Marshall's mouth opened wide, but he didn't say anything. Not at first. Then it was as if he couldn't stop talking. "Real easy to do. Real easy. Alender left. Cameron was alone. The only one drinking. Real easy for the bartender to rinse out the glass and then put it in the dishwasher. Those temperatures get so hot the evidence would be erased. Motive—jealousy. Means—any greenhouse or big-box store. Opportunity—slip it in his drink. My God, Phee! You may have nailed this murder!"

"How do we prove it? The restaurant doesn't have indoor surveillance."

"The bartender doesn't know that. Ever hear of a nanny cam? I think I can get Jocelyn to tell the bartender she was thinking of installing another one in the kitchen along with the hidden one in the bar."

"But there is no hidden—"

"Yeah. Yeah. That's the point. The bartender doesn't know that. Jocelyn will say she's still freaked out about being held at gunpoint and needs to review all the past recordings. He's bound to believe that."

"Then what?"

"We'll catch the culprit in his own act. He'll be hell-bent for leather to find that thing once she has the conversation with him. Since the bartender doesn't know Nate, he'll be the perfect undercover detective. Besides, he loves bar snacks."

"Nate. That's perfect. He can get anyone to crack. I

can hear him now. 'Looking for something? Surveillance perhaps?' Oh my gosh. That's ingenious."

"Give me a few minutes. I've got a zillion calls to make."

By eleven that night, a plan was in place and we sat down to watch the evening news. No sooner did I lean back and relax on the couch when the human-interest segment came on. I all but had a coronary. "Oh no! Oh no! I can't believe it. That's me. On my butt. In the snow. What the heck?"

It was footage from today's event at Sun City West's Precious Pooches Holiday Extravaganza. I never even knew someone was filming it.

"I'm afraid to change the channel," I said. "More than one station could've been there."

Marshall was laughing so hard he almost choked.

"Don't say anything to anyone. Those retirees go to bed earlier. Chances are no one will see it. Unless—Oh no! Herb probably archived it to his digital video recorder."

I switched channels to the weather station and buried my head in my hands.

On Monday morning, Augusta told me she never would've thought I'd be one for winter antics in the snow. I was used to it by then. My mother and the book club ladies had all watched the news. There was no escaping it.

Marshall called it the Tumbling Tower after some board game he used to play as a kid. I called it Strategic Planning and it involved the deputies and the Tempe police. Thank goodness Jocelyn cooperated and the plan to catch a killer went off without a hitch a few days later.

The bartender was no match for Nate and confessed to putting crushed sago palm seeds into Cameron's drink. Years of obsessing over Jocelyn had pushed the guy over the proverbial edge. It had nothing to do with the seafood industry, the fraud, or Alender's desire to keep his side business hush-hush. Unfortunately, it still didn't solve the other part of the equation—Elaine Meschow's bout with the same toxin. The bartender was off the hook on that one. Since the actual crime took place in Tempe, their police department got the credit. And, to make matters worse, Ranston and Bowman were also credited in the arrest.

Nate and Marshall took it in stride.

"A paycheck's a paycheck," Nate said, "and our consulting fees pay well. Don't sweat it."

I didn't. I had other things on my mind. Kalese was set to arrive the day before Christmas Eve and the first day of Hanukkah. That was only four days away. My mother was ecstatic her granddaughter would be staying at her house, even though I felt a tad guilty. And Marshall felt much worse. Maybe next year my daughter would stay with us.

"Darn it," Augusta said the day before Christmas Eve. "What a way to start the morning. I've got toner ink all over me. I hate when that happens. That stuff flies all over the place. Worse than those grass clippings that get all over shoes and socks."

I had just popped in a K-cup of eggnog-flavored coffee and was waiting for the blue light on the machine. The image of grass clippings made me stop in my tracks. "What did you say? About the grass?"

"Huh? You're from back east. You know. When you're done mowing the lawn your shoes and socks are green."

"The clippings. Oh my gosh. Clippings."

"I don't understand. What are you talking about?"

"It was a long time ago. I met a guy in the dog park

who lives next door to Phyllis Gruber. She clipped off his sago palm near her driveway. And I remember something else. Geez! I think I know who poisoned Elaine Meschow."

The eggnog coffee began to pour, but my mind was elsewhere. "He didn't mean to do it. He had no idea."

Augusta gave me a strange look. "Who didn't mean to do what? Honestly, you're getting as bad as Nate. Half sentences and all."

"Alender. The delivery guy from The Bountiful Life. The one who was running that illicit brothel business. Jocelyn's brother. He was the one who poisoned Elaine."

"I'm confused."

"Okay, I'll try to slow down. Phyllis and Elaine both ordered flash-frozen fish, fresh fish products, and health supplements from that company. Alender delivered Phyllis's order first and then went to Elaine's. Only once was the schedule switched, and Phyllis put up such a fuss it never happened again. Anyway, Alender cleaned up the sago palm clippings on Phyllis's driveway before he went to Elaine's house a few days before that Halloween pet parade. He had the remnants on his hands and that stuff got all over the food he delivered."

"I don't understand how. Shouldn't the food be wrapped?"

"Normal stuff, yes, but, according to the directions on some of those things, they had to be soaked in water first and then put in the fridge. I remember hearing him tell Phyllis that. He also offered to do it for her. It didn't mean anything to me at the time. Quick! Where's the nearest phone?"

"On my desk. Where it's always been."

If I sounded incoherent with Augusta, I must've really sounded as if I'd been hit over the head with a sledgehammer when I got Elaine on the line. I asked her a series of questions that made sense to me but confused the daylights out of her.

"Soaking salmon roe? Yes, yes. It was something the delivery guy did. An extra service. Why? What are you getting at?"

When I finally explained, she shrieked so loud I thought my eardrums would burst.

"Prince! My little Prince! He could've been poisoned to death. Thank goodness I was the only one who ate that stuff. Usually I give him table snacks, but not fish. It's a good thing that would-be murderer is locked up or I'd make it a point to have him put behind bars for life."

I told Elaine it was only a theory, but in my gut, I knew I was right. Marshall and Nate believed it was probable, too, and insisted that Ranston and Bowman have Elaine's freezer tested for any remnants of sago palm toxin. Something, in my opinion, that should've been done months ago.

The results arrived two weeks later. Kalese was already back home in Minnesota. Three degrees below zero as usual. She and Marshall had hit it off and she said she'd love to stay at our place next year if we'd have her. My mother looked as if she'd lost her best friend, so we agreed to split the time.

It was Saturday morning, and I was wedged between Cecilia and Lucinda at Bagels 'N More for the monthly Booked 4 Murder brunch. My iPhone vibrated and I checked to see who it was. Marshall.

"Excuse me. I need to take this." I listened carefully and then let out a "whoop." Not the best thing to do under the circumstances.

My shout of glee was met with, "What happened?"

"What's going on?" "Did you win something?" and "Did Marshall propose?"

"I'll ignore the last question," I said, "but I do have good news. Very good news. We found out who poisoned Elaine."

My mother all but jumped from her seat when I told them who was responsible. "Can't they arrest Phyllis Gruber? If she hadn't clipped those palms, Elaine wouldn't have gotten so sick."

"That's really stretching it. It was unintentional. It's up to Elaine if she wants to press matters further, but I doubt it. And, getting back to that last question, Marshall and I are quite happy the way things are."

"I guess that means he didn't propose."

Shirley immediately came to my defense. "Lordy, Harriet, that daughter of yours is the best darn investigator in the valley, even if she's employed as an accountant. And if and when her boyfriend does propose, I'll make the wedding gown."

"Um, er, uh . . . all of you are moving way too fast. No talk about weddings. Or gowns. Or anything. Thank you, Shirley, but I think you'll be plenty busy making costumes for next year's doggie extravaganza."

Lucinda put her hand on my shoulder and spoke softly. "Oh dear. I guess no one told you. The committee decided not to hold another extravaganza. Something about liability. But that won't deter your mother's little showstopper from taking first place in the St. Patrick's Day Doggie Leprechaun Look-Alike Costume Contest. The Irish club is sponsoring it. Isn't that right, Shirley? You'll be up to your eyeballs with that green fabric."

Shirley nodded as if someone had presented her with front seats to an execution.

Then Myrna spoke. "Tell her the good news, Harriet. Go on, tell her."

I know. The St. Patrick's Day prize is better than a pot of gold. "Tell me what?"

"I was waiting until dessert, but you might as well know. Streetman and I got an anonymous gift certificate for three nights and four days at the JW Marriott resort and spa. It was signed by a fan, who said Streetman was the real winner. And they sent a gift certificate for Shirley, too. Looks like the three of us will be enjoying that spa vacation after all."

"That's wonderful! Absolutely wonderful." *And I'd better thank Nate the minute I get out of here.*

Epilogue

The hiatus between the last of the fall pet parade contests and the St. Patrick's Day Doggie Leprechaun Look-Alike competition was a short one. Thanks to the genius of Shirley Johnson's imagination, Streetman was decked out in the fanciest, most extravagant leprechaun outfit anyone could have imagined. Glittered belt, sparkling green Swarovski crystals that formed shamrocks on his vest, and black pantaloons with ruffles. It was surprising he didn't bite my mother when she dressed him.

The contest was held the week before the actual Sun City West St. Patrick's Day Parade in March. The winner and his owner were to celebrate the victory on a special float that was the jewel of the parade. Secretly, I prayed Sir Breckenthall the Third would win so that I could be spared another agonizing event in my mother's retirement community. I should have known better.

No one could match Shirley's mastery with a needle, and Streetman won the pot of gold. Or in this case, enough gift certificates from local merchants so that my mother could dine out for the rest of the year and pamper the dog as well.

Streetman's winning status meant Marshall and I would be coerced into not only attending the parade but riding on the float, too.

"The contest committee wants the entire family to be part of the celebration," my mother said when she phoned me a few days after the competition. "All you and Marshall have to do is sit there and wave. Streetman will be on my lap like a perfect gentleman."

Yes. Those were her exact words. "Streetman will be on my lap like a perfect gentleman." *In whose world?*

Weather-wise, it was an absolutely splendid afternoon for a parade. Temps in the high seventies and abundant sunshine. A perfect Saturday for the year-round residents and the last of the snowbirds to enjoy the final hoop-dee-lah before the summer heat kicked in.

My mother, Marshall, and I boarded the decorative float that was pulled by a neat little T-bird, compliments of the Automotive Restoration Club. My mom and the dog had the seats of honor up front, with Marshall and me directly behind them. Our entourage was four floats down in the lineup and headed to Meeker Boulevard, a major street that crisscrossed the city. The book club ladies were all on hand to watch the event, including my aunt Ina, who had managed to convince my uncle Louis that he couldn't afford to miss Streetman's claim to fame. In addition, Nate came as well. According to Marshall, "the poor guy simply ran out of excuses."

Everything went smoothly for the first fifteen minutes or so as the float made its way down the street. Residents who lived on Meeker Boulevard had set up chairs along the sidewalk to enjoy the show. Still, I had this unsettling feeling that something was about to go wrong. I couldn't pinpoint it exactly, but by the time we reached the intersection of Meeker and 135th Avenue, my stomach was in knots.

The parade continued down the street a few yards past the spot where the book club ladies and Nate were gathered. That was the moment when Streetman lifted his head in the air and began to sniff.

I poked Marshall in the arm. "The dog's sniffing the air. This can't be good."

"Relax, hon," he whispered. "It's a gorgeous day. He's probably enjoying the fresh air."

The float moved gracefully past the rows of attached houses to the section of the street with single-family homes and large side yards. More fold-up chairs along the street and even more people.

The dog's nose was still in the air, but he hadn't budged from my mother's lap.

"Maybe you're right," I said to Marshall. "Besides, the parade ends at Stardust Boulevard and that's only a few blocks away. It's not as if he's about to—Oh my God!"

In that instant, Streetman jumped from my mother's lap and onto the side of the float. The structure was only a few feet from the ground and the dog had no problem taking the next leap to the road. From there to the sidewalk and over to someone's side yard.

"Stop the parade!" my mother yelled. "Stop the parade! Streetman is loose!"

Shouts of "Loose dog!" could be heard everywhere, and without wasting a second Marshall and I bolted from the float. My mother was already on the sidewalk screaming for her dog. By that time, Nate had charged down the street followed by Shirley and Lucinda.

"Look," I said. "He's headed to the house with the row of agaves in front."

Just then my mother shrieked, "Streetman, *no*! Streetman, *no*!"

Streetman had made his way to the side yard and tugged furiously at a tarp that was covering what looked like a barbeque grill. Marshall, my mother, and I were only a few yards away. All of us shouting at the dog. Unfortunately, Streetman had developed selective hearing and ignored us.

Nate, Shirley, and Lucinda were now in our immediate vicinity.

"Lordy, Harriet, can't you do something?" Shirley asked.

My mother shook her head and grabbed Shirley's arm. "He's found another crime scene. That's all there is to it. Streetman has found another dead body. He's become a regular cadaver dog."

In that second, a portly-looking man in gray Under Armour sweats literally flew out of the house and over to the tarp. It was too late. Streetman dove under it and emerged with something in his mouth.

My mother was inches behind the man and her voice permeated the air. "What's he got? What's he got? Don't tell me it's a body part!"

I widened my eyes and took a good look. Streetman's mouth was clamped into the middle of a very large fish. The tail appeared at one end of his face and the eyes and fins at the other.

"My salmon! My freshly imported Alaskan salmon!" the man bellowed. "I set it under the grill in a pail while I got ready to grill it."

By now, the fish had broken into two halves that fell on the ground. Streetman snatched one of them and growled. The last time I had seen him do something like that was in the Stardust Theater when he rooted through some old costumes.

"Um, I don't think you'll be able to retrieve your fish,"

I said to the man. "The dog's kind of territorial when it comes to food."

"Whatever that salmon cost," Marshall said, "we'll be happy to reimburse you."

The man looked at the four-legged leprechaun and burst out laughing. "Nah. I'll just grill a steak. Besides, I haven't had such a good laugh in ages. Looks like that little dog found his pot of gold, huh?"

"Think we can get him back on the float?" I asked my mother.

"Grab that other fish part and wave it in front of him."

"Ew!"

"It's just a dead fish, Phee; it could've been worse."

Actually, it was. We appeared on the evening news since one of the parade spectators videoed everything and sent it to KPHO, where it also appeared on their Facebook page. The photo showed me dangling a large fish tail and the caption read: "That's a leprechaun, lady, not a trained seal."

At least they got the *not trained* part right.

Don't miss the next exciting (and hilarious) novel in the Sophie Kimball Mysteries:
Broadcast 4 Murder,
coming in
November 2020.

And don't miss the last Sophie Kimball Mystery,
Molded 4 Murder,
available now from your favorite bookstore and e-retailer.

Turn the page for a sneak peek
at this delightful mystery!

Chapter 1

Office of Williams Investigations, Glendale, Arizona

Augusta, our receptionist/secretary at Williams Investigations, looked up from her computer and straightened her tortoiseshell glasses. "Hey, Phee, two ladies called while you were at lunch and wanted to schedule an appointment with you for this afternoon."

"With me? Did you tell them I'm the bookkeeper and not an investigator?"

Augusta sighed. "They already knew that and said it didn't matter. Said they met you on a plane a year or two ago. They couldn't remember."

Two years ago. That sounded about right. My mother was insistent I use vacation time from my job at the Mankato, Minnesota, police department and fly out to Sun City West, Arizona, because she was convinced the members of her book club were going to die from reading a cursed book. The only thing cursed was my trip.

I moved closer to her desk. "Oh my gosh, Gertie and Trudy from the Lillian. It's a residential resort hotel of sorts. Very elegant."

"Don't know about that, but those were the names they gave. No last name."

"I think it's Madison. Did they mention what they wanted to see me about?"

"Theft. They said someone's been pilfering things from their retirement complex. So much for elegance, huh?"

"That sounds like something they should be taking up with the Lillian's management company, not me."

"I got the feeling there was more to it. Anyway, I scheduled an appointment for two thirty. They want to be back at their place in time for the four o'clock seating for dinner."

"Four? That's almost as bad as my mother's five thirty. What is it with these people and their obsession about eating at a certain time? Sure, I'll see them, but only as a courtesy. Geez, when Nate retired from the police force in Minnesota and started this firm, I came on to do the books, not the investigations."

"And yet . . ."

"I know. I know. Things sort of happened."

"Uh-huh. By the way, Nate got called a little while ago to confer with the Maricopa County Sheriff's Office on a recent homicide. They didn't come right out and say 'homicide,' but you know that's what it is or they wouldn't have insisted he rush over to Sun City West."

"Sun City West? Yikes! That's where my mother lives. I'm surprised she hasn't called. She usually gets that news long before it reaches us."

"Yeah. About that . . ."

I let out a groan and waited for Augusta to continue. "She called all right. I was just about to get to it. Good thing I remembered my shorthand from high school. Here goes. 'I left you more than one voice mail, Phee. Arlette from the Cut 'N Curl is going on vacation for three weeks. She didn't say anything to me when I was in last week. Myrna found out about it this morning when she went in for a trim. Three weeks! Who's going to touch up my hair? Are there any good salons near you in Vistancia? I refuse to have Cecilia drag me to one of those cheap seven-dollar haircut places. God knows what kind of color I'd wind up with. Call me. And don't forget to mark your calendar for the Creations in Clay on June thirtieth.'"

Augusta read the entire message without pausing to take a breath. For that matter, I didn't take one, either. I expected to hear some awful news that would link Nate's possible murder case to someone my mother knew. The last time that happened, my mother and her friends hired Nate to investigate because the sheriff's department was "moving like geriatric slugs." I prayed to the gods that whatever Nate was called to consult on wouldn't involve my mother or the Booked 4 Murder book club.

"So that was it? Hairdresser on vacation and the Creations in Clay?"

"Yep. That's all she said. You can breathe again. So, if you don't mind my asking, what on earth is the Creations in Clay? Some sort of exhibit?"

"Sort of, with tentacles. The Creations in Clay is the annual pottery and clay event in Sun City West. It always takes place right before the summer heat kicks in. It includes a juried art show and lots of booths where the clay club members sell their creations."

"That sounds nice. I didn't know your mother was interested in juried art."

"Up until a few months ago, she wasn't. Then one of

her book club ladies read this article about people whose artistic talents don't begin to show up until they're in their seventies or eighties. Like Grandma Moses. Or that lady from the seventeen hundreds who discovered decoupage. Anyway, one of my mother's friends convinced her to join the clay club because, and I quote, 'Molding clay could be the conduit to our hidden artistic talents.' "

"Really? She said that?"

"Actually, if you want to know the real reason, I think my mother intends to make dog bowls for Streetman. Don't ask."

Augusta tried not to snicker, but we both started laughing.

I finally caught my breath. "It's only May, so she has lots of time to make that spoiled Chiweenie of hers a complete place setting. Well, I'd better get back to my accounts before Gertie and Trudy get here. And especially before Marshall returns from that missing person's case in Buckeye. I don't want him to think I stand around gabbing all day."

"So, how's it going between the two of you?"

"Geez, you're beginning to sound like my mother. Seriously, for someone dating in her forties, it's going great."

It was hard not to smile and get all dreamy eyed. I didn't want to jinx anything by saying it out loud, but boy, was I glad Nate hired him. Imagine, Marshall and I worked all those years for the Mankato Police Department and neither of us knew we were both interested in dating each other. Maybe Nate figured it out all along and that was why when it came time to hire another investigator for his firm, Marshall was his first choice.

"Glad to hear it." Augusta clicked the mouse and looked at her computer screen. "I'd better get back to work, too."

Within seconds, I was working on my billing and filing. The time went by so quickly I hadn't realized it was two thirty until Augusta knocked on my door frame.

"The ladies who called are here to see you. Do you want me to send them right in?"

I stood up and followed her out. "I'll get them."

Gertie and Trudy were facing the window and turned when they heard my footsteps. Their hairdos looked a bit different from the last time I saw them. Short silver curls with hints of blue. Perfectly styled. Same could be said for their identical outfits. It almost looked as if the two of them were standing at attention.

I rushed over immediately. "Hi! It's nice to see you again. Can I get you some coffee or tea?"

Gertie shook her head. "No thanks. We'll be eating soon and we don't want to ruin our appetites. The Lillian has a marvelous master chef and tonight is tilapia night."

"It's always tilapia night, Gertie," Trudy said. "They have that on the menu every night."

Augusta, who had returned to her desk, sat bolt upright and gave me one of her unmistakable looks.

I turned the other way and ushered the sisters into my office. "Please, take a seat."

There were two chairs in front of my desk, and I moved my chair to the right of the computer so it wouldn't obstruct anyone's view as we spoke. "So, tell me. What's going on regarding the thefts? I understand that's why you came to see me."

"It is," Gertie said. "It most certainly is. You show her the list, Trudy."

Without wasting a second, Trudy opened a large floral handbag and took out a folded piece of paper and began to read it.

"Mildred Kirkenbaum, one spool of purple yarn, Emily Outstrader, two cans of tuna, Warren Bellis, one jar of olives. The green ones without those red things in them. Mabel Leech, one fountain pen and some paper clips, Norma O'Neil, a five-dollar bill, Sharon Smyth, a small clay jar she bought from the last clay club art show, and Clive Monroe, a box of tissues and his lifelong membership pin to the Elks."

"Uh, is that it?"

Trudy nodded as she handed me the list. "As far as we know. And we've been asking. From the minute Mildred told us about the purple yarn."

"What about you and your sister? Are any of your items missing?"

"Not that we know of," Gertie said. "But sometimes you don't know if something's missing until you go to use it."

I had to agree with her on that one. I'd spent entire afternoons looking for stupid things like razor blades, the extra packet of dental floss I swore I had, and my reward card for a local restaurant that I only frequented once in a while. Most of the time the items in question turned up days, weeks, or months later, in places I never expected. I wondered if the same could be said for the residents of the Lillian, but I didn't want to sound as if I was dismissing the two sisters who had made a point of coming to our office.

"Is this the first time something like this has happened? Or the first time people felt it should be reported?"

Gertie and Trudy glanced at each other before Gertie spoke.

"The first time. We're certain. Those residents, who happen to be friends of ours, have lived there much longer than my sister and me. That's why we're so concerned."

I edged forward in my chair. "A theft is a theft no matter how small or valuable the item is, so why didn't your friends report it to the management?"

"They didn't want to get anyone in trouble," Trudy said.

Gertie gave her sister a poke in the arm. "Tell her the real reason. Go on."

Trudy started to fiddle with the strap on her handbag. "If we reported it, the manager would think the thief was one of the staff members. I mean, they have keys to our apartments in order to clean them and change the linens. Not to mention the regular maintenance. The staff members do all sorts of extra things for us like helping us put groceries away if we go shopping or move furniture around. Some of them even help residents with their hair if they have time. All of that will come to a stop if they get hauled in by the residence director."

"My sister's right," Gertie said. "I wouldn't go so far as to say the staff plays favorites, but those of us who remember them during the holidays or tip them once in a while get better attention, if you know what I mean."

I bit my lip and waited for a second. "Is it possible these thefts were committed by another resident and not a staff member?"

The sisters shrugged simultaneously.

"Maybe, if someone was careless enough to leave their door open or unlocked. That happens sometimes. But the people we mentioned, the ones on the list, were all insistent they locked up whenever they left their apartments, even if they were only going down the hall to get their mail," Gertie said. "And it isn't as if any new residents have moved in lately. The last one was Florence Shiver, and she moved in at least nine months ago."

"Well," I said, "this is troubling. Look, as you know, I'm the office bookkeeper and accountant, not an investigator, but I would be willing to speak discreetly with your residence director, without letting on you were the ones who called me. I'd be doing this unofficially. As a friend. Would that be okay with you? For all we know, maybe the director is aware of something going on."

"Do you have to show her the list of names?" Trudy asked.

I shook my head. "No. I'll type up a list of the items and go from there. How does that sound?"

Gertie opened her handbag and took out a twenty-dollar bill. "We're willing to pay you."

I honestly felt as if I was about to blush. Talk about feeling uncomfortable. "No. No. Please put that away. It's not necessary. I'll get in touch with the management and I'll let you know what I find out in a few days. Did you need me to call a taxi service for you?"

"Heavens no," Gertie said. "We told our residence driver to pick us up in a half hour. His car is probably out front."

Sure enough, a sleek white limo was parked a few feet from our entrance. I escorted the sisters to the door and reassured them I'd be in touch.

Trudy grabbed my arm and whispered, "There's one more thing."

Here it comes. Whatever it is, I can only imagine.

"Sharon Smyth is beside herself over that clay jar she bought. The woman was in tears."

"I know for a fact the clay club is having another sale on June thirtieth," I said. "That's coming up pretty soon. She can always buy another jar."

"That's what we thought, too, dear, but Sharon was still distraught."

Wait until she sees my mother's creations. It'll give a whole new meaning to the word "distraught."

"Yes," Gertie added, "you'd think that silly jar was worth a fortune the way that woman carried on. Wouldn't you say so, Trudy?"

"I would. Indeed, I would. She's still carrying on. And acting strangely, too. Refusing to go out on excursions like shows or shopping. If it keeps up, she'll be a regular recluse. So, you see, it's really important, Miss Kimball, that you find out who stole these items."

"I'll do my best."

The two sisters, with their matching teal capris and polka-dotted blouses, went directly to their limo.

"So, what did you find out?" Augusta asked when they left.

"Not much. Sounds like the usual stuff that probably happens in college dorms and all sorts of residences where there's a large population. Petty theft. I mean, if I were to add up all the stuff that was taken, it wouldn't even equal twenty-five dollars, but that's not the point. The residents are feeling very uncomfortable and one woman is taking it to the extreme."

"Yeesh. So I guess that means you'll be on the case, so to speak."

"Not a case. A favor for two elderly sisters. I've got Saturday off. I'll drop by the Lillian and have a word with their director. See what I can find out."

"You're a good soul, Phee. Just don't get too deep in the mire. Makes it hard to wipe your boots."

Just then the phone rang and Augusta grabbed it. I could hear her customary greeting of "Williams Investigations. How can I help you?" But instead of the usual banter that follows those calls, all I heard was, "Uh-oh. Okay. Okay, I will."

I hesitated to return to my office. Something was off.

"What's the matter, Augusta? What is it?"

"Looks like the mud you're going to be wiping off your feet is waiting for you in Sun City West. That was Nate. I was right all along. It *was* a homicide the sheriff's department was investigating. Some guy found dead in his garage."

Suddenly the corned beef sandwich I had eaten for lunch wasn't settling too well. "Not anyone I know?"

"I don't think so, but Nate wants you to call your mother and go over to her house."

"My mother? Why? What's she got to do with this?"

"The guy they found was holding a piece of paper with two names on it. Your mother's was one of them."

"Oh my God! Did he say who the other one was?"

Augusta shook her head. "No. All he said was for you to call your mother and go directly to her house. If she's not home, wait there for him."

"And here I thought the worst thing I was going to deal with today was a bit of filching."